Bad Books

...and other stories

h d munro

Author: munrohugh@aol.com

CONTENTS

Out of the Elephant

'Allah taught us to lie so that we can save ourselves at moments of difficulty and confuse our enemies' (Muhammad Naab-Safavi, 1985).

It is London in about six years from now. Islamic fundamentalism is a prominent and militant culture. The economy is in recession. Closed circuit T.V. and information technology have formed a grid of steel across the cityscape. For public servants life is reduced to function. The metropolis is sterile. Crime is managed, but only just.

1.

On Friday January 8th, 2025 there was nothing out of the ordinary happening in the Major Crime Unit at Paddington Police Station in West London. It was 06:15 and the recorded call to prayer echoed from the top of the mosque which was once the Green Man pub.

The MCU is housed in three separate but adjacent open plan offices. The description 'nothing out of the ordinary' covers a multitude of sins. One of the sins covered by the MCU is of course murder. Another is rape. Detectives work around the clock on a shift system analysing data, taking witness statements, preserving exhibits for forensic examination and, most exhaustively, collating information for the retention and consumption of the Predictor. The Predictor is not an unimaginatively – and some would say disingenuously – named machine that is supposed to tell the cops when, where and by whom the next and subsequent major crimes will be committed. Of course it comes nowhere near to doing so, but nonetheless creates a lot of work for the officers who have to satiate its unquenchable thirst for data.

So, 'nothing out of the ordinary' that winter's morning included the work of three female uniformed police officers, one in each of the three rooms, reading rape victim statements from paper forms. The Predictor listened and silently converted to text which appeared on screens. But the visible text was merely a useful by-product. The actual data hurtled off into the cyber-bowels to be sifted, shuffled, sorted, compared and reshuffled a thousand times per second.

Human listeners in each case were CID officers, time-served detectives of which two were male, one female. The victims were all Asian Muslim women. The statements were all in great detail, often repetitive. The first uniformed woman police officer began by briefing the supervising detective, a Detective Sergeant Soraya 'Dez' Fernandez.

'The victim is called Sophie Khan. She comes from

Pakistan, her accent is strong but she is articulate. She lives in a woman's hostel in Ilford, east London; she is 47 years of age. Shall I start sarge?'

'Yes please, carry on.' The uniformed cop did not see the rather harassed Fernandez glance at her watch.

The uniformed cop inhaled and began.

'My name is Sophie Khan. I live at the address that I have given to the police. I wish to report that I have been raped. I have been examined by a doctor and I gave my consent for this to take place. It happened today just after I got off the tube, I was walking up the side alley when he grabbed me from behind...'

In the next room another uniformed police officer read from a written statement to DS Stephen Yip. The Predictor absorbed every word.

'Her name is Temma Shernaz. She's a 53 year old grandmother, sergeant, she lives on the Tuitt Estate in Notting Hill with her son, his wife and their two children. They are devout Muslims. She was on her way back from a late trip to the shops when it happened....'

Yip was a tall, irascible Londoner of Chinese extraction, always impatient for meaningful facts; he hated the system and its obsession with analytics.

'What do you mean 'late'?'

The policewoman looked through her notes.

'Er... twenty forty, or thereabouts.'

'Go on,' urged Yip.

'She was found collapsed in the street and someone called an ambulance, otherwise she would never have reported the rape. She doesn't speak English. The interpreter's draft isn't ready yet but I've listened to the Autolinguist and it's pretty accurate. Er... the....'

Yip tutted, but was mindful that the officer had had a long night.

'Okay, let's hear it, but don't go, stay in case there's anything I want you to clarify, where's the victim now?'

'Gone home sarge, wouldn't even accept a lift.'

The officer touched a screen a few times and a staccato computer translation of the victim's statement began through an unseen speaker.

'I have been raped by a white man. I do not wish my family to find out, nor will I willingly attend court. I give this statement, along with a medical examination of my body, so that the man will be caught. It happened last night. It was late. He came up from behind. He was very strong. He....'

In another room a third uniformed officer was reporting and the overseeing detective was Detective Inspector Charlie Filmer. The police constable appeared nervous but spoke loudly and clearly, almost as if giving evidence.

'She's thirty eight but looks ten years older. Having sustained severe facial burns as a child in Lebanon she had to come to London to find work. She lives in a cheap

Hounslow hotel which she cleans daily for her keep.'

The reporting officer then launched into the actual statement, Filmer and the machine listened.

'I am 38 years old. I was born in Lebanon. I came to this country seven years ago. My name is Umza Farouk. Tonight I have been raped. I do not wish my family to know about this. I was walking from the underground station in Hounslow. He came from behind me. He was very strong. He pulled me down backwards and I felt something sharp in my ribs. He told me he had a knife and that he would kill me if I screamed. Then he pulled off my head dress. He looked closely at my face, like he knew this would be bad for me. He was very rough with me. He made me talk to him. In my own language….'

2.

An hour later and all three detectives were in Filmer's office. He was worried.

'Okay. Keep these jobs under your hats. I don't want panicky reports of a serial rapist on the loose. Just get the details onto the system and the analysts….'

'Phwuh!' The only thing predictable about Steve Yip was his rudeness and disrespect for rank. But he was a good detective and Filmer sought to placate him.

'Steve, the system is here to help us, just play the game and it'll work.'

Then the DI turned to Fernandez, 'Dez, can you get all the CCTV product onto the machine and... why are you shaking your head?'

Fernandez was ahead of the game. 'I've done it. It didn't take long ...there's bugger-all there. A few muffled screams on the audio but all the action seems to have taken place in the blind spots. It's like he knew where the cameras were.'

Filmer accepted this. 'Christ, those cameras stick out like donkeys' dicks all over the place. You would think that with the technology these days....'

Yip saw an opportunity for another dig. 'Civil liberties, we can't argue, our masters say that we must not spy, no covert CCTV and....'

Filmer's patience was being tested. 'Yeah, all right, alright. What about DNA?' he asked generally, 'Samples off to the lab yet?'

Fernandez was ahead again. 'Done. No trace on any recently released sex offenders. They're running through other possible categories now.'

Filmer started to sum up. 'This has all the hallmarks of a....'

But Fernandez interrupted. 'Sterile semen.'

This stopped Filmer in his tracks; 'Eh? Do what?'

'Zero sperm count.' Fernandez was enjoying this, and Yip though it time for a funny; 'That was a waste of a morning-after pill then, wasn't it!'

Filmer finished his sentence '...all the hallmarks of a fucking nightmare job.' He sighed before going on, 'Right.

Let's get what we've got properly inputted and see what comes out of the other end. You never know, somebody might find the 'solve' button!'

All three allowed themselves some ironic laughter as they rose to leave.

3.

Martin Plante, ex-detective constable and current free-lance journalist staggered from the toilet and back into the bedroom of his squalid flat. His prime intention was to answer the phone, which had been ringing for some minutes, but he was distracted by the need to locate the bottle of whiskey he had been tucking into throughout the night. But he gave up on the distraction and resentfully picked up his phone.

'Yeah?'

Steve Yip was on the other end and knew his voice would be unmistakable, as would his tone.

'Breakfast, 8, tomorrow. Usual place.'

'Okay,' said Plante, knowing this was not a request.

4.

The next day Filmer got a call from New Scotland Yard. The analysts had done the not too difficult job of guessing that the rape of three Muslim women in the same geographical area within 24 hours was something that very senior management should know about. Much more senior than Filmer.

The caller was none other than Deputy Assistant Commissioner Reza Choudhary, a man Filmer hated with a vengeance. Choudhary had once chaired a disciplinary board of one of Filmer's favourite detectives and had sacked the lad – for nothing more than voicing his opinion in the closed environment of a police canteen about the possible virtues on a ban on the wearing of burqas in public. A Muslim officer had overheard him and had reported it, and the rest was history. Filmer had always thought that the sacking was nothing more than a political stunt by Choudhary, to curry favour with the liberal elite.

'Charlie! How you doing?!'

The bonhomie did not fool Filmer, and probably was not meant to, but rather was sarcasm. He recognised the voice and instantly became guarded.

'Good morning, sir.'

'Yes, good morning to you too Charlie. What are you doing about the serial rapist of Muslim women on Five Area then?'

'Well sir, we're….'

'Let me help you, I'll tell you what you're doing. You've got a meeting here in my office in an hour's time with our head profiler, Dr Suzannah Seymour. Byeee.'

And that was it. On one hand Filmer was annoyed, ruffled at being treated like this by a politician in uniform who had slithered up the ranks with a total disregard for others. But on the other hand he was a bit relieved. Choudhary wanted to hijack the job for his own purposes – well, he was fucking welcome to it.

5.

An hour later and Chaudhary had an audience in his opulent 10th floor office on the Thames embankment. Photographs of himself adorned the walls, obscure trophies crowded the bookshelves. The carpet was an inch thick and topped off with a massive Persian rug. The desk was nearly two metres wide, and there was not a scrap of paper on it. Chaudhary stayed seated behind the massive plinth as three of his visitors were shown in by his staff officer. Two further visitors were already there, seated at a conference table. They were Professor Suzannah Seymour, a large, 35 year old peroxide blond with a big voice and big hair, and Dr Bobby Koor, a 25 year old Asian woman with good looks and short black hair.

'Charlie, come in, welcome to my little broom cupboard.'

Filmer walked across the Persian rug wearing a grim smile.

'Oh, you've brought your team along, I should have ordered a bigger pot of coffee.'

'That won't be necessary sir, we've all just had one in the canteen downstairs,' Filmer lied, 'Allow me sir to introduce DS's Fernandez and Yip, both on this enquiry.'

'I should hope they are Charlie,' said Chaudhary, without even looking at the two sergeants. Then he rose from his sumptuous leather chair and motioned toward the conference table.

'Now my turn to make an introduction; 'DI Filmer, this is

Professor Suzannah Seymour and Dr Bobby Kaur, two of the finest criminal profilers in the business.'

'Koor,' said Koor.

Chaudhary frowned, 'Pardon?'

'Koor, not Kaur, Koor,' corrected Koor, again.

Chaudhary was dismissive and insincerely apologetic, 'Sorry, Koor.'

Nodding their acknowledgements, the three detectives selected chairs and sat down at the opposite side of the table. Chaudhary sat at its head.

There was then an uncomfortable silence, which Seymour broke;

'It's okay Reza, she's a bit pernickety, perfectionist, aren't you darling.'

Koor glared at Seymour. The detectives hardly noticed, being somewhat stunned by Seymour's use of Choudhary's first name and the inappropriately affectionate reference to her colleague. The Deputy Assistant Commissioner resumed control.

'Er, right, anyway, let's get on with it. Suzanna has all the stuff and her profile is on line, fully assimilated. Already there are some interesting things coming out. I've called this meeting as an informal kickabout, really, er, just so as we can actually talk to each other face to face. It's agreed that all three rapes are the work of one man and that they will continue; the seriousness of the attacks increasing until he kills. He has a career to pursue. He has threatened at least one victim with what she thought was a handgun. We have to assume he's armed.'

At that point Seymour jumped in.

'He's a racist. He has knowledge of the Muslim community and will already have a history of sexual offending. He's sterile, he's clinical, methodical and silent. Your kinda guy, Bobby?'

Any trace of hostility between the two civilians had evaporated. Koor saw this as a cue to contribute.

'Absolutely darling. Very firm but never leaves any marks. Not yet, anyway. He has probably been married before and abused his wife. She has now left him or may have even been killed by him. He may have recently been released from prison. His victims, the ones that we know about that is, have all been poor, underclass Asian women. Our man is familiar with the cowed body language, covered or semi-covered faces, black headwear, dark or black clothing, *etcetera*, of such women. He may even be Asian himself.'

Yip saw his chance and took it.

'Except that he's white.'

Filmer next, 'A white man with experience of Asian women?'

Yip; 'Rare.'

Koor; 'Very rare.'

Koor and Yip stared at each other across the table; a hint of familiarity.

Koor continued, 'Always during the first week of the month; always within half a kilometre of the Piccadilly Line. Always the same sterile semen. HIV negative.'

Chaudhary stepped in, keen to maintain control. 'Forensic testing has so far drawn a blank on the semen... er... no pun intended... so it's a decoy operation. Next week. Here begins Operation Willow.'

Filmer just sat there open mouthed, this bloated administrator in uniform had just started, even named, an operational strategy without consulting him, the senior operational detective, and there was nothing he could do about it.

Choudhary enjoyed the embarrassment he had caused. 'Okay, Charlie, I'll leave the rest in your capable hands. Let me know when you get a result,' And with that the Deputy Assistant Commissioner stood up and went back to his desk. The meeting was over.

6.

Charlie Filmer was a Freemason, a member of the St James Lodge, which was mainly for police officers who hope to enhance the promotion prospects by rubbing shoulders with influential high rankers. It did not actually work, but once you were in you were in and leaving was something no-one did. Filmer was dressed in the customary black suit and Lodge tie; he walked into the specially hired hotel function room in Park Lane and took a readily poured drink from the bar. It was white wine, bloody horrible German stuff, he surmised.

He took a number of small sips to see if he could acquire a

taste for it and whilst doing so was approached by an elderly and senior figure.

'How are you young Charles? Keeping well I trust?'

It was Graham Churchill, a commander on the anti-terrorist branch.

'I'm well thank you sir....'

Churchill was having none of this. 'Please, you must drop the 'sir' bit in this company, Charlie. You must call me Graham. Just Graham. We're equals here.

'Oh, okay then Graham, it just seems a bit...

Churchill was keen to move the conversation onwards.

'They want this rapist caught Charlie. And quick.'

'I'm trying sir... Graham... it's like looking for a...

'Won't do you any harm Charlie, you'll get a few leaps up the ladder in this lot....'

Then they were interrupted by a call to order and they both turned to face a small but elaborately decorated podium at which another man stood in very formal dress.

'Worshipful Brothers....'

7.

Three hours later it was midnight and Filmer found himself back in his office. He was still dressed formally but with tie loosened, and was about to call his wife when he noticed his email terminal was flashing, he logged on and checked;

something told him it was important.

'It'll be next Sunday, without a doubt. Near the Dilly line so I can get home quick. Not sure what time. Depends on how much I've had. Might need a nap before I go out. Location? Oh, I don't know yet Charlie. I get on the train and that's when the planning stops. All on autopilot from then on. I'm not holding back on you, Charlie, but you'd better hurry up because this is going to get very, very big.'

Filmer hit the print button and stared at the screen. He picked up a telephone handset and spoke a number into it. This had the effect of dialling.

A few rings and the call was accepted by a female voice.

'Openness. Thank you for calling. How can we help you?'

Filmer did not known whether the voice was owned by a machine or a human, so he decided to play it safe and be civil… ish.

'Yes, 'Openness', you can help me by telling me how much 'openness' has been given to Operation Willow, that's the investigation into the serial rapes of Muslim women in London….'

The voice was too quick to be human; 'No trace on any such operational name on our system sir, bear with me... and no trace of any field incorporating 'rape' and 'Muslim' sir.'

Filmer could not resist some sarcastic humour.

'Field? What field? Has there been ... What the hell are you talking about woman?'

'Don't call me 'woman' sir. What I am talking about is that we have nothing even remotely resembling what you are talking about and, therefore, there is no Openness on it. Nil publicity. Secret. Is that clear to you? Sir?

'Very clear. Thanks. Look, I'm sorry about....'

And the line went dead.

'Shit,' said Filmer, he would probably hear more about that.

8.

Professor Suzannah Seymour's apartment was strangely located on the 13th floor of Trellick Tower. The huge block with its detached staircase and lift shafts had been built as an iconic social housing experiment and was in its heyday populated by people who seemed to be human experiments gone wrong. Like much of London's social housing it had fallen into private hands and a two bedroomed flat now fetched over three million pounds.

The big blonde lay draped voluptuously over a settee, large scotch in one hand, menthol vapestick in the other. She was entranced by the soundtrack of Clockwork Orange and the doorbell only just made it through the booming Beethoven.

She sighed, rose and glided to the door without turning down the volume. The blast of sound hit Filmer in the face, along with the sight of what looked like something out of a 1960's B movie.

'Charlie, *entre* my darling man, what a pleasant surprise.

Seymour stood dramatically aside and waved in the

policeman. Filmer felt like he was stepping into a parallel universe. The place was minimalist open plan and the view from the panoramic window was stunning.

'London by night Charlie, beautiful isn't it?' She joined him at the window. 'Seething.'

Ludvig van was making hearing difficult.

'Soothing?' frowned Filmer.

'Seething!' she raised her voice, and turned to the volume control.

Her choice of adjective made his frown deeper and turned his head slowly toward her as she came back from the hi-fi control.

'With what?'

'Crime of course Charlie. Whiskey?'

'Eh? Er… yeah, go on then, just a small one please.' His gaze went back to the cityscape.

She poured a very large Scotch and handed it to him, he took it, looked at it and did not say a word. She sat down on the sofa and patted the cushion next her. He did as bade, awkwardly, his coat still buttoned up.

'Right Charlie, couldn't trace the email I gather?

He was not surprised that she knew about the latest development and decided not to appear so.

'Nah, you're joking. They go about twice round the planet

these days. Could have come from anywhere.'

'Run it. But be very careful. He's got his eye on the big one. Perhaps unconsciously, but it's there. A - decoy. Unless he already knows. B - He will want to take her. It's happened before. C - He won't mind being caught; shot, even. Just as long as he rapes or kills her. Preferably both. Run it. Be a bit of sport. Careful though, careful.'

Filmer was lost for words. How did she know all this? He had been thinking that a decoy job was the only way to progress this job, but, apart from Yip and Fernandez he hadn't discussed it with anyone.

'You're thinking how I knew what you've been thinking, aren't you?'

Again, he decided to play it cool. 'No, not really, bloody obviously the only way, isn't it.' He drained his scotch in one and hoisted himself out of the sofa.

'Where are you going Charlie?'

'Home.'

'No, please don't, your surprise visit presents us with an amazing opportunity.'

'What?'

'Bobby will be here any minute now, and we'd love to discuss the case with you.'

Had Filmer's visit to Seymour been planned he would have suspected a trap. Nevertheless, he did not like the sound of this one bit.

As if on cue, the doorbell rang. As Seymour went to answer Filmer got up and walked over to the window and resumed a thoughtful gaze outwards. Seymour came back into the room with Koor at her side.

'Here he is Bobby, our very own Detective Inspector…' then she quickly added 'Charlie Filmer' before the introduction sounded proprietary.

Filmer tuned round and said, 'Hi'.

Koor said, 'Hi, we met at the Yard, didn't we.'

Seymour motioned her visitors to sit at a hardwood dining table, they did as bid and she offered more drinks. Filmer declined and Koor chose a glass of cranberry juice. Once they were settled Seymour took the lead.

'He's afraid. He's afraid of fear. He wants everything out in the open but it's much too big for him. He's getting out of his depth. He does not know how to use fear. He is beginning to freeze.'

Filmer did not hear a word of this; his attention was completely taken by the expression on Koor's face as she fixated on her pontificating mentor. It was one of infatuation, bordering on erotic.

She maintained this countenance when she spoke.

'Do you think fear freezes the victims like they say it does?'

Seymour did not miss a beat; 'Probably mostly maybe. In some cases the fear causes partial asphyxiation, blocking oxygen supply and heightening pleasure.'

'Heightens pleasure? Surely you mean lowers pain?'

'Same thing. If something that is meant to hurt like fuck goes off painlessly then any residual pleasure is amplified a thousand times.'

Then the women stared adoringly at each other in silence. Filmer struggled to suppress a mischievous smile.

9.

The following day Seymour and Koor were together again, this time in their shared office. One of their machines let out a Skype sound and they both turned to a shared screen. Filmer's face appeared.

'Ladies, we have a problem. The job starts in two days from now and the decoy has gone off sick. We cannot find another suitable female Asian officer. This will give us more time to consider your input, I've called another....'

Koor was straight in, 'I'll do it!'

Koor looked back from the terminal at Seymour. The professor remained calm, half smiling, Koor's eyes were wide, manic.

Filmer decided to act stupid.

'Do what?'

Koor was determined, 'The decoy. I'll be the decoy.'

Filmer was having none of it. 'No you will not. It's a job for a trained police officer. Besides, you're not insured....'

'I know him, better than any of you lot. I'm right inside of him.'

The DI could not resist it; 'Yeah, and he'll be right ins-...,' then he thought better of it.

'No. No. Suzanna, talk some sense into her will you. In a few days I'll have another....'

But Seymour liked the idea. 'No, she's right. Anyway, what if you can't find an Asian officer, you can't use a European, he'd smell that a mile off....'

Filmer did not need this, he had to get control of these two weirdos.

'Ladies, ladies. I'm not going to argue with you. Civilian members of staff do not get involved in operational police work....'

'Nor do police officers by the sound of things,' interrupted Koor gleefully, 'I bet you don't get another volunteer. Then you'll have to suspend the operation and the next thing you'll have is another rape... come on, I could get this bastard, I have his scent, I know how he thinks. I'm a Muslim.'

This stumped the cop, made him think. They had a lot of Asian females on the force, but not many of them were followers of the prophet Mohammed, and certainly those who were would not be permitted by their families to engage in anything that could jeopardise their purity.

Koor knew she had him, she smiled and moved her face nearer to the webcam, then she cut the connection.

Seymour smiled also. 'Lucky you. He'll come round to it.'

Koor agreed, 'He has to.'

10.

Another 32 hours flew by during which the game of politics was played at Champions League level. This culminated in a big meeting at a Yard briefing room. At 4pm it was full of all forms of police life, including uniformed top brasses, plain clothes officers and TSG armed operatives.

Charlie Filmer had worked all night and was visibly shattered. But he was on good form and steamed in with aplomb. As he spoke he manipulated a large CGI screen.

'Good morning ladies and gentlemen. Welcome to Operation Willow. My name is Charlie Filmer and I'm the DI responsible for this deployment. The object of the operation is the arrest of a man believed to be responsible for at least three brutal rapes in which all of the victims have been Muslim women. You will be aware that this fact alone gives rise to the need for the highest level of discretion. There is a press blackout on all but the most general details of the whole investigation. Tonight's deployment will consist of static surveillance on a decoy, and at this point I would like to introduce Doctor Bobby Koor, an accredited offender profiler and, as you can see, of suitable appearance to fit the victim profile. She, er, will, of course, not be dressed as she is now....' There was some polite laughter, as Koor was dressed rather sexily in tight jeans and tee shirt. She smiled knowingly, clearly enjoying the attention.

Filmer continued. 'Full teams 19:00, on ground assigned.

Full monitoring of all CCTVs. Dogs, heli, firearms. The decoy plot is broken into sectors. Each OP team has a sector, the usual rules apply. Sector leaders are as follows....'

11.

DS Steve Yip had made excuses about his wife being ill and was not at the briefing. Instead he was in a café in Warren Street, London, talking to an astounded Martin Plante.

'Don't just go barging in for fuck's sake. I'll keep you genned up on where and when. Stay off of the email. All the modems are being watched. Same with the phones... that goes without saying. Filmer's good luck message from our man means he has someone on the inside.'

Plante thought Christmas had come late. 'Wow. This is a big one.' Then he paused and looked down, embarrassed; 'Look, I really appreciate this Steve. I will, er... I haven't got....'

Same old story, thought Yip, Plante was always skint. 'Don't be stupid mate. Don't worry, I'll call all these favours in one day! We're all sailing close to the wind. 'There but for the grace of God' and all that, eh?'

12.

Three hours later Koor and Filmer were in an unmarked police car in the carpark of Hounslow Underground station. Hounslow is a bleak, dysfunctional place at the best of times, but on a bleak and dysfunctional January night it was beyond the pale.

Filmer regarded his fellow passenger. She was wearing dark clothing from head to toe, topped off with a full face niqab.

He feigned academic interest; 'Is that a burqa you're wearing?'

'No, it's a niqab,' she answered flatly, 'the terms niqab and burqa are often incorrectly used interchangeably; a niqab covers the face while a burqa covers the whole body from the top of the head to the ground.'

Filmer frowned, still looking at her. 'Are you nervous?'

'Yes, I'm fucking shitting myself actually. Not that you seem to care.'

As she said this she seemed to be adjusting her get-up, making sure her covert comset was readily positioned.

'Of course I bloody care,' Filmer was genuinely alarmed by her rather offensive stance and his hackles rose. 'If you're in any way worried that you haven't had or are not getting enough support or safety cover then say so and I'll call the whole fucking thing off now!'

'No, I'm fine, sorry, I didn't mean to be rude, yes, I feel safe, you have my back, as they say.'

Filmer switched on a monitor in the vehicle and flicked from one visual to the next and then to a map on which a tracker spot pulsated.

'I'll go through it again. Here you are now, that's the tracker on your phone showing you here in the car. And these are the views from the observation points, those are the places where we think he's most likely to strike. Armed response units have got telescopic sights on those as we speak. Stick to the route and you'll never be out of sight. Even if you do stray the alarm will sound clearly and we'll be with you in under 3 seconds.'

'You'll be 2 seconds too late. He'll have this in his belly.'

With that she produced out a 6 inch flick knife, the blade shot out and glinted in the sodium light.

Filmer could not believe his eyes. 'Jesus Christ you must be fucking joking! Give me that now!' But it was back in her copious clothing before he could even think about trying to snatch it. It was too late to do anything about this; if he called off the job he would have to state why and then she would have to be charged with possession of an offensive weapon. What a nightmare, but he would just have to run with it.

'Look, we'll have him long before he gets to you, there are sensors all along the route, not one blind spot, Steve Yip's checking them now.'

'Yeah, well, you're not getting 3 seconds to find out. You'll have to get him before I do. First come first served.'

Filmer sighed, 'Okay, okay. You're on!'

If it came to it he would deny ever seeing that knife.

13.

Filmer tapped a microphone switch and secured a series of readiness responses; 'Alpha three, ready to go?' *'Affirmative'*, 'Alpha four, ready to go?' 'Affirmative' and so it went on, he counted them in, all set. He turned to her. 'Okay Bobby, we're ready when you are.'

'Okay,' she smiled, 'Tootle pip.' And she was out of the car and gone.

Filmer set to work watching the screen, he flicked from one camera to the next, keeping her in sight at all times as she walked along a tree lined street. In addition to the static cameras in place along the designated decoy route, Koor was wearing a body camera. It was positioned halfway up her chest, between her breasts. This gave the viewer her POV as she walked. It was this camera that Filmer had engaged on his screen in the car when it happened. Quite suddenly the picture went haywire, it jerked skywards and then went blank. The other cameras were engaged and flipped frantically from screen to screen, but Koor had disappeared.

Filmer shouted into the radio mic, 'Decoy, decoy, where are you? Location decoy, we've lost you....'

He needn't have worried about the safety of the decoy, but had he known what was happening at that instant they would certainly have other concerns. Koor was being passionately kissed by a darkly clad male, this was just out of sight of the fixed cameras and her body cam was blinded by the chest of her assailant which was pressed hard against her. After five very long seconds she broke away and spun round sharply.

'I'm... I'm okay - I fell.'

Without letting the bodycam focus on her assailant in the shadows she turned and gave him a fleeting glare. It was

Detective Sergeant Steven Yip. He was laughing silently as he retreated backwards, further into the darkness.

The bodycam refocused and the static cameras resumed contact as she emerged back onto the pathway. Normal service had resumed and Filmer hissed rather than breathed a sigh of relief. Thirty seconds later Yip returned to join his assistant at his observation point; he pretended to be fastening his fly. 'Sorry about that, got caught short, anything happened yet?'

14.

Filmer let the job run for another 40 minutes, during which time Koor walked an uneventful 2 miles along the designated route. Then he called it off, pulling up alongside her he leant across and opened the passenger door. She stopped walking, appeared to hesitate, but got in. She was furious.

'You didn't give him time. He's out there. Now he'll try to get me.'

'What do you mean he'll try to get you?' Filmer frowned as he pulled the car away from the curb and glanced across at her for a response. 'What are you talking about?'

She remained silent. 'Bobby, what the fuck are you talking about – he'll get you? Are you holding something back? Do you know who this bastard is?'

Koor shook her head vehemently, 'No, but I think he knows who I am.'

Twenty minutes later Filmer drove the car into the back of

Paddington Police Station, Koor rid herself of her comset and body cam and threw them into the footwell, got out of the vehicle and marched across the station carpark and got into her own car. She was still in Islamic dress, but her niqab was pulled down beneath her chin.

As she drove out of the security gates and turned left onto the Western Avenue dual carriageway she noticed another car pull out of a backstreet and tuck in behind her.

15.

Still distracted by the sudden departure of Koor, Filmer set about debriefing the twenty-odd personnel who had returned to the station following the stand-down.

He had just about finished when he was called to the phone by Fernandez, 'Intel for you guv, need your voiceprint, won't speak to me.'

The voiceprint system ensured that spoken intelligence could only be listened to by certain recipients identified by their voiceprint. Filmer took the receiver and introduced himself; there was a click, followed by a recorded message.

'Reported at Ealing Hospital A&E by a Muslim woman. Victim's description very vague. Reported about 20:15 hours. Minimal co-operation from victim. Photo refused, address refused, refused to be seen by police. Reported to police by hospital. Only sparse details given. Told the doctor that she would return to see him when she felt better, possibly to make a statement to police if and when she felt like it. All she wanted was anti-pregnancy medication. The doctor is also a Muslim. Not to be disclosed to press. Not in the public interest - spurious source would cause disproportionate undermining of public confidence in police. Full data on crime report XD 4573. Autolink to DI Filmer at One Area HQ, reference Operation Willow, any queries to....'

Filmer cut the connection and looked really tired.

16.

Filmer and Fernandez arrived at Police HQ at the same time on the following morning and parked their cars in adjacent spaces. Always cheery and slightly spaced, the young woman was the first to speak.

'Morning guv, we weren't far off last night, a mile farther north and an hour later and we would have had him.'

Had Filmer heard this from someone else he would have taken it as sarcasm, but Fernandez wasn't like that. 'Yeah Dez, but we weren't a mile north or an hour later, so we've spent four and half grand of the budget and got fuck all.'

They walked into Filmer's office and sat down. Filmer logged on to his terminal and Fernandez started talking.

'It's just incredible that all four victims go on the missing list. All different parts of London, we just don't know enough about them. If this is some sort of politically motivated stunt then we could be in real trouble. How can the rapist be confident that this victim trend will continue? He must know that, sooner or later, one of these women is going to help us....'

Charlie Filmer was accustomed to these streams of consciousness from the young detective, and he had learned to listen.

'Hold on a minute. What do you mean 'politically motivated stunt'? You reckon he's trying to cause some sort of revolution or something? A Muslim uprising?'

'Why not? They've started over less. And our Jihadi friends, or some of them, are just waiting for an excuse.'

'Sounds wonderful stuff, but who are you digging around for? Have you got the details of a political fanatic or something? You need a suspect for that sort of line, get me one and we'll follow it. We've got four racially motivated, extremely serious sexual attacks on women, one of them an hour after we did a decoy operation to catch the bastard, and you're fucking about like this! Stay on track Dez, for God's sake...we haven't got time... just get on with the actions as directed by the system!'

Fernandez was taken aback by this outburst, and visibly hurt. It was well known that she had the DI's ear, and was used to being listened to. And she was often right – a gifted cop. She could not believe he'd turned on her like this. She left his office, red faced and head down.

17.

Booby Koor stood in her bedroom with her back to the wall; she faced the French windows and held the full length shotgun at the ready. It was loaded. She had heard the ground floor veranda gate being slowly opened and knew what was coming, although not who. Then Martin Plante walked almost casually through the French window and into the room.

There was enough light for him to see her and his eyes widened in horror, he had been told she would not be there.

'Don't shoot, it's... it's alright, nothing personal….'

She sensed his fear. 'It never is, so goes the cliché. Who and what are you?'

'No, no, no, please. All you should be interested in is who and what I am not. Why d'you have the gun?'

I'm expecting a visitor. And I like guns.'

'Who?'

'You. What do you want?'

Plante tried to be conversational. 'I'm a writer, a journalist. I need a story. A good story, and I can smell one here.'

'So why didn't you just call me?'

There was then three long seconds of silence. Then Koor lowered the weapon and expertly flicked out the two cartridges. Plante exhaled, not realising he had been holding his breath. Koor spoke quietly.

'Okay.'

18.

Filmer did not get the bollocking he expected and got back to Paddington from the Yard in a reasonable mood.

'They're extending the budget, provided we keep a lid on it.'

Yip and Fernandez were already waiting for him in his office, he sat down and Fernandez wasted no time.

'The Ealing victim has disappeared, there's a surprise.'

Filmer had been thinking and wanted to focus. 'Look, let's just leave the Ealing victim out of the picture for a minute, she's given nothing, hasn't been seen by police even. Concentrate on the first three; why won't they come back to us? The care officers are trying to get hold of them for follow ups but all of them are playing hard to get, it seems the phone numbers they gave were all duff or out of order, occupants at the addresses say they don't know them...'

Fernandez was sitting forward, her elbows on her knees, frowning at the floor. She interrupted, but not rudely, 'Perhaps..., perhaps they know each other... acting together....'

Yip contributed; 'How? They all live miles apart....'

'No, I mean through some sort of organisation, like a political....'

Filmer needed to head this off. 'Oh here we go, we've had all this. These women are poor, oppressed even, they don't have any clout and, what's more, I've ran SB checks and there is nothing to....'

But Yip was impressed. 'She's got a point. They're all Muslims, they read the same stuff, listen to the same stuff, watch the same stuff on the TV, they may be under control, they don't act as individuals, they....'

'Ooh, listen to it! Mr Victim Profiler, okay then clever

dick, what do you suggest, we all do courses in Islamic studies or something?' Filmer was being silly now, unprofessional.

Yip ignored the DI, he was on a roll and Fernandez was loving it.

'Spin them.' Yip said this like he was delivering a final decision, and Filmer didn't like it.

'What?'

'Search warrants on all the addresses. We've got powers to search for evidence of serious criminal offences, the warrants would be no....'

Filmer's irritation faded as he became more interested. 'Yes, thank you Steven, I'm perfectly aware of our powers, but these are victims, we would be criticised for just steaming in....'

'The flak we're getting now'll be nothing compared to what'll happen if we don't get a result soon....'

Filmer stood up. 'I know, I know, I know! Okay. Let me... let me think about it. I never get time to think any more!'

19.

Very often Charlie Filmer found himself regretting the extent to which he let those in his charge get close to him. Familiarity often bred contempt. It was not some sort of deliberate strategy on his part to instil trust or good working relations, it was just that he hated being distant or officious. They were often disrespectful to him, sometimes rude even. But now and again good things happened, they would tell him things without fear of sanction or ridicule, and the ideas would flow. This was one of those times.

The following morning search warrants were executed at the addresses of the first three victims. Filmer, Yip and Fernandez took one each, accompanied by junior detectives, forensic teams and the uniformed officers who had seen the victims initially.

At the Ilford address the team met with hostility and entry had to be forced. The victim had never been heard of and the search bore a negative result.

At the Notting Hill address the police were met with dumbfounded shaking heads, but no resistance. Again, the result was negative; no-one answering the description of the victim had ever lived there.

These were interesting outcomes, why would rape victims give false addresses when reporting to police? Why would they bother reporting to the police if they didn't wish to be contacted subsequently?

Filmer was told about the first two results as he knocked on the door of the Hounslow address. It was a 'half way house', a cheap hotel that would accept cash payments from customers wanting only short-term stays.

The turbaned hotelier admitted the police team and listened to Filmer politely. Fulmer handed him a piece of paper bearing the victim's name.

'Yeah guv, I know the one, badly burned face, bit of a nutter, a mozzer, come out of the Lebanon or samink I fink. Why what's she done?'

The west London accent threw Filmer for a few seconds, it was like this guy had voice-over standing behind him.

'Oh, nothing, but she may have left something behind, we have a search warrant, can we see her room please?'

The hotelier was pleased to assist, the room was searched and nothing found.

20.

The search teams met back at Paddington, the uniforms were dismissed back to their mundane duties, Yip and Fernandez went to the canteen for high cholesterol breakfasts and Filmer went into his office and closed the door behind him. A voicemail awaited. He tapped the screen and listened.

'Time's up for your pretty little decoy. I'm watching her. I'm building up to it. She's had her looks or her life. Not sure which. Bored with the rape, aren't you Charlie? We need to graduate before this whole thing goes stale on us.'

And then silence. In a weird sort of way Filmer had been expecting this, expected the psychopath to be ahead of him. All through that morning's operations he had felt like he was being watched, that he was acting out a play written by someone else, going through pre-determined motions. He had never experienced such helplessness. He slumped in his chair. There was a meeting that afternoon.

21.

At 14:00 hours prompt the meeting was opened by Deputy Assistant Commissioner Choudhary.

'Mr Filmer has told you, no doubt, about the email from someone purporting to be the rapist. Personally I don't believe it. Probably just a hoax. The Muslim press know about the operation and know that it's being run from here. The details of the offences and their locations are still classified.'

He sighed, theatrically.

'However, we can't take any chances. Dr Koor, you will from now on have a close protection unit with you.'

'No way.' Koor was sat at the back of the room and everyone turned round to gape at this impertinence.

Choudhary smiled, 'I beg your pardon.'

'I said no way. There's no way I'm having a guard with me. If you do that I'll resign.'

Choudhary maintained control; 'See me after this meeting Doctor Koor. Mr Filmer, take over please.'

And with that the Deputy Assistant Commissioner left the room and Filmer rose wearily to recount the empty details of that morning's search operations.

22.

An hour later and Koor stood in front of Choudhary in his massive office.

'Sit down Dr Koor.'

'No thank you.'

'Very well. We need you on this enquiry Doctor, we need you with us in the police service. But we do not have the capacity to take unnecessary risk….'

'You allowed me to act as your decoy….'

Koor was keeping her cool, Choudhary was losing his.

'Yes! And I wish to Christ we hadn't! I'm sorry. But that was a managed risk. We had you covered. There was no way you could have come to any harm….'

'Then why did the Service take out extra life insurance for me just for that day?'

'Simply to bring you in line with the cover serving coppers get, you're a civilian, remember. Anyway, that insurance policy is no longer in force, so you need extra protection... look, at least let us put some guys outside your home. They'll be out of sight and won't follow you, just watch your back whilst you're indoors, would you agree to that?'

He did not let her answer. 'Actually, that was a rhetorical question, we've been keeping an eye on you and we'll continue to do so, and if you don't like it just go ahead and resign. I can find another profiler and another decoy in less time than it takes me to explain you getting raped and possibly murdered, now get out of my office!'

23.

And another 24 hours slipped by. Detectives plodding away in the main CID room were distracted by a row going on in Filmer's adjacent office. They had seen the DI summon Steve Yip who had entered and closed the door behind him.

They heard raised voices but it was fortunate that they could not hear what was being said.

'He's your man Steve, always bloody has been!'

'Fuck all to do with me guv, I haven't spoken to him in months!'

'You've got 24 hours to get some answers, otherwise he'll be coming in.'

'What the fuck for? What offence?'

24.

Less than an hour later another meeting was taking place in a café in nearby Warren Street.

'I went to see if she would do a feature on offender profiling, that's all, it has nothing to do with Willow.' Plante was hissing his words earnestly, like many pressmen he really believed in his God-given right to pursue a story by any means.

'Bollocks!'

'What, yours or clean ones?!'

'It's me you're talking to! You're up to something. I can smell it. Why don't you visit her in her office; make an appointment through PR? Like all the other feature writers. As if you could ever be a feature writer. Offender profiling my arse! You're trying to get the Willow story from her….'

'It covers you Steve, if I get it from her it covers you, protects you or they'll think you're leaking classified information....'

'How did you find her? I didn't give you her address.

'You gave me her name, come on, I'm not a total cunt....'

'You do a fucking good impression... She's only just moved there, it's well under wraps....'

'Look, you don't know what I'm looking at....'

'I don't give a fuck what you're looking at! It's what I'm looking at that bothers me and that's the fucking sack! Now, how did you get her address?'

'I followed her.'

'Where from, Area HQ? You couldn't have got near....'

'It was late. From the car park. After the decoy deployment.

'You did what? I told you to stay away. Especially on that night. You dangerous bastard, you could have... You're going to get me in such deep shit!'

'How d'you make that out? Nobody knows about....'

'Come on! We went to training school together, we served together, as soon as your name goes in on a check mine pops up....'

'Yeah... yeah... alongside about fifty other coppers!'

'But I'm the only one of them on this pissing operation you daft twat. All I ask is that you're careful. That's all I ever asked Martin. And you can't even deliver that!'

'How was I to know her place was under surveillance? Why didn't you tell me? You've told me nothing but the bare bones. What d'you expect me to do? Sit around waiting for you to give me the go ahead? Eh?'

'You'll get the front seat at any press conference, you'll get the nod as soon as a collar is felt, but you've got to stay out of the fucking way until then, not fuck things up like this!'

'You lot are really worried about her aren't you. Why is that? I've touched nerve, have I not Stevie-boy?'

'Yep. You certainly have, you certainly have.'

25.

That evening the lighting was subdued in the Trellick Tower apartment. Seymour and Koor sat facing each other over a Chinese takeaway. They picked their way through a conversation as they slowly ate their food.

Hypothesis followed hypothesis as they engaged in gentle verbal sparring.

'The similarities are not only in what we know but also in what we don't know. The system never really recognises the negative. It merely virtually recognises it. De-emphasises. The positive gets the limelight treatment though. I ran an action programme the other night. It screamed for victim profiles, not offender profiles which is all we're being asked for.'

Seymour did not disagree.

'We know that the victims are all shy, innocent, Muslim non-entities. But that's only because they've chosen to give us that impression and the system doesn't encourage us to question them further. They are, after all, victims of a terrible crime and their dignity and privacy must be respected. And of the politics; God help us if we ever found anything wrong with these women, like previous convictions or illegal immigrant status. We just cannot afford to be seen to be looking at that angle.'

Koor took the baton.

'But this dignity and privacy bit, victims charter and all that, just gets absorbed as part of the system; victims end up as constructs, even more so than the offender. Even the crime is just a simulated version of our own assumptions but, because we put it through a computer we get to believe in it, know what....'

Seymour was suddenly bored or feigned it, 'Yeah, Yeah, and we believe everything we are told by the system which, in this case, is very little about the victims, blah blah blah - the times I've heard this sh....'

Koor resented this and raised her voice.

'This is the first time you've heard it from me! We know lots about the suspect, except of course who and where he is. We don't know that about the victims now either, now that it seems they were all giving false particulars. I don't know why the police just don't drop the whole thing. If these women are so reluctant to identify themselves they're hardly going to turn up at court to give evidence, are they?'

Seymour countered. 'Oh, but they would have to! If the police made an arrest and the CPS launched a prosecution they would drag the women to court. Use special measures and all that. What happened after that wouldn't matter. They could all drop dead in the witness box if they wanted to. It would not be of any real consequence, the system would have achieved success, clear-ups, that's all that fucking matters! Why are you talking to that journalist?'

Koor did not bat an eyelid.

'I'm not. He's talking to me.'

Seymour took a slug of wine, and concluded in an unaltered tone.

'Please be careful.'

26.

It was getting late and the MIU suite was deserted as Filmer walked into his office, his tie was unfastened and he had been drinking. The blinking light on his terminal told him of a waiting message and he knew who it would be from. He slumped into his chair and tapped in his user id.

'Well then, that was a turn up for the books, eh. Right under your very nose. You would have got me if you'd hung around. And the cheek of it. I wasn't really going to do it until I saw her. Then I couldn't resist it Charlie. The decoy I'm talking about. After I'd seen her I just had to do one. Pretty girl your Bobby Koor. You could get done for contributory negligence using her. She's not going to be pretty for very long though!'

Filmer smacked the keyboard with his hand and stared at the screen. He snatched up a phone and punched in a number whilst hardly taking his eyes off the monitor.

'Modem 468, get me trackback now!'

A tired human voice answered. 'It takes us 4 to 6 minutes, at best.'

Filmer tried to be patient, reasonable.

'It's hooked up, 468, it's on the hook, get it tracked back now... please, you've got about another 90 seconds before the eraser moves over. Call me back without fail.'

He replaced the receiver carefully, calmly, still staring at the screen.

27.

The next day saw London's Harrow Road at its worst. The pissing rain accentuated the knife edge desperation of life along that tortured varicose vein of the capital's mutating physiology. Bankrupt Asian shops selling bankrupted stocks of cheap jewellery, defunct computer devices, chipped mobiles and poisonous fast food. People trundled around like zombies wearing dull clothing and duller expressions. And it was a dull expression on the face of a tired and bored DI Filmer as he gazed resignedly at a screen on his desk through which the contents of an antiquated DVD, seized that day from the Aziz Internet Café, a shabby outfit nestled on the Harrow Road between a filthy chicken burger shack and a cut price mobile phone shop, was being played.

Notwithstanding his hangover, Filmer's eyes widened as something he recognised came into view. He hit a button and froze the frame. It was the fuzzy but unmistakable picture of Martin Plante leaving the premises.

28.

Meanwhile Koor was cutting her hair; she stood naked in front of her bathroom mirror. Having finished with the scissors she picked up an electric clipping machine and began taking her thick black crowning glory down to 4mm. Through the door in her tiny flat her TV was playing a Tehran newsreel. There were subtitles showing but she did not need them.

`Every single lock of hair that shows from beneath a Chador carelessly worn is like a dagger aimed at the hearts of our martyrs` (Hashemi Rafsanjani, 13.6.86)

29.

Back at Paddington MIU suite an irritated Charlie Filmer was trying to keep his temper as he spoke to Yip and Fernandez.

'We have a problem, Steve. Just a little one. You're matey with him. Not a problem, you worked together when he was in the job. Trouble is he's seeing Bobby Koor, we've seen him leaving her place. He's on security video. She's a civvy contractor and she can speak to who she likes within the terms of her contract. You've spoken to him and he says he's doing an article on offender profiling in general, no problem. No problem at all except that I don't fucking believe it!! I reckon your little hack is in on this, we traced one of the messages back to his drop address on the Harrow Road, he's taunting me, he's in on it Steve!'

Yip was always ready for this sort of challenge, and this was no exception.

'Oh come on guv, that's only a drop address, there must be thousands of wankers using that place, plastic anoraks, know what I mean, Plante's a sad bastard at the best of times,

it's the sort of place you find the likes of him, he hasn't got his own net connection - he's so broke - and he lives around the corner from that place, probably uses it for accessing porn on the web, that's all, but it doesn't mean he's a ....'

Filmer was having none of it.

'I reckon you're underestimating him ... I want him nicked and samples taken. By force if necessary.'

Fernandez felt she had to say something.

'He's right Steve, Plante could be....'

Filmer butted in.

'He's talking to the profiler's assistant, she says she hasn't told him anything about Operation Willow, you say you haven't told him anything, so how the fuck does he know just about everything that's going on, on the inside? He's either doing the rapes or he knows who is and he's running the show. Well handy for a down at heel hack short of a good story - direct your own!

But Yip was still on the front foot.

'And aren't you just going to give him a serious leg up! He's got legit reason for visiting Koor. He's got legit reason for using that drop address and you can't prove he sent you those messages. Yet you're going to nick him for rape - a crime writer - he'll fucking love it!! You'll make him a fucking fortune!!'

Filmer looked like he'd been punched the face, Fernandez looked down and wished that she was not there.

30.

The hotel room curtains were heavy and drawn tightly closed. Not that it mattered; it was only 6pm but already dark outside. The bedside light was on and Yip lay wide awake. As was Koor - lying beside him.

The post-coital conversation was a tad unconventional.

'What are you telling him about?' he asked, staring at the ceiling.

'Who?'

'Our little friend from the press.'

She was on her side, facing him. On hearing this she rolled over and tried to get out of the bed. He grabbed her by the shoulder and pulled her back.

'Don't worry, its only general stuff, nothing about Willow as such, not that that's much of a secret any more. He's more interested in Filmer. Wants to know what makes the DI tick, the sort of pressures he's under, a sort of human interest slant on the man in charge of a major police investigation.

Yip sneered. 'Yeah? Really? And then, more conciliatory, 'Just you be careful. He's a weasel.'

'I know what I'm doing.'

'Yeah, I bet. How much are you getting?'

'Nothing. I wouldn't take money from him. Not like some people I know.

Yip did not like this. He rolled over, nearly on top of her.

'What do you mean by... what d'you know?'

She wasn't fazed, she knew she'd hit a nerve.

'He pays people for information – he pays coppers for stories, that's how he makes a living, they all do, everybody knows that….'

'Yeah, I know that. You shouldn't be getting involved in it though, think about your career.'

'I am. Oh, I certainly am.'

'Yeah I know. C'mon, out of here, you're due home soon, your watchdogs'll be wondering where you've got to.'

31.

Filmer was south of the River in an anonymous office block that served as the headquarters of the Policing Standards Agency. He sat in a bare room with two men. They were smart, young, middle class types, graduates recruited from the campuses. They spoke in clipped, Etonian accents. They listened, Filmer spoke.

'He's getting something out of it. Steve does nothing for nothing. He's friendly with the bloke and they've just got to have something going between them.'

One of the smart young men asked a question.

'Have you suspended him from the investigation?'

'No. What good would that do? He'd soon find out what was happening. If I took him off the job I'd have to lose the rest of the team. Besides, he's good - and I need a result on this, badly.'

The same smart young man spoke again. 'So what do you want doing? Not exactly being very specific....'

Filmer got annoyed, his voice rose a few decibels.

'What I do want is for you to start having some fucking respect! So stop talking to me like I was a piece of dirt - it's cunts like me that are doing the job that you fuckers feed off.'

A few seconds of stunned silence followed, the two smart young men looked at a Filmer like a couple of student doctors would regard a patient with a new disease they were just learning about; with a sort of academic regard. Filmer reddened, and continued, trying to recover his composure.

'Right. I want a life-style analysis. I want his bank accounts looked at, his e-mail checked, his phone checked, the full works. I want to know him inside out. Is that clear?'

'Okay Guv, we'll give it the full works. You can leave it to us.' The police slang in a posh accent sounded ridiculous and the sarcasm was not lost on Filmer.

'Are you trying to be funny?'

'No guv, course not.'

Filmer stood up and walked out of the room. The PSA men looked at each other, exchanging smirks.

32.

On his return to Paddington Filmer walked through the general office and saw half a dozen officers crowded around a television showing a London Islamic cleric being interviewed.

'We cannot assist the police. It is up to them to find the rape victims. Statements have already been given. What more do the police want?'

Filmer's attention was grabbed as the interviewer pressed the cleric.

'But the victims seem to have gone missing, the police are concerned for their welfare….'

The cleric was typically anti-authority, anti-Britain, anti-everything except the Islamist agenda.

'The police are concerned for their own welfare. They have raided three addresses looking for the victims, why are they not raiding addresses to look for the rapist?'

'Presumably because….'

'Presumably, presumably, why do we have to presume? I presume other things. I presume that the police have deliberately lost these victims so that they no longer have to investigate the rapes!'

The cleric raised his voice and this last sentence was spoken directly to the camera.

The camera shot changed abruptly to that of the interviewer who hurriedly went on to announce the next topic.

Filmer was livid. 'How the fuck did that get out there?'

'It's everywhere guv, ever since we visited the victims gaffs.' Fernandez was trying to be reasonable to calm the DI down. She knew what he was thinking.

33.

Filmer walked into his office, closed the door and shut the blinds. He sat down wearily. When would this ever end? Twenty eight years in the job, the last ten as a DI. He spent his days in a continuous state of anxiety. Although looking healthy, his blood pressure was sky high and he had constant lower back pain. His doctor had told him to take more exercise and cut down on his drinking. Joke. He sat stewing for about an hour, doing nothing in particular. Then there was a rap on the door. The rapper was Fernandez who did not wait to be invited to poke her head through.

'Come and see this guv,' and she was gone, back into the main office where the TV was still blaring. Filmer followed her and his jaw dropped when he saw the breaking news.

The scene was one of an east London street burning, a reporter in a flak jacket was shouting at the camera.

'What began as a fairly peaceful demonstration about the

perceived lack of police action regarding the recent spate of rapes of Muslim women, has become a running battle between police and Young Jihad members. Nine officers have been injured and twenty seven people have so far been arrested.

Considerable damage....'

34.

That bulletin sparked off a media storm. Filmer's phones and inboxes went white hot; by 6pm he was out on the street, walking, he's had an idea. He walked North West along the Harrow Road, an hour later he was just north of Shepherds Bush, under a tangle of flyovers, at one of the rape scenes.

Police tape remained draped around the area which had been forensically examined. He stepped through the tape and looked around, his eyes jumping back and forth, searching. He looked at the ubiquitous CCTV cameras, a feature common to all of the scenes. Then he started taking photographs on his phone. Haltingly and hesitant at first, but then he got into a sort of rhythm and developed a method, picking up speed. He knew what he was looking for; he had a theory and was testing it. And he visited all three scenes.

35.

Having taken about 60 photographs Filmer could hardly wait to get back to his office. But as he walked through the doors of Paddington Police Station his pace slowed. What if he was right, he thought. What happens then? He walked up to his desk with a feeling of dread. He sat down and navigated his way into the CCTV system, using his workstation to view the scenes through the cameras. Frowning, but his eyes darted around each screen.

Then he sighed and sat back. His expression was one of tiredness, sadness and resignation. The only way to find the camera blind-spots was through the cameras themselves. He reached down to his bottom drawer and pulled out a half full bottle of grouse and the large crystal whiskey glass that had been a present from his wife.

A couple of slugs and he was back at it, working feverously, using the keyboard and roller mouse to delve the shoals of data, zooming in on graphics, columns of figures, video clips, maps. He clicked on some video footage and frowned. It was grainy war scene reportage. Gulf. 1991. Rows of bodies.

He moved on, transfixed. Then a beep sounded and the screen changed to show the face of the senior PSA3 man.

'Mr Filmer, just thought I'd run something past you before close of play today, are you....'

'Yeah go on.'

'Well, it's not much but that seems to be the point. Your main man is giving off revealingly little. All his credit cards have been cancelled in the last three months, he's ditched his mobile; he runs his personal comset from Pacific Rim. Looks like he's unplugging himself, going invisible....'

This did not surprise Charlie Filmer.

'Okay, thanks, er, call it off now, I think he's okay...'

'Can't do that sir, got Snifferdog on it for another three days yet... you'll get the virement bill at the end of the week.'

Filmer could not resist a dig at this stupid jargon shit.

'*Virement Bill*, who's he when he's at fucking home?'

'Your Area Headquarters have to finance this sir, it's part of...'

'Yeah I know, I know. Thanks.'

Filmer cut the connection and muttered to himself, 'Stop the fucking world, I want to get off.'

36.

Liz Yip sat on her expensive sofa in her impeccable living room; she was dinking a glass of red wine. Wearing a black silk dressing gown over which her long black hair cascaded, she was perfectly still, and remained so as she heard the front door of the large suburban semi open and then close.

As he walked through the door of the living room Steve Yip's eyes went down; he could not look his wife in the eye – he was late, again.

'Where've you been Steve?' she asked, coldly.

He sighed, trying to sound tired, 'Working. As usual.'

She had anticipated this. 'No Steve. It's not as usual. Did

you keep the appointment today?'

'No. I've been very busy. I had to cancel.'

With that Liz Yip stood up and walked out, Yip followed her.

'Look, those tests are never 100 per cent... Liz... listen to me.'

37.

When Charlie Filmer walked into his office the next morning he found one of the PSA men waiting for him. He did not like this; the whole office would have seen the idiot and he probably would have been recognised.

'What are you doing here? What's wrong with a phone or secure link?' demanded Filmer.

The PSA man offered no explanation for turning up unannounced.

'It's nothing really, just one thing came up.'

'Go on.'

'His home number came up in a free ad. He's selling some furniture. Has all the signs of a bit of a domestic if you know what I mean.

Filmer was interested. 'Okay, wiz me a scan of the ad. Today. Now fuck off. This lot can suss you buggers a mile off!'

The PSA man smirked, turned and walked out, just as Yip

walked into Filmer's office.

'Yes?' asked Filmer, deciding to front it out.

'Who was that?'

'National Crime Squad, why, you not happy? Anything I should know?

'Plenty.' And then Yip turned and walked out also.

Filmer slumped into his chair, hit a button and spoke to the terminal.

'Give me the links display.'

The screen image faded and was replaced by a graphic chain sequence, linking numerous keywords, dates, names, places. Filmer scanned these, talked to the machine as he did so, swapping streams of consciousness with the machine.

'Islam. Anti-Islam. London. Women. Woman. Mosque. Flyover. Friday. Friday Prayers. Rape. Sex. Break stream. Re-commence. Islam. Sex. Rape. Purify. War. Jihad....'

Then the machine beeped and a chipvoice cut in:

'Request from Fernandez to break in.'

'Yeah, go on.'

Fernandez's face appeared the on screen. 'Great minds Guv ... you just bumped into me.'

Filmer did not try to hide his frustration.

'I don't understand... I don't understand where we seem to be heading.'

Fernandez concurred. 'Not sure meself. I reckon it's political. Positive. The databases are full of cross references to allegations of racism. Every time something bad happens to a Muslim one of their leaders starts screaming conspiracy by the authorities....'

'Yeah, Dez, for Christ's sake stop going on like this, you sound like... I dunno what's got into you. We know all this shit, we know the Islamists are milking it, but wouldn't it be nice to know where the victims are and, another minor detail, who's fucking doing the sodding rapes!' Filmer was stuttering and spluttering his words.

Fernandez tried to recover some sort of order.

'I know, look guvnor, you don't have to talk to me like this, I'm doing my best, it's management that forces these systems on us in the first place, we're only playing the game by your rules, the system clearly....'

Filmer was having none of this.

'Don't lecture me about the system Dez. The system is there to *not* solve crime, it's there so that when we're getting bloody nowhere we can say we are doing our best with the best equipment that spares no expense. The actual results, when we ever get any, are got through us lot... you lot... having ideas. Same as it always was. Now just....'

The young woman interrupted. 'Alright alright alright alright. I'll get on with it!'

And with that she was gone. Filmer just carried on at his terminal as if the heated conversation had never happened, such was its ordinariness. Then his eyes and mind were jerked into focus by something on his screen. It was a shot of a small ad.

'miscellaneous items of furniture, chair, stool, highchair, cot'

Filmer frowned at the screen and muttered to himself, 'Cot? Cot? I didn't think he....'

Then he swung round and picked up the phone. Scrolling through an options menu he chose a number and gave the dial instruction.

'Personnel? Yeah, DI Filmer, 6 Area OCU. Can you dig me out your file on DS Steve Yip and tell me his date of joining the service... what...I don't have access to that...can you just ring me back? Okay, thanks.'

He cut the connection and continued staring at the screen until he glazed. He switched to television news.

Not only were there scenes of more demonstrations and headlines in the Muslim press claiming that police were ignoring rapes, the news stream featured shots of banners proclaiming that the police themselves were the rapists.

38.

'89? Thanks,' Filmer was talking into his desk phone, hands free. He continued, 'When did officers have to start giving DNA samples on joining the service?'

The voice at the other end replied immediately,

'August first ninety one. Officers joining before that time were not required to submit. But many did it voluntarily. Yip is one of them.'

Filmer remained silent for a few seconds before cutting the connection.

Yip was walking south down Edgeware Road when he felt his smartphone vibrate. He did not even slow down as he pulled it from his pocket, smiling as he viewed the screen. Ducking into a shop doorway to get out of the drizzle, from another pocket he extracted a second phone and stabbed out a number. A few hundred yards away a public booth telephone rang and a waiting Bobby Koor smiled and picked up the receiver.

39.

Plante lay on his bed, a cigarette held between his teeth. Smoke shot upwards with each powerful exhalation.

He surveyed his walls, covered with newspaper cuttings of Islamic militancy in London. It was coming together.

And there was certainly something coming together. Less than two miles south, an Uber cab crept through the traffic across Vauxhall Bridge and turned left along Kennington Lane. The two rear seat passengers were enjoying a joke.

'Nice one,' said Yip as he peered out into the gathering darkness. 'Where are you taking us Bobs, come on, even the driver has more idea than me.'

'Don't worry sweetie, I'll take care of you,' replied Koor, smugly. 'I'm the caring sort, aren't I Mo?'

'Certainly are, Miss,' replied her regular driver.

A twenty second silence followed and a frown appeared on the detective's face.

'Oi madam, what's going on, you setting me up or something? Not sure if I like the feel of this shit....'

But she interrupted, 'Okay, we're here. Stop panicking you wimp. Thought you had a sense of adventure. What's the matter with you?'

She leaned forward and gave the driver a note as the car drew to a standstill. He did not attempt to either look at the money or give any change, just fingered a button on his steering column causing the nearside rear door to swing open. The passengers alighted, the door closed and the cab re-joined the traffic.

Yip decided to remain silent as his escort led him across the pavement to the entrance of a large, semi-derelict looking building. She was grinning as she took out a key and opened the wide, heavy black door. They both entered, side by side.

Had Yip been able to see the building from the other side of the wide avenue he would have seen that its roof was a cupola dome topped with an Islamic star and crescent.

40.

Charlie Filmer leaned heavily against the bar, nursing a pint of strong lager. He was slightly drunk and deep in thought. Vaguely aware of his dishevelled countenance, he made the effort to pull himself together. He straightened up and looked around, blinking to gain focus on his surroundings. Then something caught his attention from behind the bar. It was the barmaid; she was Asian or middle-eastern. She had her back to him as she mixed a drink on the worktop beneath the optics. Between the worktop and the optics was an ornamentally fragmented mirror in which the detective viewed her face. She suddenly stopped working as her black eyes, reflected many times as downsized images in the numerous glass facets, met Filmer's gaze. He looked away quickly, almost guiltily. But something stirred within him; an unpleasant feeling which snaked slowly but determinedly from the pit of his stomach to the front of his brain. He left the bar, and his pint, and walked out. Nobody noticed the haunted look on his face.

Filmer walked a little unsteadily to his car. He got in and put his thumb on the printlock. A chipvoice announced an excess of alcohol in his blood. He hit a button to override this and the car started.

41.

Koor strolled around the dimly lit room; it was spacious and untidy; there were rolls of material, crates, boxes of files, everything stacked haphazardly. Yip stood still, slightly nervous, occasionally glancing around him.

'Come on then, ask me why we are here,' said the woman.

But Yip was on to her, or so he thought.

'No. You're obviously trying to scare me with some psychobabble shit. I'll wait for you to tell me why we're here.'

She stopped suddenly and stared at him coldly. He returned the stare, cocking his head to one side. And then his watch buzzed. He looked at it and then looked up and around.

'I need a phone, Filmer wants me.'

'Where's your mobile?'

'Ditched it. Don't want her indoors tracking me. Not when I'm seeing you, anyway.'

Koor threw him her mobile.

'Here, she can't track you on mine. Unless you've given her my number, that is.'

'What the hell would I do that for?'

He tapped a number, taking care to withhold that of the phone he was using, or so he thought.

Filmer, dishevelled and still half pissed, was back in his office.

'Where are you Yippy? Something's come up. I've had a thought... is that bloody journalist mate of yours still seeing Koor?'

Yip did his best to respond professionally, which was somewhat difficult with Koor stood right next to him.

'How would I know Guv, I'm not in touch with her - him.'

Yip's strange little slip did not go unnoticed by Filmer and a silence ensued.

'Guv?' Yip was keen to keep the conversation going,

knowing that he had just screwed up.

'Yeah Steve, I heard you. See you tomorrow. Cheers.'

'Yeah okay Guv, I'll be in early.' But before he had finished this last sentence Filmer ended the call. Yip took Koor's phone from his ear and looked at it and realised that it was a Government Issue device.

He frowned. 'Does the withhold caller option work on these?'

'No idea darling, never tried.'

He looked up at her; she was sneering at him.

42.

Filmer plugged his mobile into the console on his desk and hit the keyboard. A few seconds elapsed before the assignee details of the phone from which he had just received the call came up on his screen.

SUBSCRIBER DETAILS METPOL 76590 --- CIV STAFF

KOOR NSY

He sobered up instantly. 'Jesus Christ!'

He punched a fast dial number onto his screen, a chipvoice answered instantly, 'State your requirement.'

'Get me central eleven three five, urgent!' A radio burst into life as Filmer was being patched through to a mobile unit.

'Central eleven three five, what's the position with your subject – is she at her h/a?'

The reply came from the bored and supine voice of a typical surveillance officer.

'Negative. Left h/a alone 35 minutes ago, we think in a mini-cab. All quiet at h/a.'

Filmer was incredulous, but asked the rhetorical question anyway,

'Anyone follow her?'

'Not that we could see from here,' came the answer.

'No, you - I mean any of you lot - did you get in behind her?'

'Negative. Not in the brief. Static op for subject's security only. Sorry.'

Filmer banged out instructions on his keyboard and stared intently at the screen.

'Come on, come on, where's that phone.'

A chipvoice responded, 'Geographia reference 54 4B Dunlop Street, 200 metres south of Elephant and Castle station.'

Filmer tapped another button and spoke, 'MP from Bravo Delta Seven, give me station to car with all units Central South!'

43.

Koor sensed Yip's anxiety and sought to distract him. She put one arm around his neck and applied her free hand to his crotch. It worked. Looking over her shoulder, his hands dropped to her rump slowly then, very suddenly he lifted her. Her knees bent either side of him and he had her supported on his hands. She arched back, holding his lapels and grinning at him.

'C'mon then darling,' she oozed, 'Rougher than ever. Rougher than ever before!'

Then she arched herself farther backwards and slammed forwards, her forehead delivering a crushing blow to the bridge of his nose. He dropped her, holding his face, blood gushing through his fingers. He staggered back, wide eyed, as she stood and laughed, hands on hips.

'You don't know what rough is, mate. Do you know why I've brought you here?'

He just stood there, weak kneed and speechless, both hands still to his face. She answered her own question.

'To show you something. To show you how uncosy life can be.'

'What the fuck,' he managed, weakly.

'You know perfectly well who is raping my sisters, don't you.'

'What?'

'You heard. You know exactly what I'm talking about

Steve.'

He gathered himself, a bit.

'No I don't. But you're probably talking shit, as usual, you're fucking out of your….'

She raised her venomous voice. 'You know all about these rapes Steve, a lot more than I do.'

'Are you saying I did them?'

'I may be. You wrecked the decoy operation. That must have been deliberate.'

'What, when we had a grope in the bushes? You're fucking joking! If you've been that worried why haven't you said something before now?'

'And let you know I suspected you? I'm not that mad.'

'Oh, so you admit you are mad then, eh?' Yip let out a manic laugh, 'You're a fucking psychopath, you bitch….'

Koor remained calm, assertive, keeping control.

'No. You are mad for thinking the world takes you seriously. I don't actually suspect you of committing the rapes. But you are responsible. The Metropolitan Police is responsible, corrupted by cowardice.'

Yip threw back his head and let out another cackle of laughter, which looked bizarre coming from his bloodied face. Koor continued, raising her shrill voice.

'Stupid, ambitious, frightened people running around like

headless chickens!'

Yip steadied himself, concentrated on his breathing and examined his blood soaked hands, feigning nonchalance. He looked up, cocked his head to one side and said,

'Finished?'

She was wrong-footed by his sudden composure.

'What?! What?!'

'I said 'Finished'. Are you quite finished?'

'No,' and with that she produced another phone and tapped out a number without losing eye contact. It was answered almost immediately. Yip could hear the chipvoice on the other end.

She spoke, 'You have rape, corruption. Add a mosque. Come out of the Elephant on the north exit and turn left. You'll see lights. Hurry. Now.'

44.

Martin Plante frantically dressed and literally crashed, rolling and somersaulting, down the staircase from his flat to the street below as if his life depended on getting somewhere.

Three miles south, Yip and Koor were now seated opposite each other in the dilapidated mosque, about ten feet apart. He had not needed her to tell him not to leave, which in turn told her she was onto something. He was sailing to the centre of the storm. 'Call who you fucking like,' he had told her, 'I've got fuck-all to worry about.' And so they had just sat there for a full 15 minutes, glaring at each other, she motionless, he smoking.

Neither flinched when the door came in with an ear-splitting crash. Uniformed, gun-toting police piled in with blinding flashlights and loud shouts of 'Armed police, don't move!'

'Hands on your head, come on, get them in sight!' This was from the squad leader to Yip.

Yip did as he was told, and began to sweat profusely. Two policemen frisked and cuffed him. Then Charlie Filmer walked in, tie loosened, hands in pockets.

'Got you Steve. You're under arrest. Rape.'

Yip grinned, 'Thank fuck for that guv. I thought it was something serious.'

Filmer continued, 'Times four. You do not have to say anything but it may harm your defence if you fail to mention….'

Yip wasn't having anything of this, 'Yes, yes, I know the caution guv, I also know about evidence and I can't wait to see what you've got on me.'

Filmer resumed, '… anything you may later rely on in court and anything you say be given in evidence against you.'

Yip shrugged, 'Righto. I'll say fuck-all then,' and then, pointing at Koor, 'But what does she have to say?'

Filmer raised his voice. 'All she has to do is thank her

lucky stars we got here….'

Yip was quick to counter this, 'No. I'm thanking *my* lucky stars you got here. She's off her fucking trolley!'

'Thought you were going to say fuck all.'

'Just trying to help,' replied Yip as he was handcuffed and led away.

'We don't need any help,' shouted Filmer, but Yip was again having the last word,

'She made a call just before you got here. Watch her, she's got all the answers. Watch her Filmer, watch your fucking back!' And with that Steve Yip was pulled out of the door and out of sight.

Filmer looked across the room at Koor who was leaning against the wall like a mildly curious bystander.

'Who did you call?' asked Filmer.

'Press.'

He was incredulous, 'Press? What the hell for?!!'

Koor shrugged, 'Make sure you lot did your jobs properly. Anyway, what about me? I was nearly a rape victim, wasn't I?'

Filmer was reminded he was dealing one very dangerous person and decided to play safe, 'Yeah, course.' He turned to a uniformed sergeant, 'Er, give her... give Dr Koor a lift to Area Headquarters, make her comfortable...' then something hit him like a sledgehammer. He broke off mid-sentence and turned slowly back to face Koor. His voice was measured, controlled.

'What jobs, how did you know we were coming?'

She remained calm, almost casual, shrugging again.

'I didn't. But it was a good guess, wasn't it.'

Filmer was struggling to process this rapidly changing matrix. But he kept his breathing steady and looked around to regard his surroundings. When he spoke he did not try to conceal his confusion.

'What in God's name is this place? Did he bring you here?'

She smiled, 'Nope. Other way around. And it has nothing to do with God. See you back at your office.'

And with that she stood up and allowed herself to be escorted out by the sergeant who gently put a foil blanket over her shoulders. She had successfully adopted the role of victim.

Filmer continued to survey the scene around him. His officers were conducting a search of the building. He gathered himself and addressed two of the search team supervisors.

'Okay, Mr Miller, Mr Wort, careful what your chaps are doing, this may be a scene of previously unreported crimes, seal all this off once the search is done. Preserve anything you find for the Forensic Science Unit. And get a photographer here….' He was then interrupted.

'Will this one do?'

Filmer swung round to see Martin Plante walking in through the door, accompanied by a youth with a camera.

'Get out Plante. One flash of that camera and you're banged up for a fucking week! Anyway, the real press are probably on their way. Get out of here!'

Plante was unfazed and continued walking towards the livid DI.

'Wait Mr Filmer. She called me here. She brought him here. D'you know the full picture? I don't. But there is a picture and it's a big one. Bigger than me. And bigger than you.'

A similar perception had been dawning on Filmer over the preceding few minutes and his next words were half to Plante and half to himself.

'She brought him here. She brought him here. Why? Knowing that we'd...' his voice trailed off.

Plante hadn't quite caught this, 'What?'

Filmer continued his reverie; 'Yip, he's... look, just.... No. You're coming with me.' He indicated to the photographer, 'Send him home. Come on.'

Filmer sat in the driving seat, a puzzled Plante his only passenger. They fiddled with their seat belts.

'Am I under arrest Charlie?' laughed Plante, nervously.

'You know damned fine you're not under arrest – and it's Mr Filmer to you.'

'So where are we going then – Mr Filmer?'

'Shut the fuck up. You've got lots of questions to answer….'

As he started the engine there was an urgent rapping on the driver's side window, which Filmer wound down. A uniformed sergeant peered in.

'Guv. You best get back in there. We've found something.'

Filmer got out of the vehicle but before he slammed the door he turned to Plante. 'Stay here. Don't fucking move or speak to anyone.'

'Okay, okay,' replied the hack, 'Take it steady.'

Filmer followed the uniform back into the building, the interior of which by now was brightly lit with search unit arc lamps; the forensic team was giving it the full treatment. Filmer was led across the open space in which they had found Yip and Koor, and towards a door leading to the rear of the makeshift mosque.

The uniform walked through the door and stood aside to watch Filmer's face as the DCI took in the scene before him. After nearly 30 years in the job nothing really surprised the old detective, and what lay before him was no exception. Surprise was not the word. Surprise is the effect of something contrary to expectations. What he was now seeing could never have been expected and therefore did not give rise to surprise. But the tidal wave of possibilities engulfing Filmer over the following thirty seconds weakened his knees and rendered him breathless.

The centrepiece was a three-paned theatrical mirror bordered by light bulbs, all lit up. Filmer walked towards it, mesmerised by the illuminated, triptych reflection of his own haunted face. His eyes fell to the table beneath the mirror, littered with makeup paraphernalia. He slowly took in the rest of the scene. A chair and wig-stand. Items of black clothing, including a chador. A long black wig. A vague awareness of something strange about the face of the wig stand nagged him. His eyes began to dart from one item to the next, speeding up, widening with realisation.

Outside in the car Plante was making a call.

'What's going on, where are you?'

'In police custody,' replied Koor, as if it should have been obvious. 'Well, not quite, but I will be very soon. Where's Filmer. They found my little den yet?'

'What are you on about? Have you been arrested? What 'little den, what are you on about?'

Koor was sitting in the comfort of the victim suite at Old Kent Road Police Station. Stood beside her on her own phone was DS Fernandez, she was listening to a very aeriated Charlie Filmer.

'Don't let her walk out. Take her into custody, under arrest, do you hear me?'

'What offence guv?' Asked Fernandez, quite reasonably.

'Er, perverting the course of justice, that'll do for starters, I'll explain to the custody sergeant when I get back, and don't let her speak to anybody – incommunicado, d'you hear me?'

'Yes guv,' and with that Fernandez snatched Koor's phone from her, put a hand on the grinning woman's shoulder and gave her the news. Koor threw her head back and cackled,

'Now there's a fucking surprise!'

45.

Half a dozen or so phone calls later and the shit was really hitting the fan. It's not often that very senior police officers turn out for duty late at night, but a seriously perplexed Deputy Assistant Commissioner Reza Choudhary rose to the occasion and was in his office in full uniform at 3 o'clock in the morning. Stood in front of him was an exhausted Charlie Filmer.

'Are you quite serious? She's been faking rapes. How?!'

'How? Because she knows the bloody system, that's how! The question you ought to be asking, guv'nor, is not how, but why!'

Choudhary was stressed enough as it was without being spoken to like this.

'You bloody tell me, Filmer,' he shouted. 'You've been co-ordinating the enquiries - or rather you obviously haven't!! Christ man. She was working for you. She's an employee of the Metropolitan Police. What in God's name has gone wrong?!'

Filmer paused and momentarily eyed Choudhary with interest; he liked the fact that the pompous twat was sweating and had spittle on his lips. He decided to play cool, take charge.

'Let's keep the lid on it sir. We'll manage. We'll turn it round. She's infiltrated us - that's the fact of the matter. She probably never was a genuine service employee. She's a sleeper, and now she's active and ripping us apart. We have to limit the damage....'

Choudhary was having none of this. 'No! No whitewash Filmer. I want this fully aired in public. Whitewashes back fire. We're not in the nineties now. It's hearts and minds these days. We have to bend over backwards and apologise, openly and fully....'

Filmer interrupted, laying on the theatrics,

'Please tell me you're joking, sir. If we do what you're suggesting then every rapist convicted with the help of Koor's evidence will be released. She's profiled scores of sex attackers. And murderers. They'll all lodge appeals. Her evidence will be discredited by this shit and all the convictions will be quashed as being unsafe. Don't do it, please.'

Bullseye. Choudhary visibly crumpled in his big padded chair, his eyes dropped, unfocused, as this scenario hit him. Filmer stood in silence, waiting.

'Get out.' The order was barely a whisper but Filmer complied, knowing he'd won.

46.

The night wore on and by daybreak the search team and forensics had finished their work in the mosque; the exhibit list had been posted electronically to the supervising ranks and the corporate mood was one of stunned disbelief giving way to a groundswell of political manoeuvrings and realignments. Conversations were hushed, eyes were down and heads were shaking.

The two policemen sat a few feet apart facing each other in the small room. There was no table between them; instead lay a pile of transparent polythene exhibits bags. Steve Yip wore the white paper overall of a detainee.

Yip turned one of the bags over in his hands, peering incredulously at its clearly visible contents.

'A mask? A fucking mask?'

Filmer explained, 'Fake scar tissue, bottles of makeup, wigs, the lot. She's faked the fucking lot. Using your semen. There haven't been any rapes Steve.'

Yip eyed the other bags on the floor and then looked up at Filmer.

'Christ. That'd explain the one at Ealing hospital. She must have gone back there straight after she acted as decoy.'

Filmer nodded, slowly, 'Yeah, that's probably right.'

Yip looked back at the bag he still held and stared again at the prosthetic burned face within.

'She must be some sort of nutter, she….'

Filmer interrupted, 'How long have you been giving her one?'

Yip sighed, 'Couple of months, three maybe... I'm in...' he sighs again. 'Fucking hell!'

'Well, I suppose I have to ask you what you were doing in that dilapidated mosque with her.'

Yip shrugged, 'She took me there. It's been good.'

'Yeah, I bet it has.'

The two men looked at each other for 5 seconds in silence, an understanding forming between them.

Filmer broke the silence, 'Go on. Go and get some sleep.'

'I'm going sick guvnor. I'll be at my home address.'

'Okay mate,' comforted Filmer, give me a call when you feel up to it, we're going to need one big witness statement from you.'

Yip pondered this for a further few seconds, then stood up and left the room.

47.

Yip was back in his own clothes when he walked unsteadily down the steps from the big, modern police station. Once on the pavement he looked up to get his bearings and something caught his eye. That something was Martin Plante sitting alone in a car parked on the other side of the road. Yip steadied himself and focused his reeling mind. Any attempt to control his temper was nipped in the bud when he saw the smirk on Plante's greasy pockmarked face. He straightened up, looked left and right and then marched across the road. Plante stopped smirking as he tried to activate the central locking system. He was too late and Yip yanked the door open and took hold of the reporter by the hair and collar.

'You fucking knew about this shit! Didn't you! You fucking knew all the time you total, out and out scumbag!'

Plante didn't offer any real resistance, allowing himself to be pulled from the car.

'Steve behave yourself! Behave yourself...I didn't know...I still don't know what's going on! All I know is you've just been locked up and released...there has to be a funny story there....'

He was interrupted by a hard punch in the kidneys. But the reporter continued his quest for knowledge.

'What the fuck... has happened, just tell me... s'nothing to do with me....'

Yip spun him round and punched him square in the mouth. Plante's eyes rolled with the force of the blow, bloody saliva flying into Yip's face.

'You're lying. You were with her on the night of the deployment. You told me. You boasted to me that you had followed her home. You must have seen her do something. On that night!'

Plante was frightened now. He was being seriously assaulted by a copper not twenty yards from a police station, surely this would be stopped. Wide-eyed, he looked around, no one came. He decided to talk, rapidly.

'The hospital. Ealing Hospital. I asked her about that...

she... she told me she had a friend in there... night worker on the psycho ward... she said it had nothing to do with....'

Yip interrupted. 'There was another rape reported from there that night - we kept a press blackout on it. So now think!'

Plante was certainly doing that. 'You've... you mean she....'

Yip kept up the coaching. 'That's better. Now you're using your mind. Remember detective training school. 'Use of mind and memory' Martin. Do it and you will get answers from seemingly nowhere. A good detective needs no knowledge, only experience, from that grows instinct and wisdom! Now go and think hard and publish your fucking story. Blow the fucking lid off of it!'

And with that Yip released his grip and the reporter slumped backwards against the car and slid to the ground, bloody and exhausted by his ordeal, but nonetheless struck by an idea, a revelation.

48.

Koor had slept well. Filmer and Fernandez had not. The psychologist faced to the two cops across a table in a small interview room. She had insisted that she did not want a legal representative. She was relaxed, eyeing her interlocutors with an almost academic interest. The room was brightly lit and recording apparatus was running.

The exhausted Charlie Filmer began proceedings. He cautioned Koor, who feigned a stifled yawn.

'I am led to firmly believe, Doctor Koor, that you are involved in a series of serious offences. These will be itemised throughout the following interviews, when we will go into the evidence in more detail. First of all, it should be recorded that you are an employee of the Metropolitan Police Service, you are now suspended from duty pending the outcome of this enquiry....'

Koor butted in, 'I bet you're finding this really difficult.'

Filmer ploughed on, 'If at any time you change your mind about not wanting a solicitor present you may....'

Koor shook her head and leaned forward across the table.

'Look, Rob. I admire your tenacity, if that's what detectives like to have, but all you're going to get from me is abuse. No co-operation. Just abuse.'

Then, as if to exemplify her message, her demeanour changed abruptly. The calm, considered tone deserted her, the academic aloofness vanished. Her face became a mask of sheer hatred.

'Just fucking abuse! Abuse and lies! It is my right to abuse and confuse you. I am Fedayeen. I am a sister of Islam!'

This did Filmer a favour, woke him up. All these years of facing psychopaths across tables in interview rooms had equipped him to deal with this. He suddenly found himself in his comfort zone. Accordingly, he just stayed silent for a few seconds; it was his turn to regard his opponent with considered interest. And then he gave it to her.

'You are nothing but a stupid, dangerous person. You have

found nothing else you're capable of but being dangerous and destructive. It's all you are good for. First of all I accuse you of the most serious charge against you. It is what you have been arrested for. You have wasted over three hundred and fifty thousand pounds worth of police time. You have behaved corruptly as a public servant. Would you like to tell us why?'

The psychologist regained control of herself.

'I have done a lot of good work for the Police. I have helped put many bad men in prison. You cannot say that I am corrupt. You have nothing on me. You'll probably just end up getting a doctor to say I'm mad then end my contract on medical grounds. That's all that's going to happen, a bit of probation perhaps, but nothing more. You know that as well as I do.'

'Why did you fake the rapes?' came the question, evenly.

Then she lost it again.

'To show you people up for what you really are! Arselickers. Stupid arselickers with electronic toys and cameras and statistics and careers and fast cars and theories. And by God I have done it, haven't I! How can you now deny that you never really investigated those rapes properly? It's going to come out in tomorrow's papers that the police claim that there were never any rapes in the first place. That they were all made up by a Muslim woman! A single Muslim woman who just happened to be working for the racist, cross-worshipping filth of the Metropolitan Police!'

What happened next made Dez Fernandes consider her

boss's mental health. Charlie Filmer burst out laughing. And then, as if the scene was not bizarre enough, the door crashed open and in stormed Suzannah Seymour. Red-faced and chaotic of hair, she launched herself at the startled Koor.

'You fucking bitch!! What have you done to me? What have you done to me?? You were supposed to be mine. My girl who was going somewhere. You've destroyed me - you've….'

Filmer and Fernandes were up and around the table, they got hold of Seymour and dragged her out of the room. Koor just sat there, smirking.

49.

And Steven Yip, dressed in suit, shirt, tie and leather shoes, ran. He kept a steady pace, his face glistening with sweat, eyes fixed on a point in the distance. His face that of a man on a mission.

As Yip ran Plante wrote. His words appeared in capital letters on the screen as he stabbed the keyboard.

MUSLIM RAPES - DID ROGUE POLICE FAKE THEM?

Meanwhile Filmer and Fernandez were also busy. They sat on either side of a table in a small conference room. A chaotic pile of papers and photographs was spread out between them.

'Where the hell did she come from?' Fernandez asked the question for both of them.

Filmer felt a breakthrough coming on. 'I think you've just

answered your own question, look.'

He selected and passed her some old photographs of scenes of middle-eastern devastation, depicting torn down buildings, bodies lying in streets. Hell on earth.

'These were found at her place. She called herself a 'fedayeen' in that interview... look.'

He picked out and handed her a typed transcript of the interview, pointing at the relevant text.

Fernandez read and then tapped in the word on her phone. She read out loud, 'Fedayeen - the first real Islamic fundamentalist organizations in the Muslim world... demanding strict application of the sharia and assassinating those it believed to be apostates....'

She was interrupted by a young detective bursting through the door.

Guvnor, sorry, you'd better come to the briefing room. Best you come too sarge. There's been another one.'

Filmer was baffled.

'Another what?'

'Another rape, sir, up on Hammersmith's section. The uniforms have got the victim coming in here. They figured as you were here....'

The rookie didn't get to finish. Filmer and Fernandez jumped to their feet and barged past him through the door. They marched along a short corridor and into the main briefing room. A number of officers were already assembled and there was a tense, expectant atmosphere. Filmer headed directly for the small ante-room in the corner from which a uniformed woman police officer was just emerging. She barred his way for a moment.

'She's going to help us, sir, she's going to stay the distance.'

The DCI nodded and entered the ante-room. It was dimly lit and a large colour screen was showing a video link of the rape victim being interviewed. The sexual offences officer was not visible, but her questions were audible. Filmer only had ears for the victim's replies.

'My name is Hallee Shirat.'

'I am 44 years old.'

'I work at West London College.'

'Yes, as a teacher.'

'He was about 6 feet.'

'Chinese. A Chinese looking man.'

'A London accent.'

Filmer just stood there, gaping as the hijab-wearing woman gave an articulate and detailed description of Detective Sergeant Steven Yip.

***

Horses Mouths

You may shoot me with your words,
You may cut me with your eyes,
You may kill me with your hatefulness,
But still, like air, I'll rise.

Does my sexiness upset you?
Does it come as a surprise
That I dance like I've got diamonds
At the meeting of my thighs?

Out of the huts of history's shame
I rise
Up from a past that's rooted in pain
I rise
I'm a black ocean, leaping and wide,
Welling and swelling I bear in the tide.

Leaving behind nights of terror and
fear
I rise
Into a daybreak that's wondrously clear
I rise
Bringing the gifts that my ancestors
gave,
I am the dream and the hope of the
slave.
I rise
I rise
I rise.

Maya Angelou, 1978

Prologue

My mother died in childbirth. Instead of casting me aside

the big momma midwife thrust me into my horrified father's arms like a consolation prize. Nor did he dash me to the floor either, holding me tight instead as he witnessed his wife's last gasps. Then soon I was on the *Windrush*, bound for the mother country. It wasn't the *Windrush* really, that boat went out of service ten years earlier, but it sounds good, and nobody checks.

There must have been a lot of blood spilled that night; most of it on the bedsheets and floor. There's a lot of blood being spilled right now, the difference is that it's going into a bottle. I clench and unclench my fist, the cannula in my arm hurts, the blood ebbs and flows, the bottle fills.

1.

Detective Inspector Sasha Bensen sat opposite Abdul Reza in the small, spotless interview room in a central secure unit of Belmarsh Prison. Beside Reza sat Peter Glass, his solicitor. Beside Bensen sat Detective Sergeant Paul Gates. A silence had befallen the meeting. Bensen broke it.

'Think about it. Mr Glass must have told you about the possible prison sentences you could attract - 15 to 20 years. It's my duty to inform you that a system exists for you to help the authorities and help yourself, by way of a text – a letter – to the judge'.

Reza turned to look at Glass. 'What's she mean… what's she on about?'

The solicitor began to explain to his client. 'She has a point but it's a matter for you. There is a system in which the sentencing judge can take into account help given by a defendant to the police. But there are no guarantees that it will have any effect and it does depend on you pleading guilty.'

Reza had listened but was less than impressed.

What sort of help? If you mean I could get favours for giving information to the police you must be fucking joking! I could get....'

Bensen interjected, 'the ball is in your court really Abdul, it's up to you. Your pleas and directions hearing is at the Old Bailey on the first of next month and we'd....'

But Reza was ahead of her, 'Would a number do?'

The copper was flatfooted by this, 'Pardon?'

Reza repeated his question, 'I said would a number do'?

Bensen shrugged, 'Depended where it led to.'

Reza countered, 'That's up to you, innit. I'll think about it.'

2.

Marc Lassiter sat behind his big, ostentatious desk. He wore cufflinks but no tie and was fond of saying if the tieless look was good enough for Richard Branson then it was good enough for him. The window was behind him and he liked that; he liked that anyone in front of him would be looking at little more than a silhouette. On this occasion the man sat in front of him was junior solicitor Peter Glass. Standing at Lassiter's side was the practice manager, a fat and sweaty man called Paul Phelan.

Glass had been called in to see his boss and knew he was in

trouble, because it seemed that he was always in trouble. Glass was the only black brief at Lassiter and Co and suspected he had been taken on so that the firm could tick the diversity box. But Lassiter had never liked him.

'I gave you a golden opportunity, Peter, and you've thrown it back in my face. I think we'd better call it a day while we're both in front.'

Peter Glass felt his stomach turn. This was not totally unexpected and he'd considered the disastrous consequences of being sacked. Getting another job would be far from easy; his pride deserted him, anger and the need to feign disbelief replaced it.

'But… I don't understand Marc. I thought I was doing okay… only last week you said….'

Lassiter cut in, raising his voice, 'Never mind what I said last week. Last week was last week. This is now. You've been mixing it downstairs. Since you had that display of temper with the practice manager others have been jumping on the band wagon. You've….'

Glass got off the ropes; it was his turn to raise his voice.

'What? You're joking, I never said anything about that to anyone… you're just making this up so you can get rid of me… why? Not enough work coming in, eh?'

Lassiter jumped to his feet, propelling his chair backwards against the window. He was shouting now. 'Right. On that remark alone get out of here!'

Glass, his heart thumping, became outwardly calm. He

stood up, slowly, and moved towards and to the side of Lassiter's desk, a manoeuvre deliberately made to make his sacker nervous. It had the desired effect. He spoke slowly, quietly.

'Oh, so what happened to the progressive, straight talking law firm then?'

Phelan decided to show loyalty to his boss.

'Settle down Peter, settle down....'

Glass did not take his eyes off of Lassiter, who he saw was starting to tremble. He maintained his calm, laced with a hint of menace.

'Settle down? Settle down? Do you realise what you're doing to me? I'll fucking sink....'

Despite his nerves Lassiter managed to keep control.

'You should have thought of that. Get out. Clear your desk and get out. Now. Stay with him, Paul, I don't want him sabotaging the place.'

Phelan stepped forward and got in front of Glass to stop him getting nearer the senior partner. The fat practice manager put his hand on Glass's shoulder.

'Come on Peter, we don't want any trouble, let's go to your office and I'll help you pack your stuff mate.'

Glass did not take his eyes off of Lassiter, who although now sweating profusely, was maintaining firm eye contact. Glass turned and walked out of the room, Phelan waddling behind him.

3.

Back to me then. So, I walk across Waterloo Bridge in the wind and rain, carrying a heavy pilot's case containing the contents of what was my desk. It's still only midday on a Monday, a weird time to be suddenly out of a job. I've been at Lassiter and Co less than a year and so have no employment rights, no recourse through the tribunal system. Oh, I could complain to the Law Society, but that would be a spectacular own goal, *'back o'the net'*, so to speak. Might just as well leave the legal profession altogether if I do that.

So I just walk, and walk. In Soho when the weather really takes a turn for the worse. I duck into a pub and buy a large scotch, down it in one and order another one. And then another one. My thoughts get deeper and darker. And an idea begins to form.

4.

Back in the offices of Lassiter and Co the senior partner was pacing about barking orders at his fat practice manager who sat at a conference table eating pot noodle out of its canister with a spoon.

'Right. From now on I've got full conduct of the Abdul Reza case. Get me all the relevant files, notes, telephone messages. Everything. I'm doing nothing else from now until the case is complete and ready for trial.'

Phelen, despite his faults, was an experienced case manager. 'You're joking, what about all the….'

His boss cut him short, 'If I joke I'll tell you and you'll

know when to fucking laugh, okay?!'

Phelan nodded with his mouth full, and kept on shovelling.

'Until then take everything I say very seriously. I have to have complete control of the Reza case. I've got a good working relationship with the police officer on the job and it'll be a high profile trial and it'll do the firm a lot of good.'

Phelan continued to nod, and shovel, unperturbed. It was no good arguing. Lassiter continued his rant.

'Now, about Glass. I don't want that bastard haunting us Paul'.

There followed a pause, Phelan rammed another spoonful into his gaping maw.

'What does he know about the second LSC billing on the copyright fraud case?' continued Lassiter.

'Nothing,' mumbled Phelan through his mouthful. 'Fuck all. He didn't do anything on the case. He's only been involved in the Reza case since he got here, and he writes everything down and I see everything he writes.'

'I hope you're right... how the fuck do you eat those things all day, you make me feel ill!'

5.

Not many left these days. Had to come to Kilburn to find one. She tells me her name is Bridie. Bridie McNernie, an

Irish landlady, one of the last of a dying breed.

She shows me to the room I'd seen advertised in a local shop window. It was at the very top of the big terraced house with creaking stairs and ghastly décor. Crucifixes all over the place. The room is good; spacious with a boxed off loo and shower and a little electric Belling cooker in the corner. The place would fetch a fortune in Chelsea or Notting Hill.

I smile, tell her its fine and bung her a oner up front. She smiles and takes a Yale key off a bunch in her hand.

'Fine Mr Fraser, that's two weeks you're ahead. Can I ask you to remember not to come in too late at night, my husband is disabled and sleeps on the ground floor. And no visitors please, 'specially not women. Shall I make you some soup?'

I am a bit taken aback by the last question. 'Oh, no thanks, I've not long eaten,' I lie.

'Right you are then, make yourself at home and I'll take my leave of you now.' And with that she waddles out of the room and down the stairs.

I looked round at my new 'home'. Wow, no paperwork, no leases or licences or other such tosh, just a bunch of tenners and a nice smile. And me being a black man as well. But blacks and Irish had grown up together in this neck of the woods. Back in the sixties English landladies would put up signs in their windows saying 'Vacancies. No dogs, no blacks, no Irish'. Now there were no English left in Kilburn.

6.

Deborah Glass sat motionless at the end of her dining table in the small suburban semi. There was both coffee and wine in front of her. She touched neither. The flickering of the muted television did not distract her. Her athletic black face was taught with shock and the onset of worry. Her phone was on silent but as the call came in it vibrated and moved aimlessly like a stunned insect on the shiny table top.

She picked it up. 'Hello.'

Glass kept it short, he didn't want a row.

'I'm fine. Room 9, 16 Mulholland Avenue, NW6 0QK.'

The phone went dead. She had not taken in the information and tried to call back. No answer. But he had guessed what she needed and the text containing the same information followed within 40 seconds, with the additional instruction – 'delete this now'.

7.

The CID office in Bermondsey Police Station was never all that busy, in fact. Rumour had it that the manor was a high crime sink job, and it certainly was. It was also a fact that the majority of the occupants were themselves criminals and never bothered reporting to the filth when they got robbed, burgled or dealt a sachet of baking powder.

Charlie Saggs was sat at his desk talking on the telephone. 'Yeah, hello, good morning. Can I speak to Mr Glass please?'

The person on the other end asked who was calling. 'DC Saggs, OKR Police. Old Kent Road, you know, the big new police headquarters, serving the wider community and all that.'

At this point he put the receiver against his shoulder and muttered an aside to a colleague on a nearby desk:

'Dopey foreign cow.'

Then, back into the receiver:

'Yeah that one. Look I need to speak to Mr Glass, is he in?

On the other end of the line sat Miusze Li, a bright trainee, she felt uncomfortable but had been briefed as to how to respond to calls like this one.

'Mr Glass doesn't work with this company any longer. Can I ask what case you are calling about please?'

Saggs frowned, 'Case of Reza Ahmed my dear. Up at the Old Bailey on the 1st of next month, pleas and directions, who's dealing with it at your end now?'

Miusze said something that Saggs didn't catch, 'Who?' Again he didn't catch the name, but went on anyway, 'Okay, can you ask him or her to give me a call, the CPS has instructed me to discuss a few formalities with your firm about the current state of the case, that's all, the number is 020 3214 6754. Okay. Thanks. Bye.'

Saggs hung up and turned to his colleague, one Detective Sergeant Henry Gates, 'That's odd. Peter Glass has left Lassiter's. I thought he was doing well there.'

Gates just shrugged, uncaring.

8.

I'm lying here on my back at the top of Mrs McNerney's house. With the peace and privacy comes a feeling of power, it's a steady flow, not gushing, just steady. I'm getting stronger by the minute. I'm looking at the cracked ceiling and the cobweb in the corner; they're all connected you see. Even the spider has made use of the crevices in the plaster, different building materials, organic and mineral, working together like rope and steel. I let my brain make similarly unlikely connections, weaving back and forth, up and down, trying to stay random and purposeful at the same time. The sun is going down, turning everything a bit red. Dark red.

9.

A week has gone by now and I'm fitting the bill. Mrs McNerney is happy with my money and my behaviour – I rarely go out and have no visitors – and I've been shopping; bought myself a bicycle. Always wanted one. It's like a mountain bike with skinny wheels, ideal for dispatch riding, the man in the shop told me. Just what I need, together with the high viz jacket, the helmet and the anti-pollution mask which covers most of my face.

And now I'm out working, doing my new job. I've got a parcel to deliver to a very special recipient.

10.

Marc Lassiter sauntered around his minimalist apartment in Pimlico in his silk dressing gown shaving. He was thinking about the day ahead, looking forward to the evening that would follow, an evening of fine dining followed by some late night adult entertainment. It was a Friday you see; lads' night out. It had been a good week and he needed to be entertained, a few lines of the best Peruvian and a spot of dusky flesh to warm his cockles perhaps. Well, never mind the 'perhaps', he was set on it, and would therefore have it.

The intercom rudely interrupted his planning. He walked up to the apartment door, still stroking his face with the buzzing razor. He pressed the button and the small security screen lit up, revealing a masked cycle courier standing in the rain with a parcel.

Not expecting anything, Lassiter felt entitled to ask, 'Yes? Who is that for?'

The amplified voice was loud, distorted, 'Transcend Dispatch. Parcel for Mr Lassiter.'

Still feeling the need to be dismissive, 'I'm not expecting anything, who's the sender?'

'Dunno sir. Just says Marc Lassiter and then this address. Oh, it says something else too, er, in brackets, at the top, R.V. Reza. Look sir....'

'Yeah, okay, I'm coming down, it's one of my cases.'

Right, here he comes; my face mask is tight, parcel in one gloved hand, pen and clipboard in the other. The door opens and there he stands, resplendent in silk dressing gown.

'Sorry to bother you sir,' I say, as I hand him the parcel. He takes it and I proffer the clipboard and pen. He says nothing, puts the parcel under his arm, takes the board and pen and scrawls on a dotted line under the printed name and address. The paper form is A5 size, the board is much bigger, more like foolscap. I watch as his thumb makes a nice firm contact with the shiny black plastic. He hands the board back to me and makes to turn around, staring at the parcel he's now holding.

'Er, my pen sir,' I say, apologetically. 'Oh, right,' and he gives it back before disappearing. No 'Goodbye' or 'Thanks.' Rude twat, didn't even look at me, needn't have worn the mask.

I stick the board in my waterproof shoulder bag, mount my trusty steed and peddle off.

11.

Lassiter walked across the deep pile of his living room carpet, turning the parcel over in his hands, weighing it and frowning at the scrawled block capitals identifying his name and address. The bit that said R v Reza rattled him, for some reason. It was about eight inches square and an inch deep. By its weight and feel Lassiter could tell that the item inside was sumptuously packaged, probably in a layer of bubble wrap beneath the brown paper outer skin. He took it into the kitchen and began work with a pair of scissors. Thirty seconds later he had in his hand a DVD.

There were no markings on the disc. Still looking at it he made his way slowly towards the home entertainment centre located in the alcove between the kitchen and living room.

Then the telephone rang. He stopped and his head turned to face the handset on the dresser. His landline, probably just PPI, he thought, but walked slowly towards it and leant forward to see the words 'no number' on the screen. Normally he would have ignored the call and let it ring out. But something made him pick up.

'Yes?' he said, quietly.

'What d'you think of that then honey pie?' It was a woman's voice, loaded with threat.

'Think of what? Who is this?'

The voice continued, sounding hurt, 'Jennifer. It's your lovely Jennifer Marc. I want to know what you think of the video. I'll call later.'

The line went dead. Lassiter took the handset from his ear and looked down at it, and then again at the disc in his other hand.

12.

'I'm sorry, he no longer works for this firm. Can I ask which case you wish to refer to?' Miusze Li was sat at her desk in the busy general office at Lassiter's Law. There was a woman on the other end of the line this time.

'What do you mean he doesn't work for the firm, what's happening, I'm his wife and he hasn't been home for two days… I'm worried sick, when did you see him last?'

Miusze did not like the sound of this one bit. Way above her pay scale.

'Oh, I'm sorry, er, I think you need to be put through to the senior partner Mrs Glass, hold the line please, hello, hello Mrs Glass, you still there?'

She looked around the room, another member of staff had overheard this and was looking across. Miusze offloaded, 'That was Peter's wife, she doesn't know what's happened, he hasn't been home, and she hung up on me. What the hell do I do now?'

'Push the shit uphill Miusze,' advised her colleague, without hesitation.

'Yeah, I will, is Marc in yet?'

13.

Here I am in the present tense first person singular, sat in the Capricorn Club in Goodge Street. I like this place. Full of criminals, prostitutes and drug dealers. Not that I'm interested in doing business with any of the above; I just enjoy watching others do business, others who should know better.

I'm on my second bottle of Corona – and it'll be my last at eight quid a throw. Then in she walks, Jennifer Mason that was, still looks at home in this place. Takes all kinds, you see. I met her when I was cop, about ten years ago. A typical black woman, hasn't aged at all. I helped her get rid of a pimp, got him five years, put her on the straight and narrow; she went on to become a nurse. We're here for old time's sake; get her in the groove, so to speak. She's perfect; tall, slim, athletic, articulate – and deliciously mischievous. My kind of woman. My woman.

14.

Lassiter did not like the way his hand shook as he put the DVD into the player. He pressed play and took a pace backwards. What he then saw made him feel sick.

'Hi Marc, how are you?' said the black face from behind the screen. 'It's been a long time. I really think we should meet again soon. I have a problem which I need to share with you – because it's your problem too, or will be if we don't get our heads together'. The face winked, the clip ended and the screen went fuzzy.

He didn't recognise the face, but he recognised the background. He knew immediately that he was going to be blackmailed.

15.

I'm bleeding again. A nice steady dribble. If it starts to gush a bit too strongly I nip the line. I only need 20 mils. 20 mils at a time, into the bottle and then into the fridge. I must have nearly a pint now, but that's imperial measuring and we're not supposed to do that anymore. Keep it metric. I've got another problem. The fridge in my room in Mrs McNerney's house is tiny. About an eighth of the size of a normal one. When I've bled out into it enough there won't be any room for any cans of beer. Not to worry, I can always go to the pub.

16.

At just after 10am Lassiter swept into the outer office of his law firm. He was rattled by his recent movie experience. He wore no tie as usual and his cufflinks were in his trouser pocket, shirt cuffs consequently down over his hands, one of which clenched his jacket like it was a dead animal.

Miusze Li stood up, not to greet him, to stop him. If he got to his office she would not get another chance before lunchtime.

'Marc, I need to speak to you, it's urgent.'

Lassiter slowed but still tried to walk round her. 'What is it?' He was past, with her following.

'Peter's wife rang, she hasn't seen him for days.' He stopped and slowly turned. 'What?'

'She obviously doesn't know, she thinks he's gone missing, I didn't know what to tell her....'

Lassiter was walking again, through the door of his office, with Miusze in tow. He threw down his jacket and turned to face her again. 'Not our problem. He was sacked. If he's decided to go off in a strop it's down to him.'

'What do I say if she calls again?'

He shrugged as he fiddled with his cuffs. 'Just tell her the truth; he no longer works for this firm and left our employ three days ago. We've got no idea where he is.' He was now fastening his cufflinks. 'Put out an email to all staff, telling them to say the same. Copy me in.'

He was by then sitting at his desk, his eyes on his in-tray. Miusze turned and walked back into the general office, head down, frowning, thoughtful, mentally writing the email.

17.

Alone in his office, Lassiter took the DVD from his jacket pocket and put it in one of his desk drawers. He switched on his PC, activated the VR application and began to dictate a letter to the machine. 'Letter to the Crown Prosecutor, South East Headquarters, case of R v Reza Ahmed.'

18.

Three miles away, in the OKR CID office, Jim Saggs is talking to his boss, DI Sasha Bensen. She is a 35 year old career detective with an Oxbridge education and a lightning brain.

'I can't do much about it Guvnor. I've told the CPS and they're gong direct to Lassiter's. It's a shame, that Peter Glass was okay to deal with….'

Bensen interrupted him, 'Don't trust Marc Lassiter Jim, let the CPS deal with him. He's an extremely dangerous man.'

Sags didn't like this condescendence, who the fuck did this bitch think she was, advising him like he was a fresh faced PC. 'Really?'

She picked up the sarcasm and flashed a glare at him, 'Yes. Really.'

19.

Back at Lassiter's Miusze Li is at her desk, wearing a headset so that she is able to answer her phone whilst typing. A call comes in and she answers.

'Good afternoon, Lassiter's Solicitors, Miusze speaking, how can I help?' She hears a woman's voice.

'I would like to talk to Mr Glass, please; it's about my brother Abdul Reza.'

Miusze closed her eyes and delivered a short, prepared speech. 'Mr Glass no longer works for this company. Mr Lassiter is now dealing with Mr Reza Ahmed's case personally. He's not available at the moment, can I take your….'

The line went dead and the dialling tone cut in. Miusze opened her eyes, frowned and set about writing a brief email, reporting the call.

20.

Detective Chief Inspector Sasha Bensen sat in her small cluttered office. Her phone was on hands free, it buzzed and she answered by stabbing a button on the consol.

'Sasha Bensen.' Her voice was flat, matter of fact.

'Sasha Bensen.' The male voice echoed her tone. She recognised it immediately and picked up the handset.

'Keep it short. What is it?'

The familiar male voice asked a question. 'Has Reza got a sister?'

Bensen replied with a confidence she did not feel. 'No. definitely not. He has no family. Why?'

'We need to talk.'

She agreed, 'Certainly sounds like it. I'll ring you this evening.'

She closed the call without further ado. Then she sat and just stared into space. She had been through a lot to get where she was. More accurately, she had put others through a lot. But there were times when having to maintain total control took its toll on her. On these occasions, like the one she was going through now, she would just sit like a statue for ten or fifteen minutes and run through a mental mantra. Staying in total control was a state of mind she achieved by listening to each of the screaming sirens in her head and picking them off one by one until she could hear only silence.

21.

Deborah Glass sat on the edge of her sofa smoking a cigarette. She had a telephone to her ear and had just dialled a number. She remained calm as she listened to the ring tones, counting them to keep her mind focused.

After eight rings a female voice answered and asked Deborah how she could be helped.

'I'd like to report my husband missing.'

'How long has he been missing for madam?' asked the police communications officer.

'Three days.'

There followed further questions, obviously from a questionnaire, and within 90 seconds the call was over. Deborah lowered the phone and then remained motionless, save for her smoking, which she did mechanically for some minutes, before rising and stubbing out the cigarette and then turning on the television. She also felt in full control of the situation.

22.

Daly's Wine Bar in London's Strand has for decades been a favourite watering hole of the criminal bar. That is to say the overpopulated world of criminal barristers trying to climb the greasy pole whilst living on starvation wages.

The impeccably dressed Gordon MacNamara was not in that category. He had achieved senior status some years earlier and now enjoyed being bought drinks by members of the lower, arse-licking echelons. On this occasion however it was his round and he handed Marc Lassiter a large Borollo.

'You've cut it a bit fine Marc, frankly. I should have had the brief for this weeks ago. I'll need a junior, you know, and….'

The solicitor did not let him finish. 'I know, I know Gordon, I trusted a bloke to do the job and he's fucked me right up. Billed a load of shit to the Public Resources Board and not done a thing. I've sacked him but that hasn't got the work done. I'm putting the brief together personally now, you'll have it Tuesday morning… cheers.'

Lassiter took a gulp of wine before adding, 'Trouble is he's gone missing.'

Who?

'Nothing, doesn't matter. Cheers. I need a cigar.'

'Cheers Marc… well, just look at these two.'

Two stunning young women approached them and their thoughts turned to better things.

23.

Having a nice walk in the wind and rain. Four days is a long time when things are happening, and my God I'm making things happen. I can't bear to think if this is going to do me any good though, probably won't in the short term, not professionally anyway, but hey, if things go according to plan it won't half make me feel good. Christ it's freezing, might as well get myself a drink – while I can still afford one.

24.

Lassiter had an odd taste in motor vehicles. A physically small man, he was not keen on being looked down upon. So instead of the usual BMW or racy GTI he chose to drive an MPV, a people carrier. His excuse was that he could use it to ferry passengers to sumptuous events, hold on-board case conferences and entertain ladies behind the tinted rear windows. The truth was that he just liked sitting in an elevated position.

So it was in his black Mercedes MPV that he swept into the driveway of the Bamborough Club, an 18-hole extravaganza fashionably near to Wentworth. Once out of the vehicle he took the steps to the big entrance two at a time and tossed the keys to the uniformed greeter who caught them and opened the oak door without saying word.

He took off his coat and thrust it towards a second usher in the lobby before striding into the bar. Collapsing into a sumptuous leather chair he caught a waiter's eye and jerked his head once by way of summons. As the waiter approached, Lassiter's eye was caught by the entry of Sasha Bensen. The waiter got to him first and paused, seeing that he was not the focus of the member's attention. Bensen sat in the opposite chair.

'What would you like?' asked Lassiter.

'G and T please, large one.'

The waiter heard this and then turned to Lassiter.

'And I'll have a large scotch.' And the waiter was gone.

Bensen leaned back and crossed her long legs. 'Well, have we got a problem?'

'No problems, only solutions.' Christ, how she hated his smuggery.

'Oh, so cool. So cool. I'll be fucking sick in a minute. Have we or have we not got a problem?'

Lassiter was a bit stung by the prelude to her question, so simply replied, 'No.'

'What have you been up to then, bully-boy?'

This told him that she knew more than he thought she did. 'What? Come on, I don't need this.'

'Neither of us need this. So if it stops being fun we stop. Okay?'

'Speak for yourself. I lied. I do need this. I need it very much.'

Bensen continued the questioning. 'Why did you sack him? Bit cruel, wasn't it? You could've just taken him off the case. Reza hasn't told him anything – or so you say.'

He was not happy with her knowledge. 'How did you know I sacked him? He might have just left for all you know.'

She laughed, 'I know you.'

He was not laughing. 'I've a business to run. A business in which distrust is essential. It was getting to the point where I was going to have to trust him. No good. Out. History.'

Bensen shrugged, 'So, why worry?'

'Someone is trying to make contact with him. Someone pretending to be Reza's sister. Reza hasn't got a sister, according to you. And there's another thing, Glass hasn't been home for two days. His wife rang.'

Bensen became more thoughtful.

'Our intelligence is that your client has no family. But you're right about Glass. He's been reported missing by his wife. It's official, Peter Glass is a missing person.'

'What?'

'You heard. The uniforms are investigating.'

'Let's hope they do a good job then, I don't want the press hanging around my firm. Make sure they find him Sasha.'

'Don't you ever think about anything but yourself?'

'What?'

'Nothing. Doesn't matter. Reza rang me'.

'What?'

'I do wish you wouldn't keep saying that. Reza rang me.'

'What? From prison?'

Bensen was now having her patience tested by this self-centred rich boy.

'No, they let him out for the fucking day, for some fresh air and to make a few calls! Peter Glass gave him the phone cards during our last interview. Remand prisoners get three calls a day – Jesus, I can't believe you don't know….'

'Yeah, okay okay okay, leave me alone will you! Just give me a break... what did he give you?'

'A number. Safe deposit box in the basement of Selfridges, Oxford Street. Two million quid in Pakistani Bearer Bonds. Cash on demand. We just might have won the lottery my little friend.'

Lassiter took a few seconds to absorb this, trying to look calm. 'Fucking hell. What are we going to do about it?'

The copper had thought it through. 'I get a warrant for the box and we go there, just you and me, you to see fair play, I seize the bonds, take half back to the nick and you nick the other half. We have a divvy up later. Sound okay?'

Lassiter was always amazed by the matter of fact casualness of police corruption. She sounded like she was simply describing normal procedure.

He grinned and accepted, 'Yes ma'am.'

She returned the grin and with that they left their drinks, rose and walked out together.

25.

'Un-fuckin-believable, innit!' Saggs enjoyed being the bitter and twisted old detective and spent most of his time living in character. But he could not conceal his genuine love for the job and his passion for the darker sides of human behaviour.

'Bloody solicitor gone missing. On the missing list. Reported to the helmets downstairs, one of the duty skippers told me last night. It seems he's gone missing since he left Lassiter's. I reckon he's had the sack and topped himself.'

Gates sat next to him. He was used to these outbursts and only ever half-listened, picking up the key words and making the appropriate responses.

'Good enough for him. Shouldn't defend scumbags for a living.'

'You're all heart Gatesey.'

26.

A ruminative Marc Lassiter sat staring blankly at his desk. He was trying to understand what was making him do this.

He had plenty money in the bank and the business was doing well. Yet something was driving him to have a relationship with a bent cop. A beautiful and talented bent cop. And therein, he concluded, lay the reason. It was not the money that attracted him like a moth to a street lamp. It was the attraction of kindred spirits. Like him, Bensen thought she was above the rest of the human race, and he wanted to be above her, or at least be her equal. Having spent most of his life beating himself up for being a coward, he was beguiled by her audacity and wished to emulate it, absorb it as his own. The money was just an added extra.

His phone warbled and he picked up. It was Miusze Li calling from the main office.

'Marc, I've got a Jennifer on the line, won't give her surname or any other details, says it's personal, d'you want her?'

He had to take it. 'Put her through.'

He waited for the click that signified the line was open and went straight in. 'Look, I have not the first idea who you are or what you want, but if you continue to harass me I'm going to involve the police, do you hear?'

The female voice on the other end was calm, reasonable. 'Yes. I hear. But you don't. Try to think. About your little meetings. Your flash new transport. Try to think, and, perhaps rethink, about glasshouses. And stones.'

And with that she was gone. Lassiter lowered the receiver, slowly, still staring at his desk, frowning. Ten seconds elapsed before he changed over to his mobile and called

Bensen.

27.

Just over an hour later Lassiter and Bensen were together again, this time on the summit of Primrose Hill in north London. It was cold and windy and they struggled to light their cigarettes. Before he could start telling her about the call from Jennifer, Lassiter was being questioned by the cop.

'You never did answer the question – why did you sack him? You should get some answers ready for that one.'

The lawyer was straight on the defensive. 'Wasn't billing enough. Wasn't earning the firm enough money.'

She was not impressed. 'Don't believe you. Do your figures show that?'

He changed tack, 'And, he was getting too close. Too close to the staff in the office, too close to my contacts at the bar, I told you before – my game depends on a healthy mistrust, not on some Mr Nice Guy fucking ingratiating himself with all and bloody sundry. Wheedling his way into everybody's affections….'

She interrupted, 'But those aren't valid reasons, you can't give those answers to a fucking employment tribunal, they'll….'

Lassiter had the answer to that one, 'He wasn't an employee, he was self-employed, he wanted it that way for tax reasons. I could terminate at any time.'

Then Bensen got to the point, raising her voice above the

wind, 'Let's just hope Reza didn't give him the bloody magic number then!'

He responded in kind, 'I would have known if he had. Don't worry, I've got control!'

Now she was angry, 'Oh, really! How would you have known? Look, you have to show a lot of follow up on that. Your client expects help, if you can't show you did your best then the shit'll hit the fan….'

Lassiter seethed with resentment, 'Look, I know this. And I know Peter Glass. If he'd got that safe deposit box number then it would've been in his attendance notes. It wasn't. Now he's out of the firm and that's it.'

Still in charge, she ended the meeting, 'Okay. We meet at ten tomorrow morning at the store, Cumberland Street entrance. I'll be alone and I'll have the warrant to get into the box. We'll be given private access. I know the chief security guard there, used to be my superintendent, nice guy, soft as shite. Don't be late.'

And he was off, leaving the lawyer to gaze at the cityscape with the collar of his coat slapping his face in the wind.

28.

It took Lassiter nearly an hour to get through security at Belmarsh prison. Reza was being held in the high security unit; a prison within a prison. The Governor at Belmarsh had received information that a rival Turkish drugs gang was out to get Reza and had men in the outer prison waiting for their chance. Consequently the 21 year old remand prisoner was banged up 23 hours a day awaiting trial in solitary with the remaining hour spent in a highly supervised exercise yard with convicted terrorists and violent robbers.

When Lassiter walked into the sparse interview room his client was already waiting with a prison officer who left as the lawyer entered. Lassiter sat down and took out his notebook. The two regarded each other for an uneasy ten seconds. It was the first time they had met.

'Everything okay, Abdul?' asked Lassiter, cheerily.

'Yes. Where's Peter?'

'Oh, gone to a different firm. Doesn't work for us anymore. I'm taking over your case, so you've got the top man on the job now… ' The cheery countenance faded as Reza responded with an icy silence.

The solicitor continued, 'Erm… whilst I remember Abdul, have you got a sister?'

'No. Why.'

'I'll be honest with you… '

'Thanks'.

'Yes… some woman rang up our office claiming to be your sister. She asked for Peter Glass at first. Did you and Mr Glass ever discuss your personal or family background?'

'No. Apart from when he was filling in the form for the public resources. What's all this got to do with my case?'

'We have to be sure that we cover all the angles. We don't

want the police to come up with some story that you're the head of a big crime family or something, do we?'

Reza was forming a profound dislike for this patronizing twat. He moved the interview on. 'Have you read the statements?'

'Yes. Of course. I'm familiar with the case. I need you now to fill me in on some of the details. Just in case Peter didn't make notes about some things.'

Reza shook his head, 'I'd be very surprised. He made notes about most things....'

Lassiter jumped in, 'Most things, I hope....'

'Yeah, most things. Anyway, listen to me, have you spoken to Bensen lately. I rang her. She owes me a big favour – and you've got to see to it that I get it.'

Lassiter nodded, 'Yeah I know. She told me. Not the information you understand, just that you'd been cooperative. She's going to let me know the result....'

'She'd fucking well better had let you know.'

Lassiter was flummoxed, 'Yes. No. I mean I don't know what you're talking about but I know what you mean. Don't give me the information Abdul, I'll get to know soon enough after the police have done their job. Then we hit them for the big favour, okay?'

'Yeah. Okay.'

29.

Jim Saggs waved two fingers at the No Smoking sign in the CID office and lit a cigarette. He was holding court with three of his colleagues.

'Got to be dodgy. Bloody solicitor goes missing the day he's had the sack! Just happens to be representing a bloke on a 4 million quid's worth of cocaine importation charge! Just happens to work for one of the grubbiest firms in south London. Come on, lads. Who sat in his last interview with Bensen?'

Gates responded, quietly, 'Me.'

'Was it good stuff, Gatesy, or weren't you paying much attention?'

'The latter.'

They all laughed.

30.

Peter Glass stared at his wife, fascinated. The couple were sitting in a small tatty bar and Deborah Glass had just told her husband something.

'Brilliant Debs. Brilliant.'

The beautiful black woman grinned, 'I know, I fucking have to be, married to you.'

God, how he loved her.

31.

Paul Phelan sat at his desk, eating pot noodles, as usual. Marc Lassiter paced about, as usual.

'Some bitch wants to meet up with me. Says she's got some good info on Glass for me. I reckon she's more than likely to be working for him, though, trying some trick or other....'

Phelan interrupted, keen to halt the gathering tirade, 'How d'you make that out; what you on about? You getting fuckin' paranoid or sumthin'?

Lassiter bristled, 'Don't you talk to me like that, Phelan, I've taken out bigger than you before breakfast. . . shit, how much of that stuff do you eat? Must be like eating fucking worms.' Then, after a brief pause,

'Ever eaten worms, Phelan – Paul? I have. They forced us to in training. We....'

Phelan stopped chewing and glared at his boss, Lassiter stopped seeing danger ahead. He was actually quite afraid of his practise manager.

'Anyway... never mind. This woman, as I was saying, has got it into her head that Glass is going to blackmail me. Hah, that's a laugh; I don't get a chance to do anything to get blackmailed about! Hah!'

Phelan took another mouthful of noodles without taking his eyes off Lassiter. He hated him, but found special interest in observing this hyper little rich boy; how scared he was, how terrified he was that his whole little house of cards was going to coming crashing down any time soon. The prat was good at living by the sword, but the faintest possibility that death by the same device was looming sent him into wide-eyed tantrums; how dare the odds be not stacked in his favour, how dare they.

The day wore on and at close of business Lassiter was exhausted by his own apprehensiveness. He left the offices and took a cab across the river to the West End, went into the Charlotte Street Hotel, had four stiff double scotches and then took a slow and unsteady walk to the Zig Zag Club. He paid the extortionate entrance fee and lurched down the steep staircase into the dimly lit bar. It was early, a few scantily clad black girls sat around glumly chatting and a couple of heavies, the 'management' stood at the bar. They regarded him sneeringly as he slurred his request for a beer – you didn't 'order' anything in the Zig Zag, you requested it. After handing a ten pound note to the topless barmaid and declining any change – not that he was offered any – he walked slowly to a table in the corner and slumped into a chair. He sipped his beer out of the bottle and tried to look cool. The management lost interest and turned back to their muttered conversations. The girls eyed him with little interest; they would wait till he was properly drunk.

32.

I didn't see Lassiter in the cab going north over Waterloo Bridge. I was walking south you see, head down against the wind and rain. Pissed off with the weather, I jumped a cab and got myself taken down past the Elephant and onto the Old Kent Road, alighting at the Thomas a'Becket pub. I had on a brown leather jacket, black woolly hat and jeans. I didn't go into the pub (not for black guys, that one) but just strolled down the road for a hundred yards or so till I got to my old office.

So, it went like this. I walk around the back of the building and toward some large 'wheelie' bins. They stand inside a small strongly fenced compound behind the office. Never really noticed them before. Hey weren't important. They are now. The bins are full of waste papers and old files. The tops of the bins are taped over with yellow tape to stop any of this confidential waste being blown away. I put my gloved hands high up on the strong wire gates and test their sturdiness. Barbed wire across the top of the gates and wall. Can't get over. As I turn away a gust of wind blows something across my foot. I reach down and pick up the object. It's is an empty noodle carton. The sun is setting as I pop the carton into a paper bag and put it in my pocket.

33.

Twelve hours later and the same sun is rising over the Old Kent Road. Lassiter is hunched at his desk on the telephone, the receiver held close to his ear. He is speaking in unfamiliar terms to a stranger.

'I've heard about you. You've telephoned this firm before. Let me make this perfectly clear, my client does not have a sister. I've checked this and he denies having any family….'

The female on the line remained flat-toned and reasonable.

'Of course he denies it, I'm here illegally, I came here as a student three years ago and I've been here illegally for the last two of them, for this reason I cannot go to the prison to visit Reza or contact him direct, you must understand, I have something very important to tell him and you must deliver the message. Where is Mr Glass? I....'

The lawyer was struggling to maintain his cool.

'He no longer works here. Tell me what it is and I'll pass the message on.'

'My money is running out, you'll have to ring me back, the number is – have you got a pen?'

'Yes, yes go on.'

'0208 4765889, you got that?'

'Yes, I've got ....'

Then Deborah Glass hung up and remained standing by the payphone in the hotel lobby. Lassiter dialled the number and the payphone rang shrilly.

The woman answered and continued talking without preamble.

'It's a warning. I've had a warning from some men. If Abdul does a deal with the authorities they will kill him.'

Lassiter did not know how to deal with this, so reverted to pomposity.

'Look, I can't discuss cases over the telephone. If you think your brother is in danger then I will go to the police on your behalf, there are ways that....'

The woman was prepared for this,

'No. Listen. My brother is not in danger. Mr Glass is in

danger. They cannot touch my brother but if he does a deal with the police they will kill Mr Glass. Do you understand? Where is he?'

Lassiter's brain raced for cover, this was getting very messy indeed.

'I haven't the faintest idea where he is! As I said, Mr Glass does not work here anymore. In fact... erm, well, that's it really. I'll contact the police on your behalf Miss er, Reza and make a report of what you have said to me....'

And the line went dead. Lassiter lowered the receiver slowly and ran through all the possibilities. His damage limitation check list flashed in his mind's eye, the boxes getting ticked at full speed.

34.

And here I am again, back at operational headquarters. I can't get used to this bleeding business, just isn't much fun at all. The cannula hurts like fuck and the bruising is as always bad afterwards. Just half a pint this time, that'll do. Nurse Deborah should be here, but she isn't; tending to real patients at the hospital, not mad fuckers like me. I'm surprised she agreed to this, but she did, she just won't help me actually do it. Yes, just half a pint this time, that'll do.

35.

But Deborah was not at the hospital. She was walking slowly along the north footway of the Euston Road, passing the neo-Gothic architecture of St. Pancras railway station. She wore a full-length greatcoat and black high heels. Her hair was tied tightly in a bun on the top of her head, accentuating her considerable height. Her hands were warm in her pockets, but her naked calves felt the cold.

A hundred yards west of her sat Paul Phelan at the wheel of the black Merc people carrier. At his side sat Marc Lassiter. They were both dressed casually in dark clothing.

Their eyes were on the tall black woman in the trench coat, it was after 9pm, the weather was filthy and the streets were almost deserted.

Phelan was first to speak. 'That her?'

Lassiter did not have a clue who the woman was, but tried to answer with authority. 'Yeah, could be, unless it's a tom.'

Phelan responded with genuine authority – he knew how and where prostitutes moved. 'Nah. Too fast. Wrong end of the street.'

Lassiter tapped a couple of times on his mobile. The two watched as the woman's right hand came out of its pocket and up to her ear. Lassiter's phone was on speaker.

'Yes?' asked the woman.

Lassiter issued an order. 'Okay Jennifer. Stop there. We have you under control. I will approach you on my own in a few minutes. When I ring off put your phone back in your pocket and keep it there. If I see you make another call the meeting is off. Do you understand?'

The woman said 'Yes' and did as she was told. She was standing with her back to the chained gates of the British Library as Lassiter strolled up to her.

'Right, I want to know….'

She kept her eyes down, fixed on the pavement. 'Keep walking.'

He had already stopped. 'Keep on walking and turn first left, go to the Ibis hotel, there's a room booked for you in your own name.'

This shook him, 'What, what the fuck…?'

'Go and check in and go to your room and wait for me.'

'What and get sliced up by some fucking yardie boy, d'you think I'm mad?'

'You'll be mad if you don't do as I say. You'll miss the best fuck of your life.' And with that she looked up at him, unbelted her coat and gave him a lingering glimpse of her beautiful body. He looked her up and down and nodded, before walking on as instructed.

36.

As he walked into the hotel reception he called Phelan and told him to wait where he was. Then he fished out his driving licence, checked in at the desk and picked up the key to room number 127. It was a double, freshly cleaned, the curtains were open and he closed them. He checked around, looking for cameras, recording devices, spy holes. Not that he knew what the hell he was looking for, or exactly where to look. He called reception.

'Er, hi, my secretary reserved this room for me, may I ask when she made the booking please, was it today?'

After a few seconds the receptionist responded, 'Er, it was today Mr Lassiter, this evening in fact, 2035 hours.'

'Thank you.' He said, and replaced the receiver. He was reassured, 45 minutes would not have been long enough to do anything elaborate. He took off his shoes and jacket and flopped on the bed. He might as well enjoy what was coming, although the warning klaxons were screaming in his head. Years of sexual risk-taking had taught him to ignore them. He lay there for ten minutes trying to work out where this had come from and to where it was going. But the image of what was under that trench coat was dominant and he yearned for the knock on the door. And it came, two quiet taps.

He leapt up and was at the spyhole in four strides. The fish-eye view did her no favours, but it was her and as far as he could see she was alone. He put the chain on and opened the door. She beamed at him through the gap.

'What you waiting for, I'm cold from that weather outside?'

He opened up and she entered. The coat stayed on, buttoned up to the neck. She walked over to the bed, turned round to face him and sat down.

Lassiter was utterly confused; he needed to find out more.

'Never mind all that for now - talk. I want to know what you've got to tell me and how much money you want for all this….'

'Money for all what Marc, I don't want any money from you, I'm your friend.'

'Just talk.'

She sighed.

'He hates you for what you did to him. He's looking to get at you in any way he can.' Then she stopped talking but kept smiling.

'Go on, or is that it?'

'He's been using me to do stuff, like the video in the Zig Zag, I did that, and I arranged the dispatch rider to deliver it to your flat.' She stopped again.

'Go on, keep going, I'm not impressed yet.'

'He says he knows stuff about you, that you live in a glasshouse so you shouldn't throw stones. He wanted me to back up a story that you had been scoring coke from prostitutes in the Zig Zag. I work there, you see. I've seen you there. He says you could be in trouble with your profession if they found out you used the place.'

Lassiter threw his head back and laughed sincerely, he actually did find it funny. Glass was going to try to blackmail him. He walked around the bed and flopped onto it, so that he lay with his head on the pillow with Jennifer's back to him. She swivelled round to face him and to watch his reaction with calm interest.

'Hah! Pathetic! Is that the best he can come up with?! That fucking shithole, and others like it, wouldn't survive if it weren't for the legal profession. We're the only bastards in this town with any money these days. As you probably know if you work in there. No, girl, this is bollocks. You're working for him, I knew it all along. That's why I'm here meeting you.'

She smiled down at his reddening face. 'Did I argue?'

'What?'

'I need to do business with you. You owe me a job, in a way.'

'What are you talking about woman?' His hand went up to her breast as he asked this.

'I was his paid mistress, before you sacked him. Now he's broke. He hasn't even paid me for the dispatch rider. So, like a true professional, I'm offering to turn. Interested?'

37.

Phelan sat in the Merc and hummed along to Radio 4. He liked classical music, and he liked the fact that he was getting paid for sitting doing fuck all. If that woman was a honey trap and Lassiter was about to get cut up and robbed, well, that was *his* problem.

He had just finished consoling himself with this thought when he had his own rather formidable problem as a hammer came smashing through the driver's window, followed by two big gloved hands which grabbed him like a rag doll and pulled him with such force that he came out of the vehicle and was on the pavement before he could even start trying to catch his breath, and when he tried he failed, such was the force bearing upon him. He was face down and could not see anything.

The thick Jamaican accent did all the talking.

'Bloodclat! Fuckpig! I've come for a bit of you!'

Phelan managed a strangulated screech, 'Wallet in back pocket. Take it. Take it.'

'Don't want your fuckin' money you white pig! I've come for a bit of you. You gonna listen to me?'

'Yeah, yeah, sure, I'm listening, I'm listening….'

'Prove your listening – lend me your ear.'

Phelan felt like his head was being crushed into the pavement, then the cold steel of the knife against his ear and then the white hot pain as his left ear was severed. It was not a clean cut; the terrified Phelen felt his assailant actually sawing off the ear, he felt the serrated blade go back and forth. He screamed, more with horror than agony – he had just lost part of his body. His arms were flailing but he could not get his hands to his head in time. Then the assailant stood up and delivered a savage kick to Phelan's left side, the tubby clerk felt his kidney rupture, he was sure of that. And then it was over and the attacker was gone, leaving his victim rolled up in a foetal position trying to stem the blood gushing from the wound where his ear had been.

38.

'Strip.' Lassiter issued the order flatly as he lay fully clothed on the bed with his hands clasped behind his head.

Jennifer stood, unbuttoned her coat and let it slip from her body. She was wearing nothing beneath it.

'Throw me that coat.'

125

She picked up the coat and, with one arm, tossed it to him. He frisked it and then slung it to one side.

'Raise your arms.'

She complied, revealing her armpits.

'Turn around.'

Compliance, again.

'Spread your legs.'

She put her hands on her hips and did as instructed.

'Touch your toes.'

Her arms fell forward as she arched back, the revelation of her nether regions caused Lassiter's heart to miss a beat. He was satisfied.

'Now I know you're not working for him.'

39.

Here I am again, hard at work. Had to buy a hammer and nails for this little job. Would have liked to have been a carpenter, but was never any good at woodwork at school. Anyway, this little job keeps my mind off what I just know is happening right now. Well, it isn't really, but I'm trying to put a brave face on. Never out of her comfort zone, my Deborah, always prepared to go the extra mile. But I married her, for better or for worse.

40.

It was just as well that Glass did not know the extent to

which his wife was going the extra mile. At that very moment she was straddling Marc Lassiter and her insisted use of the condom would have done nothing to appease her husband.

She arched her back and locked her lips on his as she felt him reach climax, and then it was over. She rolled off and lay beside him, her arm across his chest. She watched his face, keen to gauge the effect she had had on him, but he remained self-consumed, stony faced. Not much effect at all she feared, but to not have gone the full way would have amplified any lingering suspicion or doubt in his mind, so it had been a worthwhile precaution.

41.

Out in the Surrey countryside a car sped through driving rain. Its lone occupant, Sasha Bensen, gripped the wheel tightly and squinted through the thrashing wipers. Her head was splitting.

42.

Deborah held one of the purple sheets around herself and stared at the ceiling. Lassiter came out of the shower, looked at his watch and began to dress, hurriedly.

'Well?'

'Well what?'

'Do I get the job?'

'What fucking job?'

'The job of being your mistress. Your black bitch.'

'I'll call you.'

Then he left the room, closing the door quietly behind him. Deborah lay still for a few seconds then rose slowly. She removed the pillow case from the pillow and placed it to one side. Then she walked to the shower.

43.

The CID office was busy, it was 'expenses day' and a dozen or so detectives, rarely seen together, were busy conspiring and cobbling together embellished and often totally fictitious cash and mileage claims.

Saggs, his usual laconic self, sat at his shambolic desk. He was stirring himself to respond to some polite urgings by one of his more organised colleagues, DS Marion Carter.

'Yeah. I'll think about it. Do some actions. Cover my arse I suppose. One thing Glass's wife told me, he's got sickle cell anaemia. Maybe he checked in at some clinic. But there's nothing else. His phone is dead, no use on cards, no use of vehicle….'

Carter was not to be mollified, 'This needs to go to MIT Jim, it's too big for us.'

Saggs knew she was right, but dreaded the work entailed. 'Oh fucking hell Marion, I suppose it's down to me to write the fucking report to the MIT management to persuade them to take it on, it'll be quicker for me just to hack away at the job myself.' He paused, but she didn't speak, just looked at him. He sighed and went on. 'Yeah, okay, I'll do it today. Fuckin' hell!'

Carter shrugged and walked away, quipping over her shoulder, 'Hope so, I've got two tickets.'

44.

Detective Inspector Bensen was sitting in a steam room with a towel wrapped round her glistening body. Beside her sat Lassiter, similarly attired. They were alone.

The lawyer was the first to speak. 'Is it safe? As they say.'

'Yeah. S'pose so.'

'Good. He knows absolutely nothing. I've made sure of that. If he did he would be using it by now.'

The copper frowned, turning to face him, 'Using what? What are you on about?'

'His knowledge. The information, he would be using it to try and have one over me.'

'How would he do that?!' She was getting annoyed.

'Oh I don't know, probably go to the press or the Law Society or something, allege that my firm was involved in corrupt practice.'

Bensen laughed, 'Fucking hell, Marc, anybody could do that!'

'But he can't prove anything,' Lassiter retorted, 'Anyway, ripping off public funds is standard practice for small firms like us, we'd go down any other way. Those allegations come thick and fast – never get anywhere.'

This exchange tired them both and they fell silent for the moment, both breathing the hot water vapour deeply.

The lawyer changed tack. 'What's the latest on Reza?'

'Still in Belmarsh awaiting trial – you should know – he's your client! Why d'you think Glass is trying to get you?'

'A little bird has told me. A little blackbird, you might say. He knows nothing of any importance. I have a spy and the intelligence is reliable and reassuring.'

'Pray tell.'

'Ah ah. Need to know. And you don't. Look, Glass isn't the problem. Not the main one anyway. There's something else. Phelan got attacked last night. He's still in hospital now. It happened all too coincidentally when I was shagging this trollope Jennifer. Phelan was waiting outside in the van for me. By the time I got out to him he was in hospital minus his left fucking ear.'

Bensen jumped to her feet. 'Jesus Christ! I thought you said she was acting alone!'

'Seemed that way, but this guy must have been following her. Phelan said he had a thick West Indian accent, built like a brick shithouse.'

'Report it. Officially. Take the high ground.'

'Already have. Fucking GBH on my practice manager. Poor bastard's deformed for life.'

45.

I get off the bed, clench my fists a few times and do some simple exercises. I go across the room to the tiny fridge. I feel like I'm watching myself. I open the fridge door and stare at its contents – it's filling up nicely. The backlight shines through the contents and bathes my face in a red glow. I close the fridge door and move over to a cupboard from which I take a carton of milk. I sniff the contents, not too bad, and take a drink. I put the carton down and return to the bed, unsteady on my feet. I feel like shit.

46.

Two days later a somewhat contrite Marc Lassiter was talking to his practice manager.

'I'm so sorry mate. What did the plastic surgeon say?'

Phelan was trying to be philosophical, 'Prosthetic lug for me. Suppose it'll give me an excuse to grow my hair long.'

Lassiter tried to put another positive spin on the incident, 'We'll put a strong CICA claim in, you'll get a whopping compensation, I'll see to it, I'll say your earnings have had to be halved due to you not being able to meet a client.'

Phelan did not reply, just glared at his boss. Trust that cunt to boil this down to money, he thought.

I'm sat here stripped to the waist in my bedsit, my 'operations room', as I call it, having some doubts. Well, a lot of doubts actually. What the fuck do I think I'm doing, I ask myself? Do I really expect this to work? In one respect the answer is no to that question. The purported objective probably won't be realized. But there's another agenda, hidden way down, and that one's bearing fruit already.

There's a knock on the door and I know it's Debs. Cannot be anyone else. But why? What the fuck is she doing here?

I open the door and say to her, 'What the fuck are you doing here?' I try to sound cross but she always stuns me, takes my breath away. It's hard to sound cross or menacing when your voice goes up three octaves.

She walks in past me, I look out of the door to check that she has not been followed (as if).

'Debs, I told you, I'm alright. We agreed, only at the hotel….'

She turns round to face me, with that smile, 'A woman has needs'.

Then she dumps a large bag on the floor and begins to undress.

47.

I kicked Debs out of my room last night before Mrs McNerney discovered her there. No visitors, remember?

And now I'm standing freezing my bollocks off on the Archway Bridge in Highgate. I'm looking down and if you follow my line of vision you'll see that my eyes are on a black Mercedes MPV on the forecourt of a vehicle hire firm.

48.

Hard work and Jim Saggs did not go well together. So the grim-faced south London detective looked a lot grimmer than usual as he toiled over the missing person file of Peter Glass. Although middle-aged, Saggs operated the mouse and keyboard quite skilfully, making quiet, expletive-free voice notes into a small microphone as he did so. His words came up on a drop-down panel on his screen.

All credit facilities stop. Verify last date of use. Confirm no use on any since August 7th. Phone use stop. Enter. Confirm no use since last billing date. Vehicle HDM 472G. No movement outside postal area since August 7th. Voters – confirm not registered. Confirm standard practice for crime lawyers. Ex-directory cable address.

He was happy to be interrupted by DS Marion Carter.

'How's it going Jim?'

'Not bad girl, not bad. Quite interesting, really. This bloke really has disappeared. It's been over a week now and not a trace.'

Sensing he was in a less bad mood than usual, she decided to push her luck. She would regret it. 'You've checked everything?'

'Look Marion, I know what I'm doing, OK. If you're so worried about this 'misper' then you can help me. Go to court this afternoon and get an order on his bank accounts. I'll give you the details, there's enough to be going on with.'

He looked at her and she held his gaze.

'Well? Have you got time to lend a hand or not?'

Carter decided to rise to the challenge, she hated going to court and knew that he knew it.

'Yeah okay Jim.'

'I've upgraded the whole thing, it could turn a bit naughty if the press get a hold of it - which is only a matter of time….'

She was feeling brave now, 'Why? You going to tell them?'

He actually thought she was serious, 'Don't be stupid. I'm in enough shit as it is. Remember the uniforms've been faffing about with this for over a week now, somebody's bound to have gobbed off. Now I'm just making sure my back is fucking bullet proof.'

'Is the family kicking up?' asked Carter.

'There's just the wife. She's been on the blower a couple of times. Spoke to her last night. Very cool, calm and collected. Wary of upsetting us, I think, obviously bloody worried though, poor cow.'

Carter was on a roll, Saggsy was actually treating her like a colleague. She stayed in 'one of the lads' mode,

'Right, yeah. Oh come on, this bloke's probably just pissed off with his bit on the side for a few days. He'll turn up sooner or later – they always do.'

Saggs played along, he felt a bit sorry for her, 'Yeah, you're more than likely right. Let's see if we can find him first, spoil his fucking fun, eh? Then we can get on the piss!'

They both laughed.

49.

Just over a mile away Marc Lassiter was in his office talking to a tall smart man who sat at the other side of his desk. That man was Detective Inspector Robert Sherrell.

'You don't have to tell me about client confidentiality Mr Sherrell. This isn't easy for me but a man has gone missing who has just lost his job. At my firm. My practice manager was viciously assaulted whilst he and I were trying to investigate the disappearance. A client of this firm may have something to do with both incidents but would appear to have very little control of what is going on – difficult as he is in Belmarsh awaiting trial.

Sherrell just sat there, applying the science of silence.

Lassiter continued. 'This woman is the link I tell you. I reckon if you traced her calls to me you'd have your answer.'

Sherrell spoke. 'Have you shared your thoughts with DI Bensen at OKR?'

Lassiter knew the answer to this one. 'How can I? She's the officer in the case. It wouldn't look right. I think it's best if we keep it separate, don't you? Tidier. I'm prepared to help you but in return I want to be kept out of it. Nobody here knows who you are and the OKR Police will get a brief report only. And there's another complication.'

'Go on.'

'I have to come clean with you. I've met the bloody woman. When Paul got knifed I was…' He tailed off.

Sherrell was, for a change, quite interested. 'What?'

'I was trying to head off… I thought the bitch was trying to blackmail me. Sent me a video of a club I'd been to with Glass, dodgy place, he took me there of course….'

'Of course.'

'Look, if I help you can we keep the fact quiet. I can't be seen to be cosy with the local police.'

'Fine by me.'

'There's more. Been contacted by a woman saying she's Reza's (that's the client in Belmarsh) sister. He says he hasn't got a sister. Anyway, she, whoever she is, tells me that if Reza does a deal with the police then Glass gets done in – ever heard of anything like that in your life?'

Sherrell had not, ever. 'Report it officially tonight, I'll pick it up on the system.' And with that he stood up and was gone.

50.

Christ this place is hot. Minus three outside so Mrs McNerney's got the heating up full wack and now I'm sweating my bollocks off. I'm working hard though, on my knees on the floor working away at some DIY. Dad would have been proud of me, always wanted me to be a carpenter, not a bloody lawyer. He was probably right.

51.

The heat in the small white interview room was also full on. A uniformed police officer stood and made notes of what Paul Phelan was telling her, his head still heavily bandaged.

'He left the company last Monday morning. We have not heard from him since but his wife did contact us complaining that she had not seen him for several days. It would appear that he didn't tell her that he'd been... that he'd left the firm....'

The copper scribbled away. 'Did you contact police at that point?'

Phelan had been well briefed by his employer. 'No. Why should we have, nothing to do with....'

The cop interrupted, 'Yeah, okay, sir, just checking, carry on.'

Phelan carried on. 'We've had information since then that he's in danger, that's all, so we've come to tell you, to be on the safe side....'

'What kind of danger?'

Phelan lost it and pointed theatrically to his ear. 'This kind of fucking danger!' He recovered his composure immediately and put his hands up.

'Sorry love, I'm in a lot of pain. Anyway, I can't say any more. Client confidentiality. And I'm not making a statement. That's it, we've told you and now it's up to you. I'm leaving now.'

But he remained standing facing the officer, as if expecting her to argue or try to persuade him to stay. She did neither. So he turned and left, leaving her to stare at the door as he closed it behind him.

52.

This is the one for me. Two hundred quid a day is a bit steep but I won't be actually paying. Just the job.

53.

Reza had one ready rolled and he lit up as Lassiter shuffled the papers on the screwed down table in the Belmarsh secure unit interview room.

The Turk took a long pull, inhaled and the smoke tumbled out of his mouth as he broke the silence.

'Why did he just fuck off like that…? Are you sure he's gone to another firm?'

Lassiter was snappy, 'Yes, of course I'm sure.'

Then Reza dropped a little bombshell, 'Right then, which firm has he gone to? I want to change to them.'

Lassiter did not want to hear this. 'I don't know. Look Abdul, you're my client. It's my job to look after you. You've got a pleas and directions hearing coming up and you haven't given me any indication yet as to how you want to play it... D'you want us to argue for bail?'

'How the hell can we? I'll get fuckin' topped! Did she get the dough out of the box? I need to know and I need to know where it is and how much. For my own records, so to speak.'

The brief leant forward. 'As planned, the police take a million and we keep a million for you. If things go wrong and you end up serving a sentence I'll put it somewhere safe until you get out.'

The Turk took another long draw. 'How much will this little service cost me?'

'A percentage of what we manage to keep for you plus the interest we make on it. That way it does you no good to blow the whistle. If you do you lose the lot.'

54.

Deborah Glass dialled the number and held the phone to her ear. She took a long toke of a cigarette, inhaled and let the smoke tumble out of her nostrils as she waited. She had masked her number; consequently the word 'unsourced' came up on Lassiter's shadowgraph wallscreen.

It was 11:45pm and the lawyer was slightly drunk, having spent the evening networking several bars in London's temple area. He stood in the middle of his living room, staring blinkingly at the writing on the wall. 'Unsourced.' The ringtone was menacingly patient, reflecting the calmness of the woman at the other end of the line. Lassiter picked up and maintained silence.

So the woman spoke. 'Well? Do I get the job?'

The lawyer felt a strange mix of fear and excitement. He tried to sound relaxed, chatty.

'Why do you keep ringing me Jennifer? Not that I mind, of course. Too much. You could have something going for you – us.'

Okay, thought Deborah, let's play along. 'Sounds good. Let's meet. I enjoyed the last time.'

55.

I always had an unhealthy liking for knives, there's just something beautiful about them. I used to collect them as a kid; sheath-knives, lock-knives, even a flick or two. Then someone told me I would end up in prison if I continued to pursue this hobby because I would graduate from a collector to a user. I listened to that advice and got rid of them all.

But now I've just been out and bought myself a new one. Nine-inch blade, stainless steel, black handle. A minimalist kitchen knife, from one of those nice Scandinavian hardware shops in Chelsea.

And I don't mind admitting that I just really enjoyed sinking the point of my new knife an inch deep into Mrs McNerney's dressing table in my room. And there it stands to attention, quivering slightly, but rigid enough for me to begin winding some shiny black electrical tape onto the handle. I'm being ever so careful, avoiding overlap and wearing surgical gloves. I should mention that I've just carefully removed this length of tape from a certain delivery man's clipboard.

56.

Deborah Glass, in full nursing uniform, examined a patient's intravenous drip. Frowning, she looked at the point at which the tube entered the patients arm and tapped it. Blood flowed back up the tube and mixed with the saline solution in the overhead bag. She shook her head in exasperation and set about fixing it.

No sooner had she finished the repair job she took a phone call from a withheld number on her mobile, for which she received dirty looks from two colleagues. It was Lassiter. He was sat on a park bench about five hundred yards away from the hospital.

'What time can we meet?'

She recognised the voice but feigned surprise. 'What? Oh! Right. What d'you want to do?'

'I'll book a hotel room, but it has to be in your name, what do you call yourself?'

'Jennifer. Jennifer… ,' She faltered, looked down and saw a name on a magazine,

'Pelham. P.E.L.H.A.M.'

The line went dead and Deborah resumed her duties, whilst overhearing her two colleagues.

'She's been told about that. Those phones can interfere with the equipment.'

'Aw, give her a break, she must be worried sick, I'm surprised she's even at work, her husband's been missing for nearly two weeks now.'

'Yeah, s'pose. Julie, did we ever find where those blood bags went, they got delivered here by accident and then just disappeared?'

'Haven't a clue. What does it matter? We weren't s'posed to have them anyway so we don't have to report them missing... Oh, Doctor Walker....' And with that the conversation ended and the busy day continued.

57.

A relaxed Jim Saggs sat on the edge of his desk contemplating the dubious contents of a polystyrene cup.

'That canteen's getting fucking worse, I reckon they're trying to poison us, fucking Boka Haram infiltration....'

Marion Carter was by no means politically correct, but slagging off Nigerian canteen staff was so seventies.

'That's so seventies Jim, you need to be careful, walls have ears.'

Saggs stood corrected. 'Yeah, I know, I know,' and then changed the subject.

'Anyway, thank Christ I can wash my hands of that now. One Area've taken it. MIT. Bloody welcome too.'

Carter frowned, 'What're you on about Jim?'

'The Peter Glass case. This bloke from Lassiter's came in

and said they'd received a threat or a warning or something that Peter Glass was going to get slotted....'

'No! Go on.'

'Yeah, this was just this morning, before you came in, the firm reckoned they've had a warning that if Reza did a deal with us then Glass, that's his brief for God's sake, was going to get topped.'

'Blimey. That's novel.'

'Yeah well, One Area MIT can have the novelty. No sooner had I updated the report they were buzzing around my head like flies. Bloke called Sherrell. DI. Never heard of him meself, seems like a bit of a keen bastard. Coming over to see Bensen later.'

58.

My beautiful wife is sat on the edge of my bedsit bed with her elbows on her knees. She looks up at me as I hand her a mug of coffee, she takes it in both gloved hands.

'I hope you're taking it easy on the caffeine,' she says. I go down on my honkers and kiss her lips.

I reassure her, 'Don't worry. I'm keeping healthy. Lots of vitamin tablets. And the Warfarin dose is steady at fifteen mil a day. Don't make a scene.'

'No,' she says, 'I'll leave that to you.' And we both burst out laughing.

Then she stops laughing. 'It's just unbelievable. What we're doing. How can it all be worth it Pete?'

Oh, here we go again, I think.

'Debs, Debs, we've been through this before. It'll be worth it. Two birds with one stone, remember?'

'Yeah, I know and it's good. So good. To rise out of the ashes like a Phoenix! We've always been up against it Pete, and we've always come through. You're right. As usual.'

She sets down her coffee and we hug and kiss. Then she pulls away, looking business-like.

'C'mon, let's have a look at you.'

'Hey, no problem. I'm an expert now.' I take off my shirt and she examines my forearms.

59.

Sasha Bensen stood behind her desk and faced the gaunt and hungry looking figure of DI Robert Sherrell.

'I'm not trying to undermine you, Mr Sherrell, but I would like to know why you think this chap's been murdered. He's only been missing a couple of weeks, what's the big rush?'

Sherrell enjoyed Bensen's somewhat nervous demeanour, she seemed afraid of him, even though she was a rank higher.

'Information. Good information. We picked up your man Saggs's work on the system, just after we had a call from a woman calling herself the sister of a man who Glass was representing, she said that her brother's gang was going to kill Glass because he was encouraging him to help the police. Then, hey, what do you know, we find he's gone missing. You've also got information that Glass is in danger from this bunch, yet you seem not to be too bothered... even though a former colleague of the missing person has just had his ear sliced off!'

Bensen felt herself flushing with anger. 'That's probably got nothing to do with anything. He was parked up on a yardie plot at the back of Kings Cross, what'd he expect? Anyway, if you're so good why didn't you tell me about your call from Reza's so-called sister, just keeping the job to yourself, fucking glory boys from MIT.'

Sherrell loved this; this stupid, over-promoted bint had bitten. He decided to take the professional high ground.

'I'm sorry you feel that way Ma'am, but we've got jobs like this coming out of our ears. I'm only here on orders from the Commander's office, if I'd had my way I'd be trying to catch up on some paperwork right now, not standing being sworn at by a Detective Chief Inspector.'

She knew she had to back down. 'Okay, I'm sorry Rob, it's just... it's been a long day.'

60.

Here I am again, hard at work. This job always looks easy when you watch someone else do it, but it's not actually all that straightforward. First I had to get the number plates made up, and that's worried me; only hope the guy in the shop hasn't told the old bill. I noticed him make a record of the job, and records are kept for reasons. Oh, well, just have to hope for the best. Not to worry though, I was dressed like I am now, oily overalls, filthy hands and a

145

baseball cap with a logo I designed, Jax Autos, Harlesden. And the bit of paper I gave the guy with the plate number written on it bore the same logo. Jax Autos is an actual backstreet outfit full of hoods; any enquiries there'll need a full crime squad with a warrant.

Anyway, I carefully unscrew and remove both plates on the MPV I just hired with cash and the driver's licence Debs borrowed from one of the patients in the hospital. Nice one Debs, Leroy Browne didn't need it whilst he was in the ITU, and now it's back in his bedside cabinet.

Oh, I nearly forgot to mention something important. I left Mrs McNerney's house a couple of days ago. Moved on to somewhere new, not far away in Shepherds Bush. I thought while I had Leroy's driver's licence I could make the most of it, so I checked in under his name at a nice little working men's hostel, paid a week up front in cash. Didn't tell Mrs McNerney I was leaving though – she'll figure that out soon enough.

61.

And a couple of days later Mrs McNerney stood on her second floor landing with two uniformed police officers.

'I never keep tabs on my tenants but he was never out of his room, never any bother, like, and he paid a month's rent up front, never any bother, apart from a bit of banging, like, said he was fixing his shoes when I asked him the other day. Only been here two weeks and now I haven't set eyes on him for four days and now there's this horrible smell. Thought I'd better call you, just in case....'

One of the young coppers was interested. 'What's his

name?'

'Said his name was Peter, didn't give a second name, paid in cash.'

'Did he have a car?'

'Not that I know of. Can't park round here anyways. Only yesterday a big black thing got a ticket, then it got moved before the removal men came. Don't know who moved it, like, but it just disappeared.'

'Yeah, we know what you mean Mrs McNerney, but this smell, er… have the drains been giving any problems?'

'No, no, none at all, but that smell is of something else not drains, officer, an' it's coming from under that door an' if you don't force the door open then I'm going to get my boy over to do it but I….'

'Look, that's up to you Mrs McNerney, it's really not a police matter so….'

At this point the other officer, an older cop, began to walk down the stairs, shaking his head. He stopped doing both when he heard Mrs McNerney's next little gem.

'And there's the moaning and groaning noises.'

The young cop was still interested, 'Moaning and groaning? What moaning and groaning?'

Couple of nights ago. Maybe three or four nights ago. Dead loud it was, like he was really in pain or something. I thought he had a woman in there with him but it wasn't that kind of moaning if you get my meaning, like, I knocked on the door but there was no reply and then it all went quiet.'

62.

Reza was not expecting anyone and sat in the high security interview room looking perplexed. Then the door opened and in walked Peter Glass.

'Peter! Fucking shit man, I thought you deserted me. That cunt Lassiter said you'd gone to work for another firm. Good to see you man, fuckin' hell….'

Glass was keen to nip this right in the bud. 'Wait, Abdul, Abdul, wait – I have moved, well, I'm self-employed now, and I'm here on the hush. Nobody knows about this visit. The screws just think I'm still working for Lassiter, nobody need know, nobody'll even check.'

'So who's paying you to be here man? I've got no dosh left, you should know that… they took it all… man you look a state, you been sleepin' rough or something?'

'Something like that. Doesn't matter about the money. We'll sort that out another time. I want some information from you, and quick, I want to be out of here fast. What did you give Bensen?'

'Safe deposit box – two million quid in Paki Bonds. I'm still waiting to hear from her. Lassiter's a wanker, I get on better with Bensen, fucking joke, man. Anyway, he's holding half of it for me. She's got the other half at the station, booked in and accounted for, proper like. I just hope she's not going to nick any for herself. The more that gets recovered for the court the better it looks for me.'

Glass was flabbergasted. 'Jesus Christ, those bonds are cash on presentation. You can change them up for Sterling or dollars without the bank having to declare it. Bombproof. Right, you got an email address?'

Reza frowned, 'Yeah, why? I can't use it here.'

'Let's have it, along with your password.'

63.

If any one of the three man forensic search team was excited by the scene at Peter Glass's former residence they did a good job of hiding it. They were not real investigators and never really owned responsibility for a case. They were called in, did the job, did the paperwork and moved on to the next assignment. The bedsit had been sealed off with yellow tape by CID detectives from the MIT who had been called in by the divisional CID from Kilburn who had, in turn, been summoned by the two uniform cops alerted by Mrs McNerney. And now all of these stood back to let the SOCOs look at the mess, take swabs and photographs and submit exhibits to the lab. After that the CID guys would return and do a thorough search, but the forensics had to have the first bite of the cherry so that scientific evidence could not be compromised by plodding policemen.

The SOCOs wore white paper suits with socks and hoods, surgical gloves and facemasks, they had been told there was a lot of blood, but on entering the bedsitting room, they were a little disappointed.

'This is just a heap of crap Wykesey, MIT sent us in at the drop of a fuckin' hat.' Ron Clark was always moaning, he hated his job, and the lead SOCO, Bob Wykes, hated him.

'Oh stop fucking whinging man! We're getting paid for it, and what's more you're on overtime so you're getting paid more than fucking me!'

The third SOCO on the team, Colin Stokes, agreed. 'Yeah, hold your tongue Ron, let's just get the job done. It's an easy one – watch where you're putting your fucking feet, look!'

They looked down closely at the carpet. There was trail of blood leading from the bathroom door to a spot in the middle of the room. Wykes approached the bathroom door. Clark and Stokes look on.

64.

Meanwhile, four large police vehicles pulled up quietly onto a Travelodge car park. From these, nine dark clad figures emerged and entered the hotel, walked past the unmanned reception and moved silently up two flights of stairs to the door of one of the rooms. On the other side of the door Deborah Glass lay in wait. Nothing could have prepared her for the ear-splitting crash as the doorframe exploded and the door slammed down as if hinged at the floor. Instantly a blinding white halogen light invaded the room, followed by the team of adrenalin charged cops all shouting 'Police!'

Deborah Glass leapt up like a shot hare, 'What the fuck!'

DI Rob Sherrell appeared like an apparition from behind the darting white light source.

'Jennifer Pelham?'

'No! Yes! Who the fucking hell are…?'

'DI Sherrell, Metropolitan Police, and I'm arresting you on suspicion of the murder of Peter Glass. You're not obliged to say anything but I must warn you that….'

Sherrell shouted the caution at the terrified woman.

65.

Thirty five minutes later the same terrified woman sat in the charge room of a west London police station facing the uniformed custody sergeant, a tired looking middle aged man. The two regarded each other in silence as Sherrell walked into the room.

Not taking his eyes off of the prisoner the custody sergeant addresses Sherrell without ceremony.

'This young lady is refusing to give her particulars, except for her name, that is.'

Sherrell was not surprised. 'Doesn't surprise me Sergeant. Let's not take too much notice of the name, either. Can we have her strip-searched and her clothes seized for forensic examination?'

The sergeant liked the idea of this. 'Yes sir – Carol.'

He called to a PC standing nearby, 'Take Ms Pelham into the detention room, strip search her and bag up her clothes. Get Linda to help you. Give the lady a paper suit to wear….'

Deborah decided to speak. 'Excuse me. Do I not have any say in this? You know, has this not got anything to do with….'

'Sorry love, if you refuse we'll have to do it by force. We can't make you tell us your date of birth or your address but we can strip search you and seize your clothes. Good, isn't it… oh, by the way, you said you didn't want a solicitor, you can change your mind at any time, don't forget that, it's….'

'Yes. My right. Good point, and I think I have changed my mind. I want a solicitor, and I want a phone call. I'll give you the details in a few minutes.'

Then she made a point of glaring at Sherrell as she rose to join the two female officers.

Once the three women had left the room the custody sergeant, not taking his eyes from his desk, muttered, 'Something strange. Something strange.'

Sherrell grunted agreement, and walked out.

66.

Wykes opened the bathroom door slowly and peered inside.

'Oh, Jesus Christ!'

He said this not in shock or horror but by way of quiet and bitter protest. He was going to be late home.

67.

Lassiter and Bensen stood drinkless in the heaving pub. It was three deep at the bar and liquid refreshment was the last thing on their minds. Bensen looked jaded, stressed.

'You're joking! What the fuck did you do that for?'

'I had to.' Lassiter made an unconvincing attempt at decisiveness.' He paused, saw the cop's mounting rage, and went on.'

'Anyway, it's true, she's up to something. All this 'Jennifer' and 'Reza's sister' shite. I bet she's the same person concocting this. And then you've got to ask why. Who is she? Press? You lot?'

Bensen let out a manic cackle, 'Ha! Now you *have* gone off your rocker!'

Lassiter went on, 'Christ where is that idiot Glass. Are you lot sure he's actually missing?'

'No,' said Bensen, with a rictus grin. 'We suspect he may be dead.'

68.

To Wykes and his men the tiny bathroom of Peter Glass's former bedsit was clearly the scene of terrible violence.

Awash with blood up the walls and lying in thick puddles on the floor. The actual bath was half full of a mixture of blood and water. The smearings and projectile spatters indicated defensive struggle and escape attempts. The stench was overpowering and flies buzzed around delightedly, but these details did not bother Wykes, he was just resigned to a long, late shift.

'We need fresh overalls and about 200 sample bottles. And get the digicam, we'll have to make a movie of this fucking mess first.'

69.

An hour later Sherrell was in his office looking at electronically transmitted images of the scene.

'Estimated six pints of blood. Six pints! It looks like a fucking abattoir!' He turned to a detective standing behind him.

'Get onto DI Bensen at OKR, find out what blood group Peter Glass is – or was. Raise an action on it and mark it as high priority.'

Then to another detective, a black female standing in front of him.

'DS Tuitt, you're going to help me interview the prisoner, OK? And it's not just because you're black and female either before you start….'

'I wasn't startin' guv! I never said a….'

'I know. I know – only joking lass. Sorry.' He rubbed his forehead. 'Go and tell the custody officer to get her a brief and feed her up ready.'

Both detectives walked out leaving Sherrell to mutter to himself.

'I wonder which brief she'll want – could be interesting.'

70.

Wykes was stressed.

'For fuck's sake, man, be careful… are you fucking

pissed... there's a fff... there's a fucking knife behind you, stop... you'll ruin this scene you cunt! Look, the pair of you, take your fucking time! This is what is commonly known as a murder scene. I know there isn't a body, but there's the next best thing in fucking liquid form so just be careful – be professional.'

Ron and Colin, suitably chastened by their supervisor's outburst became very methodical, picking items up carefully and placing them into exhibits bags, making entries in a log as they do so.

These included a knife and a purple pillow case.

71.

Lassiter paced around his apartment with his phone to his ear.

'I don't care if she's asked for me, I can't take the job... look, is DI Sherrell there, best I speak to him... yes I know, can you put him onto me as soon as....'

The custody officer was on the other end of the line with Deborah Glass sat opposite him.

'Okay, I'll ask him to telephone you as soon as I see him. Goodbye.'

The sergeant ended the call and looked up at Deborah.

'Mr Lassiter doesn't seem to want to help you Ms Pelham. Do you want to choose another lawyer?'

'Now there's a surprise.'

'What's a surprise? Look Miss Pelham, there's more to you than meets the eye. I'm not happy with your apparent state of health. I'm going to call a doctor to examine you to ensure that you are fit to be detained further and interviewed. In the meantime do you want to choose another solicitor or shall I call out the duty lawyer? It's free of charge.'

Deborah sighed and shrugged her shoulders.

'Call who you fucking like.'

72.

Lassiter and Bensen sat opposite each other in a coffee shop. Lassiter had called the meeting and he set about an explanation.

'Look, I'm sorry I didn't tell you, I was – I was embarrassed I suppose. You see I... we... her and I....'

'You'd better be fucking joking!'

'Ah, bollocks you sanctimonious bitch! I was getting to the bottom of something and I had a shag whilst I was at it. I needed to get her kit off to make sure she wasn't wired, that's all, and one thing led to another. What's your problem anyway? Jealous?'

'Hah! You? I'm surprised you could manage it, you never were....'

'Shut up. This is getting us nowhere. Anyway, I told Sherrell....'

'What?!'

'I had to. Who's she going to ask for when they offer her a solicitor? Fucking moi! So I had to set the scene for me to refuse. Anyway, I could end up a prosecution witness.'

'What d'you mean 'could'? It's a dead cert if she gets charged. Look Marc we've got some thinking to do. Where's the paperwork?'

'The what?'

Bensen leaned forward and hissed. 'Your share of the two million quid's worth of bearer bonds we, you, had off the other day. The job your client put up for us, remember?'

'Safe. Converted to US Dollars in a numbered Swiss Bank account. Can't be traced, seized or made subject to any court order.'

'I don't want to know any more. The other million – what was going to be mine - is still in the safe at the fucking police station. You just keep your head down, you could be in for some attention if she starts slinging shit.'

And with that DCI Bensen rose and strutted out onto the street.

73.

The examination of the murder scene was still in progress. Colin held out a fresh exhibit bag into which Wykes dropped an empty noodle carton that had just been found on the floor.

74.

Deborah Glass had heard of out of body experiences and

felt like she was having one as she sat as Jennifer Pelham in the windowless interview room opposite DI Sherrell and DC Tuitt.

Tuitt switched on the recording machine and delivered the caution and introductions. Then Sherrell got straight to the point.

'Who are you working for?'

Deborah was going to find this easy. 'Myself.'

'What are you up to?'

'The same as always, up to making a living, a good one, without working that is.'

'Did you kill him?'

'Why would I want to do that? He owed me money but not that much. I was just trying to hustle a few quid out of Lassiter, that's all. I'm not up to killing any fucking body! Jesus!'

'Why won't you give us your address? Why don't you have any ID on you? The way you're going I'm going to have to lock you up.'

'I don't have to give you fuck all Sherrell. You know it and you know I know it – come on how long have you been a copper? You must have met people like me before. Er, except I'm probably a bit special. Ain't never been nicked so you ain't got my DNA or nuthin', or my prints, or my photo, you know what I mean. All you got is a little black hustler who likes screwing money out of nice rich businessmen and barristers and judges and stuff. Get them down that Zig Zag baby and you got them by the balls.'

Sherrell decided to change tactics. He turned to Tuitt and gave a terse instruction.

'Lock her up.'

This took Deborah back a little. 'What?'

Sherrell continued to address his junior colleague. 'Lock her up. We'll keep her here until the samples at the scene are analysed.'

He got up and walked out, the two black women regarded each other blankly.

75.

Five thirty on the next morning found Lassiter in his untidy flat watching the news, or rather lots of newses. Channel hopping and gulping black coffee from a mug he was searching for something. He put down the TV control and walked over to his computer, logged on and began to perform searches.

GLASS, PETER GLASS, LASSITERS, 07866097906, MIL 100. Nothing of interest. Exasperated he returned to the TV and resumed work with the channel changer. Then the door buzzer sounded. Frowning, he pressed the intercom and spoke hoarsely.

'Who is it?'

'Rob Sherrell. Can I come in please? I'm alone.'

Lassiter pressed the security button and opened the

apartment door, waiting for Sherrell to climb the stairs and enter without shaking hands.

'Coffee smells nice.'

'Sugar?'

'No. And I'll have it black please. I like a bit of black.'

Lassiter ignored the subtext, 'won't be a minute. Come through here if you like.'

The policeman followed the lawyer into the kitchen.

'Do you like a bit of black Mr Lassiter?'

'What are you getting at… oh, I know you pulled in our little Jennifer, is that it?'

'Yep. That's it. Now you tell me the rest. You tell me what you think she's told me.'

'Well I don't bloody know, do I? She's the one trying to blackmail me, and she's the one claiming to work for Glass who used to work for me until I sacked him. Your call, Detective Inspector.'

'What did she tell you about the video, the one of Glass in the Zig Zag Club?'

'She told me that she had it made and delivered to my address, right here, by cycle courier and that Glass still owed her for it. That was the first time she spoke to me, rang me just after it was delivered, and my number's ex-directory so she's working with someone close.'

'Did Glass have your number?'

'Yes.'

76.

Sasha walked briskly to her car from the police station. It was dark and she had just finished an arduous shift during which she had been mercifully busy on everything but the Peter Glass case and her own corruption. She was beginning to feel regretful. Why had she got herself involved with Lassiter? Why could she not just be thankful for what she had and just enjoy her career? She knew she was a rising star would get at least another three promotions before retirement, but she just had to have more. She had always been the same, always wanted more.

Her father had been disappointed when she had joined the police, wanted her to be a lawyer. 'Waste of time you going to Roedean and Cambridge, just to be a bloody plod. Phipps-Hornby's daughter's a partner at KPMG now, got her own villa in Tuscany, they're all going out there next month….' A DCI salary never got anyone a villa in Tuscany. By the time she reach a rank that did, she would be too fucking old to enjoy it, or her parents would be dead.

Lost in these thoughts, she fumbled for her keys in the dimly lit back street in which her car was parked. Peter Glass waited until she had opened the car door before he grabbed her from behind, put a gloved hand over her mouth and hissed an introduction into her ear.

'Hi Sasha, Peter Glass. Just keep fucking still and listen to what I'm going to say….'

She was not impressed, got her mouth free of his hand and actually started to laugh.

'Fuck off, you're fucking dead!'

'That's right baby, so this cannot be happening. Now listen, this is how it goes from now on. I'll do whatever you want me to do so long as you help me put my little plan into action. And you even get a bonus because I'll keep quiet about the United Bank of Pakistan bearer bonds you've had off.'

Bensen's sense of humour deserted her instantly.

'What are you talking about, let go of me, what's going on, fuck off away from me or I'll….'

'Or you'll what, arrest me? I don't think so baby. Not a dead man. Not a dead man with no ID on him who'll call a brief to the station and make allegations that you've seized two million quid's worth of bearer bonds and only booked in half of them, eh? Does that sting a little Sasha? Eh?'

It took some long seconds for Bensen to process this information stream, but she maintained her composure.

'What do you want?'

Glass had the woman backed up against the car, he was holding her elbows.

'It's all going wrong. It's not working as planned.'

'What isn't?'

'Think about it. Think about it. And think especially

carefully about Lassiter, my old boss, bless him. Think very carefully about him. Can you really trust him Sasha, or would you not be better off with him out of the way. He's getting very pally with a certain Mr Sherrell, leading him up the garden path really. And when Mr Sherrell gets wind that he's being led up the garden path he'll get very cross with Lassiter. And then everything should work out.'

Bensen was mesmerised. Glass was still holding her arms, but this was unnecessary.

'You're mad, you're fucking mad,' she said, unconvincingly.

'Yes, that's right. Get there before Sherrell. Pull Lassiter in – you've just had information that he killed Peter Glass because Peter found out about the bonds, that's good enough isn't it?'

Her mind raced, trying to get ahead.

'Really, information? Who from?'

'Me. The victim. The horse's mouth, you could say.'

77.

The name Pelham was scrawled on the whiteboard on the cell door through which Deborah Glass was ushered by DC Tuitt who then slammed it hard behind her.

Deborah stood very still for a few seconds with her eyes closed, she then opened them and sat on the floor, lay back and placed her lower legs on the bed. She then proceeded to do a series of abdominal crunches, an exercise for the stomach.

78.

The next morning saw another door implode. It was that of the Glass residence, a modest semi in the west London suburb of Twickenham. DCI Sasha Bensen was among the flurry of police life that swarmed into the little house.

The usual gung-ho formalities were enacted with lots of shouting and posturing, but no invasive searching of storage space was needed and the building was declared safe and unoccupied.

Bensen stood still in the middle of the living room and surveyed the undisturbed scene. It is clearly one in which a violent struggle had taken place. The sofa was upturned and a glass coffee table had been smashed. But there were no signs of theft or forced entry, other than the one that her team had just caused.

Then her phone buzzed. She picked up.

'Hello Sasha. Peter Glass here. Or his ghost. Or someone pretending to be him. What are you doing in my house? You'll find nothing there, only that someone else has gone missing.'

She had not expected this but was not surprised. 'It isn't going to work. This is insane, what are you...?'

Glass interrupted. 'Oh I know it's insane, I can do insane, quite easily and it's getting easier every day. I've told you who killed me so why don't you do something about it?'

Bensen turned away from the on-looking team. 'No! I'm calling your bluff. Come in or I'm going to come and get you, and I'll drag you in screaming... what have you done with your wife? This looks very much like the scene of domestic violence to me, I think we'll have you in for that shall we, then you can make all the allegations you like about me and....'

Again. Glass interrupted, laughing, 'Got to find me first baby. Anyway, I thought I was dead. That puts you in an interesting legal position I would say Sasha, don't you agree? Has my death certificate been issued yet, should have been, or has there to be an inquest first? It's like you've got to bring me in alive to prove I'm not dead – tricky proving the negative, isn't it.'

Bensen was speechless and cut the call to save face. She turned to DS Marion Carter, 'Ok, preserve this scene and get it forensicated, I'm going back to the station.'

'Yes Ma'am,' said Carter and Bensen walked out of the house. Walking to her car she breathed deeply and tried to control her trembling hands. What the hell was happening? She felt the real fear of someone losing something that she had become so accustomed to having – control.

79.

DS Jim Saggs was working at his computer. An email popped up and he frowned, not recognising the sender, but interested in the title.

'WERE ALL THE BEARER BONDS ACCOUNTED FOR? – YOU BE CAREFUL

GATES'

Saggs clicked into the body of the message –

'BENSEN AND LASSITER HAD IT OFF, OR ABOUT HALF OF IT TO BE

MORE ACCURATE'

SAGGS

He turned round to summon Gates. 'Gatesey, come and have a look at this.'

Gates had just finished rolling a cigarette and was about to engage in the labour intensive feat of leaving the office to smoke it.

'Eh? What is it? Do I have to?'

'Just get the fuck over here – you need to see this.'

Gates knew when the old man was not to be messed with and walked over to view Saggs's screen.

'Fucking hell. Who's that from? What fucking bearer bonds?'

Saggs did not take his eyes from the screen. 'Beats me mate but I'm forwarding this to supervision – I want fuck all to do with this. Whatever this is about it's got your name on it. And I work with you. If she's been at it she can carry the can. It fucking fits in – she and Lassiter were a bit familiar, I remember thinking he was giving her one….'

Gates butted in on Saggs's panicked verbal stream.

'Where's it come from – sender's name is

rAbdul@btinternet.com - fuck me, its' Reza Ahmed, how's he sending an email? Can't do it from Belmarsh, even on remand.'

Saggs became more focused. 'Obviously getting somebody to send it for him, he's got that weird sister of his out on the loose remember.'

The two detectives stared at the email as if by doing so it would somehow reveal its origins and significance. Gates straightened and fiddled with his rollup. 'Fucking hell Jim, there's no way I'm taking any shit for this, no way, I've already got two outstanding complaints.'

Saggs was on-side. 'Same here mate, Bensen ain't gonna put this on us, we stick together, okay?'

Gates did not answer, and just walked out slowly, still fiddling with his rollup.

80.

Deborah Glass was back in the interview room facing Sherrell and Tuitt. The recording machine was running and she had been reminded that she was still under caution.

'Right then Jennifer, got a bit of bad news for you,' opened Sherrell cheerfully.

Deborah cocked her head to one side and replied, equally cheerily, 'Let's have it then.'

Sherrell stopped smiling. 'Your DNA has been found at the murder scene.'

'I don't doubt it.'

'I beg your pardon.'

'I've been locked in that cell for the last eight hours. Before I went in there you took some of my hair. You've had plenty time haven't you, eight hours, eh?'

Sherrell maintained his composure, 'Oh, I see what you mean, yes, very good but no dear, won't wash, your samples have been analysed and have been nowhere near the scene. Unlike you. When were you there?'

'Never. Where is it anyway? I don't know if I've been there until you tell me where it is.'

'Mulholland Avenue, Kilburn.'

'Never heard of it. Never been anywhere near Kilburn in my life mate. You're fitting me up you fucking cunts! She shouted the last sentence, and then lowered her voice, adopting a more conspiratorial tone.

'Is that okay?'

Sherrell was finding this difficult. 'Is what okay?'

'My reaction to your questions for the recording. Am I doing okay?'

The DI decided to play along. 'Not really. You've just hung yourself. Before I ask you any more questions I'm going to get you a solicitor and charge you with the murder of Peter Glass. Once again I must tell you at this point that you are not obliged to say anything but it may harm your defence if....'

81.

It was 3 o'clock the next morning before Detective Chief Superintendent Malcolm Taylor and Detective Superintendent Roy Tanner approached the terraced cottage in the fashionable London suburb. They were senior men from the Metropolitan Police Anti-Corruption Command and were not accustomed to working the night shift, but the circumstances were uncustomary. Tanner knocked on the door and it was answered after a minute by Sasha Bensen in a dressing gown, hair tousled.

Both men showed their warrant cards and Taylor spoke.

'Hello Sasha, we're from DPS Headquarters. Can we come in?'

Bensen nodded and stood back, holding the door open. She felt the colour drain from her face as she followed the two men into her living room. They turned to face her and what she heard next was a very reasonable offer, one that she could not refuse.

82.

Three hours later Marc Lassiter was woken by some very loud rapping on his door. He was on his back wide-eyed for a full thirty seconds. More loud rapping. He knew it was bad, he knew everything was about to go very wrong indeed. He actually thought of the fire escape, then thought better of it – he wouldn't get far. He thought of feigning illness but that would be equally pointless. Suicide? Not yet. So he got out of bed and carefully donned his dressing gown, straightened his hair and walked purposefully to the door. He opened it and was surprised, even reassured, by what confronted him.

Bensen stood alongside Taylor, Tucker behind them. He did not know the two men but their age and demeanour told him that they were of high rank.

Bensen spoke first, to Taylor.

'This is him sir, Mark Lassiter. It was his client who supplied the information.'

Taylor was next.

'Mark Lassiter, I am Chief Superintendent Taylor of the Metropolitan Police Professional Standards Directorate. I'm arresting you on suspicion of the theft of £1m worth of bearer bonds from a safe deposit at Selfridges department store in Oxford Street, London, on 4th November 2018. You do not have to say anything but it may harm your defence…'

Lassiter instinctively went for outrage.

'You must be fucking joking!'

'…if you fail to mention something now which you later seek to rely on in court…'

Lassiter continued, voice rising.

'What the fuck are you up to Sasha? You have the bearer bonds, you took them to the police station!'

Bensen was quick, she had it rehearsed.

'Only half of them. Come on Mark, it's all over, where are

the bonds and what have you done with Peter Glass?'

Taylor finished the caution. '... whatever you say may be given in evidence. My officers will now search these premises under the authority of the Police and Criminal Evidence Act. You will then be taken to Paddington Police Station where you will be told of your rights and obligations.'

And with that four plain clothed detectives appeared from the corridor and pushed past Lassiter. He did not try to obstruct them, but continued to argue.

'Really? What obligations. I haven't got any bearer bonds, search as much as you like. If there's any missing from what she took from the safe deposit box then she's got them.'

Bensen smirked. 'Not according to the evidence I'll be giving Mr Lassiter....'

'Oh! Mr Lassiter is it now! I can't fucking believe this you bent bitch....'

Taylor intervened; this was going to get messy.

'Right, DI Bensen, please leave and return to your station, Mr. Lassiter I must....'

Then Lassiter lost it. He launched himself at Bensen, grabbing her by the hair and throat, Tucker managed to get between them and one of the search officers got an arm around the assailant's neck and dragged him off the shrieking Bensen.

'Bensen's shrieking turned into laughter, 'Well done Marc,

that's another charge, assaulting a police officer in the execution of her duty!'

'Execution of her corruption more like,' hissed Lassiter whilst being man-handled and cuffed.

83.

Of course I'm blissfully unaware of all the drama, but that is not to say I'm not worried. In fact, I'm worried sick. Debs is probably festering in a cell right now and here I am boarding the Eurostar to Paris. But it's all part of the plan. I'm dressed very casually with jeans and a baseball cap.

84.

Lassiter was seated in the high security holding area of Paddington police station, west London, still in his dressing gown, rubbing his wrists where the cuffs had been.

Sherrell walked in, ignored the detainee and addressed the uniformed custody sergeant who sat at a raised desk looking down at the dishevelled lawyer.

'Sergeant, I want this prisoner fully forensicated, blood sample, DNA, clothes, the lot. Emergency analysis, turn it around in three hours if you can, I'll get transport ready to take the exhibits to the lab now.'

'Yes guvnor, no problem.'

Like all good lawyers, Lassiter had to speak.

'Be my guest. When's my interview DI Sherrell? When am I getting interrogated? You found that money yet? All those bearer bonds, cash on demand? I haven't got them, and I want to know where you got the grounds to search my home, who your information came from, lots of things I want to know DI Sherrell.'

Sherrell walked quietly over to the sitting Lassiter and stooped to speak quietly, menacingly.

'I'm not investigating the theft of bearer bonds Marky boy, remember, I'm the one investigating the murder of Peter Glass, and we don't need to talk about that. We'll let your blood to do the talking.'

85.

I haven't tried to speak French in twenty years and these fucking Parisians enjoy not speaking English. It's not that they don't, they just won't. I think they like to see an Englishman struggle, especially a black one.

Anyway, here I am in a twee Parisian internet café, just paid ten euros for an hour; this'll only take five minutes. I log in as my good friend Abdul Reza, my baseball cap is pulled down nice and tight to avoid the CCTV. (Internet cafes always have CCTV).

I type a message to the Old Kent Road CID general email address, for the attention of all, including DI Bensen. I put the caps lock on.

DO A GOOD JOB. DON'T FORGET THE OTHER ONE, THE ONE WITH HIS EAR MISSING.

And I press send and leave the café.

86.

The holding room at OKR police station was unusually quiet and the custody sergeant was doing a crossword. 'Place in danger – ten letters'. His peace was shattered when the door burst open and two detectives frogmarched in a struggling Paul Phelan and threw him down onto the bench.

Phelan was puce and still had a heavily bandaged head. The custody officer was immediately concerned, but he had it – 'jeopardise', which was what these two wankers had done to his pension. An obviously injured man being chucked about like this was not conducive to a graceful retirement.

'Right,' said the old sergeant, rising from his chair, 'You two just calm down and….'

But Phelan needed to let off a lot of steam.

'Fucking great innit! I get fucking carved up and deformed then you cunts nick me for theft of a million quid! If I had a million quid mate, I wouldn't have been sat where I was when I got separated from my left fucking ear!!!'

87.

Sherrell had left Lassiter to stew in a cell at Paddington and had travelled the eight miles across town to OKR. As Phelan was being very gently ushered into his cell, Sherrell held a briefing upstairs in the CID office.

He was smug and authoritative, clearly enjoying the occasion. The attendees included Saggs, Carter, Gates, Tuitt and a pair of civilian analysts from the Forensic

Science Service.

'Good morning ladies and gentlemen. I'd first of all like to introduce DS Saggs and DCs Carter and Gates from OKR, and Tim Thwaites and Carmen Zoob from the Forensic Science Service. Our OKR colleagues started this enquiry with their tenacity and diligence when the victim was first reported missing, and our friends from the FSS have effectively solved it with some amazing results. Put simply, hair samples and fingerprints at the scene put Lassiter firmly in play. His prints are on the handle of a bloodstained knife found at the scene. His vehicle got a ticket near the scene at the time of the killing and the vehicle was probably driven to the scene by Paul Phelan who's DNA we have also found on a noodle carton at the scene.'

Gates could not resist it, 'Have you found his ear yet?'

They all laughed, including Sherrell.

'No, but we're working on it. Anyway, they're both being charged with murder this morning and they'll be in court tomorrow. Expect the phones to get hot. Just keep silent and refer all callers to the press office.'

Fay Tuitt piped up with a reasonable question.

'What about Jennifer Pelham guv?'

'She's going to be released. The CPS say, and for once I agree with them, that her DNA at the scene was very low trace and could be explained away by the fact that Lassiter had had sex with her not long before his own presence at the scene. Basic transference of very small samples. So, our little Jennifer is a free woman. Funny old business mind. I wouldn't mind betting her and I will meet again sometime... just got a feeling... Anyway, that's it, well done everybody. Back to the mundane stuff.'

The team dispersed.

88.

Two months later the law firm known as Lassiter and Co has closed down. The reason being, that their senior partner is still remanded in custody awaiting trial for the murder of Peter Glass. I know this because I'm about to visit him. I've monkeyed up some papers and ID that enables me to pass myself off as a representative of the Criminal Case Review Board, a sort of lefty do-gooder, semi-governmental body that reviews dodgy convictions. Not Lassiter's of course because he hasn't been convicted yet, but that of Reza Abdul who was convicted last month and got ten years on a plea with mitigation. That's the pretext anyway, actually I couldn't give a fuck about Reza, he deserved what he got, but this gets me access to his former solicitor. I'm in a little waiting room and I hear a screw talking to my old boss.

'I dunno mate, the paperwork says he's from the Criminal Case Review Panel or something like that, wants to talk about one of your old cases.'

And then in I walk. My hair's a bit natty now, short dreadlocks coming through, and I've got a nice bushy beard with a few grey flecks. I sit opposite Lassiter, he blinks at me, I think he's not long been awake.

'Hello Marc,' I say, 'Don't you recognize me?'

And then he becomes very awake.

'Fucking hell. FUCKING HELL! JESUS! Right, hey, right this is....'

He swivels to address the CCTV camera in the top corner of the room,

'Hey, he's supposed to be ....'

I feel I ought to intervene at this point, lest he spoil things.

'No Mark,' I say, 'Don't spoil it.'

'Don't spoil fucking what? My chance of a life sentence for murdering you... no, course not, it's what every lawyer wants isn't it... a nice life sentence for murdering someone who isn't even dead... suppose it gives us insight of miscarriages of justice, eh?'

He pauses then, as if to consider the implications of what he's just said, how it would sound to others. He stares at me, his murderee, eyes swivelling around the room, as if searching for words. He finds and delivers them, quietly now, calmly.

'So what do you want? Why are you here?'

I reply, also quietly and calmly.

'Money of course.'

And then I lean forward across the small table and whisper into his ear.

'Resurrect me. One million pounds should do the trick.'

He remains motionless, boggle eyed. I sit back and take a sheaf of papers from the inside pocket of my heavy overcoat. I push them onto the table.'

'What's this?' He says, and attempts humour (which I can't help but respect) 'Your last will and testament?'

I'm tempted to laugh and join in the banter, but time is pressing so I have to stay on point.

'Bank documents. Instructions from you to your bank to transfer your money to my bank. Quite simple. Little birdie told me your stash is in Switzerland and I want you to put it in my account in the Cayman Islands, via another account in Paris. Just fill in the form and sign it and as soon as the money touches base I'll make another video and send it to Scotland Yard, together with a few DNA samples and a written statement.'

'So you think I'm going to trust you do you? Why would you want to spring me from here when I'm the one person who can nail you for handling a stolen million quid?

I'm ready for this, of course.

'If you don't comply then you stay where you are. And so does Phelan. There's someone with him now, telling him about this offer. If you don't sign up Mark, Phelan will suffer too. He's already lost an ear because of you, now he's about to lose his liberty. Trust me and you could both be out within a month. The CPS will offer no evidence before your trial even begins – they'll have your murder victim on a time certified DVD telling them it's all been a big mistake.'

I take a pen from my pocket and push it across the table.

'Sign up to it.'

I think I've got him under control, but I'm wrong. He takes the pen and launches himself at me across the table, which thankfully bolted to the floor. He makes a valiant attempt at stabbing me with my own biro and I just manage to dodge him. Can't get injured in here, my leaking DNA samples really would mess things up.

The door opens and two prison officers run in and restrain my old boss. I don't need to pretend to be a bit ruffled, because I am.

'Tell you what Mark, I'll go now. I'll have a colleague come and see you tomorrow. We at the CCRB understand how frustrating it can be for people like you.'

Then, quite suddenly, like a chess player seeing he's beaten, he concedes defeat gracefully.

'No... okay, I'll sign up to it, sorry officers, just a bit of a raw deal that's all, lost my temper a bit.'

The screw is not impressed. 'We're not leaving you alone with him.'

'It's okay, stay here while I sign some papers, it's okay.'

He sits down again and smiles at me. He still has the pen in his hand.

'Papers please.'

***

Causeway

The tide did now its flood-mark gain,
And girdled in the saint's domain;
For, with the flow and ebb, its style
Varies from continent to isle;
Dry-shod, o'er sands, twice every day,
The pilgrims to the shrine find way;
Twice every day, the waves efface
Of staves and sandalled feet the trace.
As to the port the galley flew,
Higher and higher rose to view
The castle with its battled walls,
The ancient monastery's halls,
A solemn, huge, and dark red pile,
Placed on the margin of the isle.

Sir Walter Scott, 1802

1.

*My name is Godfrey Driver and I am self-employed. The
job specs are always good and I can take my time. I call it
'creative surveillance'. It sort of develops itself, leads us
nowhere and everywhere. Its purpose is to learn more and
more about the target until there is nothing really more to
learn. The target is thus rendered powerless. Every myth
exploded, every mystery unravelled. The target's privacy is
systematically drained. When I'm finished, my target is
empty; has spoken all secrets, broken all confidences. Void.*

Just like me.

2.

He faced the three silhouettes and listened, or half listened, to the middle one address him. The tone was not unfriendly, but firm. The corporate mind was made up and this was a fateful day. The big window behind them looked out over an indifferent Thames.

'This board has taken into account your exemplary record, both whilst with the Special Boat Service of the Royal Marine Corps and whilst as a surveillance officer with this Service. You have on many occasions shown diligence and dedication to your duties at times when others would have been less committed. Yet you evidently have a problem and it is that which has put you in the position you now find yourself. You face this board because you were negligent whilst on a live operation in that you departed from the directed course of action in order to investigate the whereabouts and habits of a young lady to whom you were for some reason attracted. This behaviour brought you to the attention of the civilian police and you were arrested. Before arrival at the police station you had the presence of mind to disable your Service covert radio set. For this you get credit. You also get credit for managing to persuade the police that you were no more than a crank pretending to be some sort of private investigator, but we need not go into all of that. You have heard it before at your preliminary discipline hearing.'

It was not his intention to be rude but he found himself gazing beyond them and across the river. The speaker raised the volume and Driver refocused, as best he could, on the talking silhouette.

'You have been offered counselling within the Service yet have refused it. You have been put on non-operational duties in which you have, deliberately I suspect, failed to thrive....'

3.

It was about the seventh call that evening. The tall blonde woman had been drinking and had not slept properly for three days. Her world had just fallen apart and all she was getting was phone calls from people who said they were journalists. Her husband was dead; she had no children and her family, with whom she had no contact, lived in California. So the irritating calls actually provided relief, a focus for her reeling mind.

'I've never heard of you. No more than I've heard of any of the others. Look I need to....'

'Mrs Byers, I knew it was going to happen, I knew your husband. I was working on this before....'

'What did you say your name was?'

'Michaela. Michaela Tuitt. I've been working on Greschner for some time; I've met your husband, about two months ago. I tried to warn him but he would not listen to me, or at least I thought he hadn't....'

'That's enough. I'll meet you. You know where I live. Come to our house. I'm in all night.'

'No, they'll be watching you....'

'Who?'

'Doesn't matter, not over the phone, not this phone anyway. Take this number – ready – 07866 908689, ring me on your mobile – safer still buy a new mobile, pay as you go, and ring me with that….'

'What the hell's going on? What's…?'

'Oh, come on Jo, you're not stupid, and nor am I, just do as I say.'

As the line went dead the tall blonde knew that the call was significant. One way or the other. She went out to the all-night Tesco's and paid thirty quid for a dumbphone and then went for a long walk.

4.

'No, I must wait until after the ceremony. Otherwise it'll be a circus and I'll lose the moment.'

The woman paused to breath in some freezing damp air.

'I'll let you know where you can pick it up. Start driving north first thing tomorrow. You'll know where to go after the ceremony but don't attend yourself, you may be known.'

The woman switched off the mobile phone, opened it and took out the sim card and battery, placing the components in different compartments of her handbag.

Three hundred and fifty miles to the north of London the Reverend William Robson also received a telephone call in the hallway of his cold and draughty vicarage. He didn't normally hold memorial services at his isolated church, and certainly not at less than 24 hours' notice. But he had known Duncan Byers. He remembered the boy attending confirmation classes twenty five years previously as if it was only last week. A good boy, bright as a button. The woman had said that she was Duncan's wife and that he had just died of a very contagious disease and had to be cremated in London. But Duncan had stipulated in his will that he wanted to be buried in the cemetery at Kyloe Church, north Northumberland. So she wanted to arrange the next best thing. The Reverend Robson had hesitated at first, but the £3000 pledged by the woman as payment would be very handy towards fixing the leaking roof.

5.

It was just part of another terrible dream to her. The thud, thud, thud of a broken drum. Getting faster and louder, tugging her from a fitful sleep. Bang, bang, bang, bang and she was wide awake very suddenly. Sdabilla saw it through the open door adjoining the main ward. It was the man's foot or rather the heel of his foot thumping against the wooden locker by the side of his bed. Thump thump thump thump thump thump – faster – thump thump thumpthumpthumpthump – louder – THUMPTHUMPTHUMPTHUMPTHUMP – she froze at first and then sprang up out of the anti-room to be at the bedside. Her wide eyes met his which were protruding so much that it seemed that they would come out of their sockets. They started to scream in perfect unison, hitting exactly the same note and pitch. The man's was in sheer terror of the most violent death imaginable. Sdabilla's was pure anguish. His imploding body was bucking and writhing with such ferocity that now both legs had swivelled sideways and out of the bed and his heels were drumming a cacophonous tattoo on the locker. She went to go to him but a barrier nurse, masked and overalled, had got there and was dragging her back, away from this living, screaming corpse that had been, only a few days ago, her strong and supportive husband.

6.

Born on the West Indian island of Montserrat and a descendant of slaves shipped there by Irish plantation owners, Michaela Tuitt had immigrated to the UK with her three younger brothers and their mother at the age of 7. Her drunken father had died the previous year of hepatitis. The family moved to Nottingham and Michaela spent her formative years helping her mother bring up the three unruly boys, all of whom briskly found their way into the criminal justice system. The eldest, Floyd, did not make a success of it and at the age of 17 ended up being indefinitely detained at Her Majesty's pleasure following an incident in an illegal nightclub during which one man died and another lost a testicle. The other two boys managed to emerge from teenhood relatively unscathed with minor criminal records before settling down to fairly mundane lives. By that time Michaela was 21; having left school at 16 she had no qualifications and was working as an administrative clerk in a dairy. It was there that she developed an interest in journalism. Her boss, impressed by her obvious intelligence and articulacy, managed to persuade her to write a piece for the in-house magazine on the negative health aspects of pasteurisation and how these had been grossly overstated by the red-top press. Michaela was not keen but, flattered, complied and made a good job of two thousand words of propaganda. She received an extra £50 in her pay packet and decided on a career change.

Four years of evening classes later she had a 2:1 Honours in Journalism from Nottingham Trent University, was editor of the in-house magazine at the dairy and, having become somewhat of a small manufacturer's heroin, had had a number of articles published in a few scientific and technological publications on how industry was successfully discharging its duty of care in respect of ecological issues. She didn't actually believe one single jot of what she wrote, which is why she knew she was going to become a very successful journo.

7.

The woman has been here before. Over ten years ago but it had also been November and the wind, like now, had been strong, northerly and rain laden. The giant horse chestnuts, naked, swayed and hissed around the church, angrily. The old church did not hiss. It stands silent, still, unchanging, awake. Safe. Immortal. It will never be demolished. The graveyard, long since full and mostly overgrown, has in it skeletons three centuries old properly dead people, of whom no living memory exists.

She felt no cold. Just coldness. She walked around the church and faced the sea, a mile or two across a few unproductive fields. And beyond the sea, on the horizon, the Island. The Holy Island of Lindisfarne. Linked by its causeway; a narrow mile of tarmac umbilical cord to mother mainland at low tide only. She watched as it became suddenly illuminated by a series of sunrays that broke through the fast grey clouds. It is mostly sand with some grassy dunes and a village, a castle and an ancient priory, built by monks.

She walked slowly around the church, the collars of her black leather trench coat flapping in the icy gusts. As she reached the front of the old building the first of the big black cars arrived. Pulling up behind the BMW she had hired at Newcastle airport an hour and a half before. Ellis and Muller led the way, the latter allowing his superior colleague to be first with the shit.

'Jo. Jo, how long have you been here? I'm… we're so dreadfully, dreadfully sorry. We came to the hospital but they….'

She managed to keep her voice steady; menacing, hopefully. 'They wouldn't let you in. They wouldn't let you onto the ward because it was fatally contaminated. With your filth.'

'Jo. What are you trying to achieve by…?'

'Get into the church.'

The woman was similarly disposed towards the rest of her husband's mourners, as they arrived for his memorial service on that freezing wet hill in north Northumberland. She counted them in – thirty two – and followed the last one through the weather beaten old doors at which the Reverend William Robson stood wringing his huge red hands.

'Thank you, they're all here now. We can start?'

In spite of his stoop and her above average height she had to look up to him; into his watery pale blue eyes and furrowed brow. He nodded, allowed her to pass and followed her into the darkness of his House of God.

8.

Lloyd Obanga is 32. Until a week ago he supported his family. And that of his brother, Moses. Moses died last year on Christmas Day. He seemed to melt from the inside out as the Ebola virus liquidated his innards. The village had no painkillers and Moses died screaming. On Christmas day. And now Lloyd wonders when he is going to start screaming. There would be no chance of medical treatment. There are still no painkillers in the drugs cabinet. As the local doctor he is well placed to know this. Lloyd feels himself losing his life. It is not like life is slipping away from him; more like he is giving it to someone else; a wasteful, destructive, malignancy whose purpose is to kill without real purpose. A parasite which so effectively destroys its host has no purpose. Not capable of being understood.

Florence Obanga has made the journey to Monrovia. She has an uncle there who works for the government and who has a telephone which he allows her to use free of charge. When you dial the number of the London University Hospital you get a series of recorded instructions. Florence's call did not come under any of the more straightforward categories. She needed to be put through to the Soissons Virological Research Institute, part of the hospital but not on the same switchboard.

After over an hour of tearful frustration she got through to Dr Byers' extension. Voicemail. The tears, great big round ones to match her eyes, rolled freely down her face. Byers does not work there any more, his replacement, Dr Bache, can be contacted on 0207... please leave a message etc., etc. The parcel from the hospital had not arrived. Florence's uncle, David Tsaweda had Governmental Status, nobody in Liberia would dare steal from the Government. This was the second time it had happened. The Xenerferon should arrive each month at her uncle's address via the diplomatic bag. What had gone wrong? People were dying screaming. Her next call, despite her brother's protests – 'do not embarrass our country' – was to New Scotland Yard. The consignments were going missing in London. Moreover, they were not even reaching the Foreign Office for dispatch.

The system had been that every month a package containing 50 x 100mg phials of a specially developed version of the drug Interferon was despatched by motorcycle courier from the London Hospital to the Foreign Office post room in Whitehall from where it would proceed by secondary diplomatic post to the Foreign Ministry in Monrovia. From there it would be taken by car to David Tsaweda's residence for distribution to West Point's Ebola field hospital. But nothing had arrived for two months. The Foreign Office in London did not much care, saying that a Dr Byers at the London Hospital had now moved on and that they assumed that was the reason for the discontinuance. No doubt it was the reason, but only because Duncan Byers had supervised the packaging. Florence betted the consignments had been signed off in advance and that additionally a new signatory had been appointed, but for some reason the phials were not leaving the hospital. They were, she was sure, being stolen from there.

9.

'Have you heard from Florence Obanga yet?'

'Who is this?'

'Michaela Tuitt, I'm a journalist, have you heard from Florence Obanga yet Dr Byers?'

Duncan Byers had by that time heard from Florence Obanga. The African woman had managed to trace him after several more phone calls from her brother's house had yielded the doctor's current whereabouts. Greschner. He had joined the enemy. When she finally got through she did not know whether to berate him or plead for help. She did the latter – it came naturally to her. He had been the only hope of an Ebola inoculation and had now been headhunted away. Byers had listened to her faltering and distant request. He knew what had happened. He had been the driving force behind the Soissons Institute's efforts on sub-Saharan killer diseases. He had persuaded his employers of the need to be involved in relieving human beings of premature and agonising deaths. The funds going into Aids in Africa were enormous, quite rightly, but other diseases were being ignored just because they did not generally escape from the African continent.

'Yes, I have.'

'Can we meet?'

'What are you going to do? Vilify me as a traitor, the worm that turned?'

'Nice headline, "The Worm that Turned", with a picture of

the worm-like Ebola virus alongside. No, I want to warn you about something, about smallpox.'

This was madness. Byers knew what sort of firm he was working for; a 'big pharma' giant with its fingers in many pies – including probably bio-warfare. But he had chosen not to worry about this too much and had joined for fairly mundane reasons – more money, better research facilities and a London base with less travel to bloody tropical shit-holes. He knew his phone was probably hooked up to digital systems that monitored everything. The Greschner headquarters on the Great West Road in Brentford, west London, was a machine in itself, even the lift usage was recorded, swipe cards were needed on every corridor and it had to be assumed that the phones were very well covered indeed.

'No. I am not in a position to talk to journalists. Please do not contact me again.'

Just before replacing the receiver Byers scribbled a note of the mobile number that appeared on the small screen of his office phone. He would ring her from Ashington. One of the aspects of his new job was that he got to spend time in his native north east. Born and bred in Newcastle upon Tyne, Byers had lived there as a child before moving further north as his father searched for employment in Edinburgh. They had settled in north Northumberland, about 50 miles north of the Tyne and three miles from the North Sea.

He was fairly happy with the career move, as was his wife, Jo. But the call from this journo had unsettled him, even though he knew that such interest from the concerned press was always on the cards, such was the nature of the beast which now employed him.

Greschner had chosen, for very different reasons, to construct its satellite settlement in Ashington, some twenty miles north of Newcastle. A hideous relic of the once heaving coal mining industry, Ashington was now a mixture of vast featureless council estates and colliery streets, rocketing unemployment, pathetic shopping malls purporting consumer wealth, teenage mothers, drugs and boredom. A by-product of this was that land for development and the requisite planning permission were both dirt cheap. So Greschner Ashington had been born. A smaller version of its London mother, it was similarly of concrete construction and Bauhaus design. The squat, two storey block contained laboratories, archives, storage facilities, offices, a library and a helipad on the roof. Like its London mum it also featured extensive security. Razor wire-topped chain fencing skirted the periphery, guards patrolled with dogs and the building itself bristled with cameras, both externally and against its own staff inside. This attracted no concern in the forgotten corner of the country. A modicum of local labour was used during construction (though most specialist workers had been imported from the south), and some low paid full and part-time jobs were reserved for the natives. The fact that Greschner was generally rumoured to be engaged on government contracts and that the security was to ensure safety measures were complied with was sufficient to allay fears that there was something untoward going on.

Byers had been attracted by the Greschner offer; this attraction had been enhanced by the opportunity to work in Northumberland. He was given an office both in London and in Ashington; he felt more at home in the latter. The journey from the London Brentford office to the Ashington building, door to door was about two hours. The flight from Heathrow to Newcastle takes 45 minutes; check-ins and cab journeys consume the rest of the time.

10.

Becoming bored with the lack of both excitement and money Michaela Tuitt had also changed sides. Leaving the dairy she began to look for a human side to her writing, concentrating at first on environmental issues and later on unscrupulous drug companies, animal testing, undeclared side-effects of drugs on human patients and, now, the emergence of something much more sinister. And she was only 26. She had got herself onto the junior staff of a daily broadsheet and had helped with a number of speculative articles on military applications of biochemical research. Viral weaponization. She had interviewed Russian dissidents about the *Biopreparat*, a rumoured extension of earlier Soviet biological weapons programs, had travelled to post-Saddam Iraq to talk to Kurds about the ongoing effects of the chemical genocide of part of their population in the 90's and had attended Japan's police academy during a seminar on emergency procedures in the advent of nerve gas attacks in crowded places. But of all the areas she monitored the most important to her was the growing spectre of viral splicing technology - and its possible acquisition by terrorists.

Like all good hacks, Tuitt had her contacts in the emergency services, she made a point of currying favour with nurses, firemen, ambulance drivers and, of course, police officers. One such cop was a youthful detective constable she'd met at a Christmas function. His name was Guy Simmonds and he had a penchant for chubby black women. Tuitt accommodated in this department.

Simmonds worked in a busy CID office in Clerkenwell quite near to the London Hospital. Fascinated by Tuitt, her girth and the fact that she was interested in more than just celebrity scoops, Simmonds allowed her to take him for the occasional meal during which he enjoyed watching her eat copious quantities of chocolate cake after an already substantial steak or fish platter. The deal? Not much really. Simmonds just had to provide his muse on an ongoing basis with details of what and who had been nicked at the hospital lately. She promised him, and for some reason he believed her, that she would not go to print with anything that could reveal the identity of her source. Simmonds was a bright lad and a good judge of character. He'd done some research on his plump friend and knew that she was a serious journo with a respectable agenda. It was young Simmonds' agenda that lacked respectability. A single man with his own little rented London flat he could not wait to lure his admiree there with some tasty stories of stolen drugs or clinical negligence. At first he never bothered to ask why she had this fascination for what went on in large hospitals, so anxious as he was to get her into bed. But he did wonder why she was not interested in the NHS as such or the politics surrounding it, that being a particularly turbulent field and one which attracted a lot of attention from the documentary-making media. Instead Tuitt would want to know the minutia of what drugs had been stolen from which hospital and when. She took a passing interest in accidents and reports of medical cock-ups but this appeared to be secondary to her desire to know about every missing ampoules or tablets. She was clearly on the lookout for something.

'What is it you're looking for?' he said one morning as they lay on his bachelor pad bed.

'Nothing special',

'Oh come on Michaela, don't tell lies to the nice policeman, there's a good girl. Now what is it you're *looking* for?'

Tuitt paused, staring at the ceiling for a long five seconds, and then said,

'A bomb.'

'A bomb?'

'A bomb.'

'Of course,' Simmonds mocked, 'Of course, I should have spotted it a mile off. You get me to trawl every crime reported in every UK hospital over the last six months because you are looking for a bomb...?'

'Guy, don't take the piss out of me. Think. I'll see you tonight.'

She slid off the bed, showered and dressed. Before walking out of the door she turned and looked at the horizontal police officer. He lay on his back with his hands clasped behind his head.

'Think bomb,' she said, and then whispered

'Dirty bomb'.

11.

'I've got something for you; I think it's what you're looking for'.

It was 4pm on a Monday and he'd just trawled the Crime Reporting Information System for reports of theft from hospitals. Not a risky thing for DC Simmonds to do as he was often called upon to investigate thefts from the London Hospital and needed to be aware of current similar thefts in the capital in order to collate and analyse the thieves' *modus operandi*. This would help him bid for resources when he wanted to put together an operation, often labour intensive and therefore expensive, to catch a hospital sneak thief. Almost always it was drugs – heroin, morphine, amphets, anything really that would fetch a few quid up at Kings Cross or in the clubs of South London. But this time it was different. It appeared that the thief had unwittingly made off with a flask of extremely hazardous material. At least this is what had disappeared. There had been no witnesses, no stolen doctor's white coat, no security alert. No evidence of theft really. But it had to be reported as such to save red faces. Flasks of biohazardous material don't just go missing for no reason.

Tuitt was on the edge of her seat as her source milked this for all that it was worth, or all that he thought it was worth. He didn't know the half of it.

'When did it go?' Tuitt was taking notes.

'Hard to say, theft reported from Soissons Unit on Saturday – I wasn't on duty – but I don't understand it. You can't get in there very easily. It's like Fort Knox. Inside job I reckon, or an accident and they've lost the stuff down a drain or something.'

'What was it, what was in the flask?' It was the next and obvious question.

'Dunno, report didn't say – just biohazardous material, one flask, 25cl. Look, here, I've got it, take it.'

Bent cops should never do this. Hand over official documents, or even copies, to their corruptors. It had not been Simmonds' intention to do so but he really trusted her. And anyway, he didn't regard this, or himself, as bent. They never do.

The corridors of Scotland Yard were full of lower caste journos like herself lobbying for stories. And the top brass used them, burned their own a lot of the time too, just to get a sound-bite in one of the red-tops. Tuitt looked at the printout. There was nothing to tell her much about the 'theft', no details, no times, not much at all really. Except for one name. Byers. Dr Byers as 'informant'. Dr Byers was the name of the person who reported the incident over the telephone to the police. Dr Byers. Tuitt sensed this was her lead.

12.

Jo Byers was in a buoyant mood that bright sunny January day. She bounced down the stone steps of the trendy Covent Garden Gym, her hair still wet from the power-shower, a canvas bag slung over her shoulder.

I was watching her, you see. I was taking photographs of

her. I'm a good surveillance man. One of the best. I could be standing two feet away from you and you wouldn't know I was there. I'm always watching her. All that training, all those years. For this, my final piece of work before one of two things happens. Either I get what I want or I don't. If I don't, I sink.

I've been on the same job for about ten months now. A woman. 'Bottom out', I tell myself, 'Bottom out.' Anyway, it was a sunny day as I followed her along Longacre, took photographs of her as she looked in this shop and that. A reccy for the next little spending spree. Husband's got a good job. And then she stopped dead, unslung her canvas bag and reached down into it to pull out the phone. She started walking again as she answered it, quickly at first. Then she slowed down. Then, stopped. It was bad news. At once she was frantic for a cab. It didn't take her long, with that body. That hair. They appeared from nowhere and fought to get at her. She dived into the first one, snapping orders at the driver. Off she roared. Leaving me stranded. As usual. No 'follow that cab' for me. Budget didn't stretch to it.

13.

'Call for you Dr Byers, can you take it now or shall I put it on your voicemail?'

'Voicemail please Sandy.'

The young scientist was thinking. He had by now several calls on his voicemail, some of them would be urgent. Sandy Bache was Duncan Byers' PA and she was getting worried. If he didn't get it cleared by the end of the day she would end up having to stay late. She liked scientists but hated working for them – they had no concept of time, even the 'bright young things' like Byers. *Doctor* Byers.

Something clicked and he rose from his shambolic desk, eyes darting here and there, searching for an answer to some monumental question with which he had just collided. Tuitt. What had she said? What had she said? The worm that turned? That, and the mention of Florence Obanga, had been a clear reference to Ebola, and then the last thing she had said -*smallpox*. Since taking up with Greschner, Byers had steeled himself for allegations that he was now working for an outfit that had long been rumoured to be 'morally flexible' – big pharma was used to that. It took only a short leap of the imagination to expect that some sensationalist would soon accuse them, and by extension himself, of weaponizing the Ebola virus, that particular bug being his most recent speciality. But he was ready for it; confident he could deflect such nonsense with solid science. The Ebola virus was an extremely sensitive organism, barely capable of living outside of a living organism for more than a few minutes and consequently almost impossible to collect, transport and put into any sort of bomb or projectile. Even in the event of it being thus weaponized, the effects of its deployment in any population other than those lacking in basic healthcare – such as most of Africa – could easily be contained and overcome. Furthermore, an infected host was only contagious once he or she exhibited symptoms, an event that did not occur until about eight days after infection. In contrast, smallpox is one of the most contagious diseases known. It can be spread not only by contact with body fluids of infected persons, but through the air and by contact with contaminated objects.

In contrast to the Ebola virus, the smallpox virus can remain infective for days or weeks in the environment. Byers had never been involved in the study or treatment of smallpox, so why had Tuitt mentioned it with reference to Ebola?

And then it hit him and his mind boggled. He made for the door, crashed through it and stumbled, almost drunkenly, along the corridor, totally preoccupied, ignoring everyone, barging past them. Through another door and into a dark room, the lights began to flicker on, triggered by his entry. Byers stopped, in front of him was the subject of his realisation, a massive steel safe for which he had the combination. He stood before it and shook. The room was chilled by air-conditioning, but he shook for another reason. The safe was Class Strap-Alpha, the most senior level of security. He had only recently been given personal combinations which he'd had to memorise. He was about to enter the safe when he remembered that he was being filmed; also his combinations would be logged and he would, at some point, be asked to account for his actions. To hell with it. If he was right then he would be leaving anyway. At once.

14.

Based at Clerkenwell Police Station in the general CID office, Simmonds needed to justify leaving his manor. The alleged theft of the phial had been verified and, by now, officially reported. There was not much more he could really do now. A specialist biohazard unit at New Scotland Yard had taken the job on and would no doubt proceed to do exactly nothing about it. The matter was probably now already just another statistic. Now knowing what had been stolen and what Tuitt's angle was had Simmonds intrigued, beginning to share his friend's nose for something big. He drove out along one of London's western corridors, through Brentford and onto the Great West Road. He parked up in a layby opposite the Greschner building, keeping a safe distance, mindful that he was being watched. He'd done some homework and had found Greschner to be very close to the government in terms of both pharmaceutical contracts and gifts to the ruling party.

He was on nothing more than a fishing expedition and had told his DI that he was in west London forging cross-border relations with Brentford CID in respect of some burglars who lived out that way and were ripping Clerkenwell offices apart at the weekends. Travelling burglars from Brentford, Guv. That had done the trick. He would have to pop into Brentford later on to meet some of his colleagues and perhaps the subject of Greschner would pop up.

He was thinking this through when a big Citroen pulled out of the Greschner gate and headed west. Having nothing much better to do, he followed it, with about two cars between them. It had been a year or so since he'd done the surveillance course and needed to hone his skills. They travelled west for about twenty minutes before turning into one of the many Heathrow feeder routes. The Citroen was two up so the passenger, guessed Simmonds, was being taken to his flight. He guessed wrong. Just before Terminal 3 the Citroen turned left along a narrow road marked 'Urban Farm'. Simmonds could not follow; to have done so would have put him right behind the target car without cover on what appeared to be a dead end. He motored past, did the next left into a cargo holding area full of containers and parked up, got out of the car and walked over to a chain mail fence. What he saw was, as per the sign, a farm. It had pigs and cows and sheep and lots of colourful hens. There was also a very big new looking shed, and there was no sign of the Citroen.

Simmonds saw the camera move and knew that he was under scrutiny. No good bolting, no good trying to hide, they would be doing a check on the registration number already. So, time for a standard anti-surveillance technique – he took a piss. He had his back to the road and his urine streamed and splashed against on the concrete uprights. He knew he was giving a full frontal to the camera and made sure whoever was watching got a good look. The camera, high up on the corner of the big shed was of the movement sensitive variety and stayed on him throughout his performance. He zipped up, lit a Marlboro, got back into the car and did a three point turn and left the area – for about 30 seconds. He drove back onto the main road, headed north for two hundred yards to a roundabout which he went all the way round and came back on himself. Something told him that he was going to see something. He didn't believe in coppers instincts as such. It was basic deduction. Two men in a company car drive from plush offices to remote, large scale storage space near an international airport. No other visible vehicles parked in the vicinity, their car disappears into a big shed, door closes. Camera watches. Something was coming out of there, something in addition to what had just gone in. And he was right. As he drove past the turning he saw it nosing out. A Hummer H2 SUT, a beast of a vehicle, one of the ugliest and most versatile on the roads. Simmonds had deduced correctly and, whilst he was on a roll, why not, he kept deducing. Why did Greschner not want the Hummer parked at their head office? There were plenty of spaces. Why did they keep it hidden away like this? Why? Because they were up to no good. They were up to mischief. But then he knew that. It was just that the trail was getting warmer.

He flew past the turn off and did not get a look at the occupants of the H2. Only able to see that there were two of them he guessed, this time rightly, that they were the same two who had driven to the shed in the Citroen.

The digital record of Simmonds pissing against the fence was archived away without attracting attention and two men called Hasleberger and Kirkpatrick took charge of their Hummer and made their way north, unaware that they had triggered an unfortunate chain of events.

15.

I suppose I haven't given you much of an explanation. I'm like an experimental research outfit. I don't really know where the money comes from. Some anonymous benefactor I suppose. I just get contacted and spoken to. In no uncertain terms, but I don't mind because the money comes in okay; every month, on the 20th, right into my current account at the Co-op. Sometimes I wonder how I got this assignment. I don't advertise and I no longer have any contacts to speak of. Perhaps that's why I got the job. And of course because I'm the best in the business. Creative Surveillance. That's my game.

Creativity is instinctive, of course, and I instinctively knew that something big had happened that day. Big and – I had the feeling – bad. I went back to base and waited. Three and a quarter hours later she got home, in a right state.

Jesus, how I wanted to help her. I could see her face as she got out of the cab, a different cab, she told the driver to wait and she went to her front door. Dropping the keys twice before she managed to get into her block, she was obviously distraught. Three minutes later she was out again, carrying a sports bag containing – it was open, I could see – cartons of milk and an assortment of fruit, including bananas. She was white as a sheet and looked exhausted. Her hair – that hair – was like rats' tails. Into cab. Cab away, north, 2013 hours. Log closed for the day. Withdraw.

16.

'My husband believed in his work and believed in Greschner. Not only has Greschner taken his life, they have also taken his dignity. His last few days were spent in physical agony. That was nothing compared to the emotional pain he suffered....'

Jo spoke without notes, unrehearsed. She knew exactly what to say, when to pause, when to raise her voice and when to glare at certain members of her reluctant audience. The wind stopped for her and the giant horse chestnuts stood still, giving her right of way; her anger being greater than theirs.

'Greschner, you are fortunate that this is not the place for charges to be laid, not the place for strong language, not the place to feel hatred. All that can wait. But if Duncan is here in this church, the church he dutifully attended as a boy on Sunday mornings, then he will know that this service is the beginning of a journey for some of us. A journey that will end in another place, another cold stone building in which hatred *is* felt, strong language *is* occasionally tolerated and in which charges are most *definitely* laid.'

17.

The huge door swung slowly and silently open. Byers stepped inside. It was his first time and he felt that he had crossed the Rubicon. He was puzzled. Why should he feel this way? Why should he feel like he'd done something that had stripped him of his innocence? He knew everything, did he not? In which case why had he opened that door?

The system was backed up every 24 hours. As an extra safeguard DAT tapes were generated and stored alongside the system continuously. They were stacked in custom-built shelving along one side of the stronghold. The mainframe server clung to brackets along the opposite wall. Byers approached the tape racks and stared along the identity labels. Stopped at one end, taking a pen from his pocket, jotted something on the palm of his hand. He left hurriedly. He had a number. It had an 'A' prefix. 'A' for Africa. He stepped out of the refrigerated safe and closed the door, knowing that the action would be monitored and feeling the camera on him; inspecting him. He moved further along the corridor to a less secure area and entered a small library stacked with tapes and discs. The back-up store held copies of everything but was only searchable by reference to the serial numbers on the originals in the Box. So, without having gained information from the Box the library was useless. Reading his palm he moved swiftly along the shelves until he found what he wanted. It was a compact disc in a paper envelope on which was stuck a small label bearing the number he'd just discovered as being the identity of evidence that would, if he was right, indict his employers. He now had one more place to visit, one more questionable entry to make. It was a little further away though.

18.

Oh, here he comes. Nigel Fucking Broadshoulders. That's what I call him anyway. Fucking wanker. Dr fucking Byers. Ground assigned 0700 and this is all I get. On his way up to Geordieland for the usual few days I suppose, reckon he's got a bird up there, must have, must have because you could not leave a wife like his for three or four days a week unless you've got a bit on the side or you're a fudge-packer. That's just my opinion, right, and I've been wrong before. Can't put it in the log unless I mark it as 'comment'. Anyway, no comment, just get on with the surveillance shall we? Subject 2 out of h/a, left Andover St, right St Henry's to tube. Carrying what appears to be hand luggage instead of usual briefcase. Note: not using car – BS06 12kf still parked o/s h/a. No follow, return to main subject believed still in h/a.

Right Mrs Byers, back to you my dear after that little interruption. After all, you're my girl, you're the job. Subject 1. That's my speciality you see. Looking after the ladies. I got so good at it they pretended to sack me from my last job with the government so that I would appear to disappear, so to speak. But oh no, you can't keep a good man down. This is my calling; surveillance. I'm a natural born watcher. And, like I said, you'd never know I'm there. I have this ability to be invisible without even trying. Basically, it's because I'm exceptionally insignificant. Like I say I'm so exceptional that they had to sack me from the old firm. Too exceptional they said. Too much of a specialist.

Too tangential. Too creative. They weren't actually rude to me, just like, er, it had to be done before I started to show people up with my creativity. Told me the official reason was because I kept getting side-tracked with the ladies. Morbid they called it at first, obsessive. So they sacked me. I kicked up that I would kill myself and go to the press and work for terrorists and all the rest of it but they wouldn't give me my job back. But they had a specialist look at me. He said that I was extremely talented and could do much better than break the OSA.

19.

It is often said that life can be stranger than fiction. It is always so. The reason being is that fiction is just a simplistic presentation of life. Two highly trained, ruthless mercenaries planting a tracking device on an unoccupied vehicle outside a church on a deserted country road – nothing could be simpler. Oh really?

The Hummer pulled up and joined the row of parked cars, its huge wheels creating a ditch of their own in the sodden grass verge. Not out of place in the Iraqi desert or Los Angeles urban wasteland, it looked quite incongruous in the line-up of Jags and executive Lexis. Its two occupants climbed down and walked along the line to a blue BMW, hired that day in Newcastle by someone using a credit card in the name of Joanne Byers. Hasleberger carried a black plastic attaché case; he set it down on the top of an ancient milestone and opened the lid. It contained a magnetised tracking device. Simply installed on the underside of the car it could be monitored from distances of up to 50 miles. Kirkpatrick stood looking up and down the road. 'Under you get, go on.' Hasleberger knew this would rile his partner but did it anyway.

'What'

'You heard me, I'll hand it under to you, you're slimmer than me, go on, we haven't much time.'

'Yu takin' the fucking piss outa me ya cunt? Why me?'

Kirkpatrick was riled alright, he didn't like taking orders, especially off the Hun.

'Oh come on, please, pretty, pretty, please, go on, I've got jet lag, I'm so tired.'

'Jet lag? From Liberia? Don't make me feckin' laugh, it's only an hour oot… aah fuck it, giz it here.'

With that the wiry Scot dropped down and crabbed under the BMW, holding out a spare hand to take the device from the grinning Austrian. The Jock saw the grin.

'An ye can wipe that fuckin grin aaf ya face!'

Neither man had seen the little red Fiat tucked into the gateway of an adjacent field, but its sole occupant was watching them – and knew exactly what they were doing.

20.

Hywell Casey was rolling a cigarette when Simmonds slid through his door. He would not be able to smoke it until later but it was a habit that helped him ruminate. As detective chief inspector of Clerkenwell Division he made out that he had a lot on his plate. But he did not have that much to do and was, he had to be honest, bored out of his mind. Being a copper in London had once been an exciting and stimulating job, especially as a CID officer. But not anymore, not really. Unless you were a politician with a mind for promotion to the senior ranks then you really were just a dinosaur before you were halfway through your service. So Casey's thoughts were pretty bleak as he regarded this young, keen detective constable with a life ahead of him.

'Yes mate?' Despite working the underbelly of London for 30 years the Welsh accent was still strong.

'A bit of a funny one here, Guv', muttered Simmonds, still frowning at the computer printout he held in his hand.

'I know you are Simmonds, I should never have had you on this division. What's the problem matey?'

'Did a check on a vehicle this morning Guv, came back blocked. Did all the usual Intel database checks too, nothing. Current looking registration number, not issued says the PNC, yet the plates are on a Hummer being driven by employees, or at least friends, of a big drug company.'

'What the hell are you on about, son? Which big drug company?'

'Sorry Guv, I'll explain in more detail. I've got this contact at the hospital, not an informant, just a contact. She reckons a firm called Greschner, that's the drug company, are up to some serious tricks. Developing illegal drugs, animal testing, dangerous human testing, not keeping their promises to poor countries, stealing from the government, all that sort of stuff. My contact reckons....'

'Guy, you've just described every drug company on the face of the planet, son. What's the news?'

'My contact reckons – and I know this sounds ridiculous – she reckons that a man died recently from a designer disease developed by Greschner and that that man had worked in the Sassons Institute of the hospital....'

'Soissons'

'Whatever, and that at the time of his death had worked at Greschner.'

'Where are we going?'

'This guy had just found out something about his employer that he didn't like and so they killed him, or so his widow thinks, and she wants to spill the beans before they get to her.'

'You're supposed to invite your DCI to the pub at lunchtime you know.'

'Do what guv?'

'Cos that's where you've bloody been, isn't it?'

'No, I haven't.' Simmonds laughed with this denial because he knew his story sounded very far-fetched indeed.

'I know, I know, Guv, you couldn't make it up, you couldn't write the script, but this is genuine intelligence, confidential information.'

'It might be confidential information but as for genuine intelligence I'm not so sure. You're supposed to be able to act on intelligence – what the fuck do we do with this?'

What Simmonds had done was classic. He couldn't reveal his relationship with Tuitt. That would be a sacking offence at least, with a good chance of a prosecution for misconduct in public office. He was Tuitt's source, yet she had become his. Two way traffic. He could not register her as a police informant – too much paperwork and too much transparency. So she would remain a mere 'contact' at the hospital. Conjured up homely images of a staff nurse or a sweet little lab technician. Total fiction.

'Guvnor, it comes back as nothing at all. It's not a ringer – there's never been a Hummer stolen in this country – there's something wrong with that firm, Guv, and we can soon find out what, if you let me....'

The DCI was not impressed. Young London detectives could double their salaries by doing overtime, and Simmonds was one of the best at it.

'What do you want to do then Simmonds, launch a nationwide surveillance operation just because an unusual vehicle seemingly owned by a drugs company has unregistered plates?

'No, look, I was... I've got this contact you see, and....'

'Ah, one of your contacts. Never informants or covert human intelligence sources are they Simmonds? Always 'contacts', I wonder why?'

'Because you have to share snouts and CHIS's with the world and his fucking wife, all the hard earned info goes into the intel pot for lazy bastards to pick and choose from and nick your fucking jobs Guv!'

'Nick your overtime you mean. Okay then, calm down, what have you got in mind?'

21.

The Reverend William Robson, having uttered the few words expected of him at a coffinless funeral, walked along the aisle to the door to bid farewell to this congregation of total strangers. Jo walked after him, the rest allowing her to clear the premises before making their move. Not out of politeness, but fear. None of them wanted to face her. And she had no intention of hanging around outside for them either. The tide was coming in. As Jo drove down to the coast and onto the causeway she was unaware of the first car following her. Hardly her fault as it was over a mile behind her. The beacon just planted on the underside of her rented BMW gave her pursuers a clear advantage.

The six hour flight from Heathrow to Monrovia on BA0372 was delayed. An air traffic control strike in France or something. By the time Byers boarded at 11.20pm he'd had a few stiff ones airside. He slept in Club Class for the entire journey, awakening to breakfast with Africa beneath him. Two hours later he was through – hand luggage only – and was booking into the Royal Grand Hotel. The foyer was deserted apart from a couple of security guards and a group of big Americans who had just returned from a night's drinking downtown in one of the few white boozers that remained in the capital of Liberia.

The concierge was called Livingstone and had a broad head with a broad smile. He welcomed the scientist with impeccable English manners, handing him a key to a single room on the 11th floor. A bell boy offered to carry Byers' small bag, the offer was declined but the African lad got a good tip anyway. As the lift doors closed behind the latest guest Livingstone picked up the telephone.

Inside the hotel room Byers collapsed on the bed and slept for two hours longer, still exhausted despite the sleep on the plane. Monrovia, only an hour out of sync with London, does not generally feature jet-lagged Europeans – unless they've come from somewhere other than Europe, such as the one waiting in the lounge who had just arrived from Thailand.

Hasleberger had been resting in Phuket when he'd got the call. If resting is what you can call drinking a bottle of rum and having sex with at least one young prostitute each day. But business was business and he was running out of money. Liberia? Easy, after Angola.

22.

Blanchette finished her morning workout with three sets of shoulder press exercises. On her way to the shower room she paused to examine her physique in the big floor to ceiling mirrors. Not bad. After her shower she examined her face more closely, the steroids were taking their toll. Acne was appearing on her pronounced jaw line and her facial hair needed daily shaving. She was not bothered. It was what she wanted. The effect on her predominantly male peers was fascinating. They either fancied her or feared her. Nobody ignored her. This gave Blanchette an inner calm, she did not have to compete – she was unique. Her economy of speech and rareness of smiles finished the job. And her boss adored her. She saw it in his ageing eyes. She knew she possessed some strange power over him.

She saw it again in those eyes as she walked into his office with the very urgent news. He looked up and smiled across the conference table, one end of which served as his desk. He had been reading the newspapers and they were all spread out before him. Nothing of much interest to anyone. Nothing of any interest at all to Greschner.

'Yes my dear? What do you have that's so urgent?' He stood up straight, and watched as Blanchette closed the door behind and move slowly, almost menacingly towards him. He began to worry. The woman certainly knew about emphasis. She spoke in a low, husky voice.

'Byers. He's been in the Box.'

'He's been where?!'

'He's been in the secure archive, a disc is missing. That was yesterday.'

She stood before her boss with her feet apart and delivered the information from a clipboard. She wore a Tweed suit which hugged her muscular body. Ellis eyed her, as he always did, with a mixture of respect and lewdness. He had to be honest with himself – he fancied his secretary, even though she spent all of her spare time either in the gym or on the track trying, it would seem, to look like a man. Byers had been given full access to the secure archive only one month previously. It was Greschner policy to place all newly vetted personnel under electronic surveillance whilst they were in the building for the first three months after clearance. That way the security division's computer gained an 'insight' as to their habits and movement profile. This in turn could be used as a yardstick against which to assess future unusual behaviour. There was something that bothered Ellis about Byers, ever since he had been recruited three months previously from the medical community. Ex-medics always bothered Ellis because they were never really totally ex-medics. They always had a residual save-the-world attitude. The company took second place in their books. So you not only had to pay them very well but you also had to kid them that what they were doing was for the common good and not that of the shareholders.

'What disc is missing my dear?'

'Africa.'

'Keep a very close eye on him. Check the airports through friends in Special Branch, make sure….'

'Already done it sir, he's booked on the 2200 hours flight to Monrovia tomorrow from Heathrow.'

'Obviously going to check up on his old friends. Make sure we are helping them like we said we would.'

'Are we?'

Never before had Blanchette asked a question like this and Ellis was quite taken aback.

'Of course we are my dear. Of course we are. Thank you. Email me the details.'

His last words had a slight edge to them and Blanchette knew it was time to leave. She turned on her heel and strode out, being careful to close the door quietly behind her.

23.

Hasleberger

The method had been stipulated and any departure from that would void the deal. New to the mercenary but attractive all the same. No noise, no blood, no buggering about with guns.

From his stool at the bar the Austrian had a clear view of the lift lobby; such was the layout of the Royal Grand. He sipped tonic water, with ice and slice, and waited, cooled by the air conditioning and confidence in his own ability. And the fact that he was working alone. More and more these days he was being put in positions where he had to rely on others. It was agonising for the killer, especially as these strangers were always foreigners and younger than him. He hated them, with their language skills and computer literacy. There was only one for whom he had a grudging respect, he reflected. He rolled a chunk of ice around in his mouth and wondered where Kirkpatrick was these days. They shared a few clients and occasionally bumped into each other on business engagements.

24.

Yeah, they had a distinct advantage, but I didn't, so I just had to front it out. Brazen. It can work, usually does. I just belted past them. I guessed where my target was heading and, sure enough, soon caught up with her. I stayed a respectable distance behind, but didn't make a thing about it, about 50 yards. Who would do a follow on a narrow deserted road at 50 yards?

When we hit the causeway there was nothing behind me, but I could see her looking in her rear view mirror at me. So I closed in and flashed my headlamps. She kept going. A second time and her brake lights came on. We were a third of the way across the causeway. She pulled over and I flew past, as if in a hurry for a meeting with some important seagulls on an island in the North Sea.

25.

'Dr Byers, I presume.'

The sleepy and preoccupied Byers was shocked by this. Who was this man? How did he know?

'Don't worry. Your company has sent me to look after you. You shouldn't have come, you know that, don't you?'

'Who are you?'

'I've just told you, your minder, your company is worried for your safety.'

'Just keep away from me.'

'Okay but not too far. Want a drink?'

'I'll get my own thanks... why does the company think I'm in danger?'

'I don't know. This is Africa, your company has enemies here. Allow me to introduce myself.'

26.

The one bedroomed, second floor flat is cold and smells of

damp and chemicals. The heating does not come on for 24 hours. The bathroom-cum-darkroom, blacked out from the world, is particularly chilled. Black and white prints hang everywhere, pegged on lengths of string that zigzag across the room.

The living area is chaotic but clean, devoid of womanly evidence, lacking any feel of contentment. Everything seems unfinished. Half read books lay open, spine up, on cluttered surfaces. Ashtrays contain barely smoked cigarette butts, the product of an incessant quitter, perhaps. One wall has been stripped of its paper but remains undecorated – a roll of new paper stands in the corner. Just inside the window, over which one thin curtain is partially drawn, stands a powerful tripod mounted telescope. It is aimed permanently at the rear of a house on the other side of a park, almost a quarter of a mile away.

The lock is unsophisticated and easily defeated. A man and a woman enter, cautiously. David Lytolis and Sandrine Voillet are contractors. The woman is French and her slender form belies her skills and operational coolness. The man is of Latvian extraction, muscular, intelligent, relaxed.

They take in the scene. Voillet sweeps the place with a digital video camera. Lytolis, surgically gloved, searches. Their breath hangs in the bitter air. The place is a shrine to one woman, Joanne Byers. Prints hang everywhere, but there is much more. Video tapes and DVDs are stacked high and a life size statue dominates one corner, next to it sits the 3D printer by which it was built. Lytolis sits down at the chaotic desk in another corner and powers up the elderly computer, noting its many state-of-the-art add-ons. An eclectic mix of technology. Wet film processing alongside digital wizardry. Whilst waiting for the screen to come alive he thumbs through an assortment of floppy discs, USB data sticks and CDs. They are all labelled, with dates and numbers. He picks a CD at random, slips it into the drive and hits the keyboard. A moving image appears – of the woman walking along the street. Lytolis continues to sample at random and the result is always the same, always the same damned woman doing nothing more interesting than crossing the road or standing at a bus stop.

Voillet has made up her mind.

'Sicko. Sad man. He cannot be dangerous to our client. This woman maybe, but not to our client.'

Lytolis is not so sure.

'No. If he knows so much about her, if he's followed her so well, then he may have more information than he thinks. If he was properly debriefed he might be very dangerous to our client – or at least another paying customer might think so – get my meaning?'

Voillet grins and nods.

'Nice thinking Lytolis, but not with this firm, they'd not make good enemies for us.'

She walks away, leaving her partner appearing to be thoughtful. They'd been briefed on a need-to-know basis, but had been given enough information to know that the woman was of interest. All they had been told to do was search this flat and look for a CD, and there were thousands. This idiot was the woman's stalker. She would not know him. If she did know him she wouldn't trust him with top secret material, not this idiot.

Lytolis grinned and began stashing every CD, floppy, stick, video tape and negative film folder into large polythene bags. Voillet stares.

'You have got to be fucking joking.'

Lytolis turns and stares back at her.

'Not even a little bit. We take it all, and the hard drive. Someone will want it.'

He knows Voillet will refuse a share of this action. Far too straight.

27.

The bar at the Monrovia Royal Grand is a bit of an oasis in that there's nowhere really else to go, especially if you're a tired and troubled medical scientist and the company you are saddled with won't take no for an answer. Byers was mesmerised by the presence of Hasleberger and was not so tired and troubled that he didn't realise that the Austrian was a danger to him in that he would not be able to move anywhere without being accompanied. That was why Hasleberger was here; to protect the company from this rogue boffin, not to protect the rogue boffin. But poor Duncan Byers hadn't grasped the half of it. His third gin and tonic was presented to him on his return from a visit to the gents and he later reflected that it had tasted slightly different from the first two. About five days later. Far too late. He never made it to West point where evidence existed to prove that his work there had been hijacked and stolen. The latest deaths had been kept under wraps, a bit like the frozen plasma that had been extracted from the Ebola virus victims in the high security hospital he had once operated from Soissons Research Unit.

28.

Twenty four hours later the Airbus banked over Kent and headed across London to Heathrow. Duncan Byers did not feel well at all. He had a terrible thirst, ached from head to toe and felt very low. He had not effected his purpose. He had not reached West point. The organisation had prevented him from getting there. Damn them. 'No cabs to West point – Ebola outbreak, area in isolation, quarantine.' This is how the message read, the confidential message obtained by Hasleberger from the Liberian Interior Ministry. And it wasn't that confidential either. The organisation had done a good job – fingers in every pie. Watching South African TV that night at the Monrovia Royal Grand, Byers had seen a short report on an overstretched hospital in West point, trying and failing to deal with upwards of thirty seriously ill villagers. The 'mystery virus' could, said the report, be a strain of the Sudan Ebola virus carried south by war refugees. It was mysterious in that it was more contagious with carriers able to infect others before they themselves exhibited symptoms. Also, the symptoms were different from those of ordinary Ebola and featured similarities to certain strains of smallpox; fingers blackened and eyes became bloodshot within twenty four hours of exposure. The report, delivered from the safety of a studio and without film footage or witness testimony, confirmed that travel to the slum peninsula was restricted to Liberian government officials. Byers betted it was, and feared the worst; this was a designer disease – *ebolapox*. It had dawned on him on the day he had entered the safe;

Greschner had recruited him not because of his good work against sub-Saharan epidemics, but because of his former post-graduate paper on viral splicing. His intention had been to investigate the possibility of nullifying killer diseases by genetically modifying viruses so that they mutate into harmless organisms, thereby incapacitating themselves as pathogens. The research had backfired, resulting in the spliced viral pathogens becoming even more lethal. The UK government and international bodies had consequently, and understandably, ceased funding. Word got out and Greschner stepped in to fill the vacuum.

He was not picked up at the airport. This was ironic he thought, given that he'd been both imprisoned and mollycoddled by Hasleberger in Monrovia. Not surprising though, he was no danger to them now. Out of harm's way, Hasleberger had put him on his plane and had appeared very pleased to see the back of him. He had only taken hand luggage and got through the formalities at terminal three briskly. He jumped into a black cab and instructed the driver to take him to Westminster. He sat back and, as if the effort of disembarkation had taken a great toll on his health, fell asleep.

He awoke half an hour later as the taxi trundled through… where was he, he couldn't see. He was soaked in sweat and had, to his horror, urinated. His head seemed about to explode. What the fuck had happened, what had he contracted? With great effort he leaned forward and as loud as he could, shouted to the driver.

'Take me to a hospital, urgently. Take me to a hospital.' Smelling the stench for the first time, the driver did not argue and pulled the cab round to head for the Cromwell

Hospital which was about two hundred yards away.

29.

'Peter, Peter listen, I'm reading from a recent text on this stuff, if my source is good then I'm onto a biggun, listen... These viruses are single stranded negative sense RNA viruses that target primates. There are two general viruses, the Ebola virus (Ebolavirus, with four species) and the Marburg virus (Marburgvirus).'

These viruses cause haemorrhagic fevers, characterised by massive bleeding from every orifice of the body. These diseases are shockingly lethal, with very high mortality rates and infectiousness. They are classified by the WHO as BSL4, or biosafety level 4. This means that they are among the most lethal and destructive viruses known to man. But they can be controlled in modern environments. The killer news is that it looks like they're being modified somehow, spliced with a version of the smallpox virus, which would make them uncontrollable and totally lethal... You listening?'

Peter Lake listened to his young hireling. Keen as mustard. Going to put the world right, always the same enthusiasm. But occasionally they did come up with the goods, these keen young things, and his cynicism (perhaps jealously) had cost him dear in the past.

'Okay Mickey – go for it, that's what they say isn't it? Go for it? Get alongside your man and see what he has to say for himself. Can't believe he's been duped though, a doctor of science, eminent, duped by a drugs firm? Have a look though, and er... keep the expenses down.'

Chocolates. Celebratory chocolates now. Michaela Tuitt tumbled down the stairs of her tiny docklands flat and out into the sunshine, eyes squinting but fixed on the local shop. Black Magic? Terry's Gold? Both?

30.

He threw a fifty pound note at the driver and stumbled through the doors of the Accident and Emergency Unit. It was 7am and the night staff were handing over to the first of two day shifts. Huddled over a desk covered with lists and duty rosters, the three nurses looked up and when they heard Byers crash through the swing doors. Two of them rushed to help him, the third, a middle aged African lady wearing a starched agency uniform, did not. Judy Fletcher had grown up in the Democratic Republic of Congo before immigrating to the UK to marry an Englishman and work as a supply nurse. She was not fully qualified, even after 18 years, but instinctively knew not to go near this man.

'Don't go near him!' she shrieked at her colleagues. They stopped and turned, and then turned again as Byers collapsed on the newly polished floor in a pool of sweat and urine.

'Get a barrier team down here, don't touch him,' said Judy. One of the other nurses, a young male, was confused. 'We need to get him into the recovery position, if he vomits he'll….'

At which point Byers did indeed vomit – blood. His whole body convulsed and it spurted out of his mouth with such force that it decorated a wall eight feet away. Judy Fletcher was already on the phone and within minutes two heavily clad barrier porters were at the scene. They wore thick red rubber overalls, gloves and masks that covered their entire heads. Only their eyes were visible through Perspex visors. They worked efficiently, having received recent training as a contingency against the arrival of highly infectious diseases from foreign parts.

It was five hours later before Jo Byers was informed of her husband's admission. She had been at her gym, trying not to worry too much about Duncan's rushed and unscheduled trip to Africa. But she had worried a lot. He said he would ring her from Heathrow as soon as he landed. The flight Jo thought must have been delayed or even re-slotted. Not unusual from that part of the world. Duncan was never much good at phoning home at the best of times, never mind from chaotic airports. So she had tried not to worry too much.

Arriving at the hospital she asked at reception, as coolly as she could, where the Dell Ward was located. The uniformed orderly asked if she had an appointment and what her business was.

'My husband has just been admitted there early this morning, I've come to visit him.'

The orderly picked up the phone, looked up a number and dialled it. 'I've a Mrs Byers at the main entrance' he said, not taking his eyes off Jo.

A pause.

'Okay, I'll ask her to take a seat.'

31.

The big Hummer lurched off road with ease. Kirkpatrick was driving. Hasleberger smoking. They pulled up before hitting the dunes and jumped down onto the sandy soil. Climbing onto the first dune they commenced the reccy. To the south is the flat sands, pockmarked with a billion worm casts. To the north a ribbon of white beach, backed by the low dunes and dozens of concrete blocks – two metre cubes designed to stop Hitler's landing craft, had they arrived, sixty years earlier. The cubes are at three metre intervals and, every so often, are interspersed with shelters, roughly the same in appearance, but bigger and hollow with slits for machine guns. Hasleberger cannot wait to get inside one. Would they have really stopped the Fuhrer?

Kirkpatrick sat on a dune and surveyed the scene. A cold wind buffeted the long, spiky grass and ruffled the shallow sea. The tide was coming in and the island, about half a mile away, was separated from the mainland by soaking mudflats slowly disappearing beneath the water. It seemed that the wind was blowing the sea inwards, filling more space with each wave surge.

Kirkpatrick had read a little about Holy Island. How it had been inhabited firstly by mead-making monks who had farmed a few sheep on the fifty or so acres of sandy grassland and had studied and taught in a priory. The priory, or roofless ruins of it, still stood in the centre of the island's small village. A few hundred metres away from the village, on a rocky outcrop at the southern tip of the island, stood an ugly little castle. One day the Scot would like to live in a place like this. Have a couple of dogs, read books and tend a garden. He would need the dogs for company as he had no intention of taking a wife. Been there, done that, got the tee-shirt. He had married as a boy soldier. They had lived in married quarters and, after eight months she had gone over the side with his section sergeant. That had been a big turning point in Kirkpatrick's life. He'd thereafter thrown himself into his soldiering – and killing.

Hasleberger interrupted the Scot's daydream quite rudely.

'Come on. We'd better pull back. We can see the island so the island can see us.'

'So what.' Kirkpatrick responded irritably, it was not a question. He did not want to be here. The journey from London had been a nightmare. Hasleberger's endless stupid rude chatter. Kirkpatrick rightly suspected that the Austrian was nervous; but then so was he.

'We should get the Hummer out of sight; it sticks out like a sore finger.'

'Thumb.'

'What?'

'Never mind.'

With that Kirkpatrick jumped to his feet, walked to the big vehicle, got in, started the engine and reversed down into a valley behind the line of dunes. They had decided on their cover. They were bird watchers. That would explain the binoculars and maps. It would not explain the contents of a hidden compartment beneath the Hummer's floor.

Hasleberger joined his partner in the vulgar vehicle and they both studied the surveillance screen. The radio beacon had a 60 mile radius and was presenting the receiver with a strong signal at such a short distance. An Ordnance Survey map of the island was raised on the screen and a small red arrow pointed to a place in the middle of the island's village. Very near to the Priory, noted Kirkpatrick. He was not a religious man but feared God and everything associated with Him. The Scot did not want to be here, did not want to kill a woman and certainly did not want to do it near a centre of early Christianity.

Ellis and Muller sit opposite each other, the dinner table set between them. Silent, they waited. Ellis sipped a whiskey. 'Laphraog', he announces.

'What?' asked Muller, irritably.

'It's a fine Scotch whiskey, a malt from….'

'I am aware of the origins of whiskey Ellis, I own a distillery, remember; I know more about it than you know about Duncan Byers' fucking wife – not that that's saying much….'

'Look, it'll be fine, she can't get off that island until 11pm, we have it covered, there's only one route….'

Kurt Muller was growing increasingly impatient with his English partner. For five and a half years they had sparred at the helm of Greschner, resentful of each other's qualities, feigning friendship but never trust. Muller, the elder of the two, had benefited from a strict upbringing and stoic education in Germany's industrial Dusseldorf. His father, a prominent pharmacist, had insisted he follow him. The young Muller had complied and had never regretted it. Until now. Stuck one rung from the top and blocked by an

English idiot.

But Ellis was no fool. A clever bit of buying through his banking connections had made him the bigger shareholder of Greschner's British interests, and it was in Britain that they were based. Switzerland attracted too many eastern agents trying to buy for uncertain reasons and Greschner did not want to attract that sort of attention. Good Lord no. Being based in Britain kept them out of the limelight. Muller sat and quietly seethed, as usual. It did not help when one of the accompanying assistants handed Ellis a mobile phone. The Englishman took it, listened and frowned.

'Okay. Just stay there. Did you get the number of the vehicle? Oh. Okay. Just stay there.' He tapped the phone off.

'What is it?' said the German, through clenched teeth.

'Your man Hasleberger. He says the woman was followed onto an island by another car. May have just been a coincidence. They hung back.'

'This fucking island. What is there? What is she doing?'

'How the hell do I know?! Your guess is as good as mine – for a change. What do you think? Is there a funeral party going on there? Is she a member of a witch's coven that operates there? Has she got a…?'

The German was becoming reddened by this outburst of English humour.

'Fucking shut it! I only asked. We should just slot her and

be done with it. How come Hasleberger is reporting to you, anyway? He's my man, I took him on, he's the best....'

'Muller, Muller, Muller, calm down man. She drove onto Holy Island. Lindisfarne. Lovely place. It's cut off when the tide comes in twice every twenty four hours. The worst possible scenario is that she's going to drop the disc there. We can't get near her just now. There's nothing we can do about it. We'll have to confront her when she comes back to the mainland'.

'What about the disc then? What do we do? Nuke the fucking place?'

'She'll tell us where it is.'

'Ha, you going to torture her? Not very English. Against human rights Ellis, against....'

'Muller, try to use your head. She is an intelligent woman, she wants justice for the death of her husband. We must see to it that she gets it.'

'I know what she has to get! She has that disc and we have to take it from her before she passes it on.'

'How do we know she hasn't already done so... how many times have we been through this? We don't know she hasn't already passed it on – we can only guess that she would not wish to do so until after the memorial service. My guess, Muller, and let's face it, I'm usually right....'

'Fuck you! I'm usually right, I'm usually right. I am sick of your theories and indecision, you....'

'Oh shut up Muller. You bore me. Just wait. If you cannot

wait, then leave. All contingency plans are in place, we will pay her off if need be, but only if need be.'

With that Ellis hunkered down onto the leather chair and nursed his whiskey. He was not a complete stranger to executive action and didn't mind being part of a permanent solution. But he would never discuss it openly. He smiled as he privately doubted that he'd ever used the word 'killed' in his professional life.

32.

At first the woman thought the red Fiat was following her. When it flashed and overtook she was happy. Just a twit in a little red car panicking that he'd miss dry road. There were at least twenty minutes before the next tide came in. She took her time, and kept her eye on the rear view mirror. Nothing. Safe. Nice feeling.

George Niles had been the licensee of the Anchor Hotel on the island village harbour for over forty years. His wife had long since died and he ran the tiny establishment with the help of Raymond, his 35 year old son who had Down's syndrome. The little pub had few visitors in November and never any attractive women. He frowned at Jo Byers' request for a room, not knowing if to take her seriously. She wasn't a birdwatcher, nor an archaeologist. Then George shrugged. 'Fine,' he'd start warming the room up, 'dinner at eight.' He left her alone. She lay slowly down on the narrow bed. It was extremely uncomfortable. A feather filled mattress on a concave frame. But she relaxed all the same. She closed her eyes and thought of the nightmare that had been real. How she had arrived at the hospital, fearing the worst – to find far worse. To find her husband writhing around on a sweat soaked gurney surrounded by barrier staff, the fear showing in their goggled eyes as they restrained him and administered fluid and drugs through intravenous insertions which bled almost as much as his nose and mouth and... She could hardly bear it, but she had to. His last days had been agonising, he had been terrified but something had sustained him and they had talked. He had only taken hand luggage and his killer had clearly not wanted it. He had been murdered and that seemed to be the job done. All he had to do was die in Liberia. The killer had disappeared from Monrovia after their little drink, assuming his prey would travel north to West point. But the outbreak had prevented travel, ironically, and, feeling unwell he had headed home. Or that was what he told his wife. She suspected he knew what had happened soon after his fateful gin and tonic. She suspected he had realised that the company had to kill him but that he had realised too late. The company had killed him but he had got home in time to die.

33.

Christ it's fucking freezing here. How can you freeze on a beach? Approaching the island village on foot. Target vehicle outside Anchor Hotel. Take up position Lindisfarne Guesthouse. Nice one. Cheap and they're pleased to see me. I bet the food is good too. Okay. Right. Target housed. Anchor Hotel. Log closed. Stand down and withdraw. 0700 start tomorrow. This is good stuff. Brilliant tradecraft. Not one mistake, no compromise. She didn't suss me one bit. I was rushing past, no problem. Now the sea has cut us off. We are cut off Jo. All alone and cut off. I could do anything I like now. And just a few days ago there was nothing. Nothing to bring us close, Jo. Now I have you. Now we're going to meet. And you will find me to be such an interesting person. You'll love me, you really will, when I tell what I saw today. I'm your fairy godfather. Now, this is good footwork. I've got supplies in my day-sack; my transport is parked securely and away from target. Would I dare pitch up in the same hotel? Should I? No, too risky. Different had it been the summer with loads of tourists, but not just now.

34.

Well, it's a broad term. Not the sort of meal you'd expect in a part of the country known for its fresh game and seafood. But powdered potato and spam it was and she was very hungry. Raymond served it up with all the aplomb of a Dorchester House waiter. He had even tied a frayed tie around his stocky neck and a freshly laundered tea-towel lay over his forearm in true professional style. She thanked him and got stuck in. It wasn't too bad, especially once the attentive Raymond had poured some piping hot gravy over it.

As she ate she thought of her journey that day. She had scanned the plane for Greschner personnel and had been surprised that there were none. None that she recognised that was. She had met most of the 'up-highs' when Duncan had been recruited. They had made a big deal about welcoming her to the 'family'. She had been to at least half a dozen dinner parties over recent months and had met lots of WAGs. Some she had liked, some she most certainly had not. Now, she hated them all. They had killed her husband and, if they knew what she was about to do, they'd kill her too. Although she knew this she couldn't actually consciously believe it. The whole thing was like it was taking place in someone else's life. She wondered where Tuitt was. She stopped chewing for a second and glanced down at her shoulder bag, thinking of the shiny little compact disc that would be the end of Greschner. Her mind returned to her last conversation with her husband.

'I'm dying Jo', he had announced as she stood wide eyed behind the screen and shook. She had frozen when she first saw him lying there, for a long five seconds before screaming, 'Jesus Christ Duncan' and then lurching forward only to be stopped and dragged back by two big nurses. 'If I don't get through this then I've been murdered. By Greschner. More specifically by Ellis.'

Not taking her eyes from him she scrabbled about in her hand bag and pulled out her phone. One of the nurses tried to take it from her but she snatched it back and dialled her home phone number, the answer-phone clicked in and started recording, she switched onto hands free and held the phone up to Byers. 'Go on Duncan, go on,' she urged. She knew instinctively that this was what she had to do. The scene of her husband on what was quite obviously his screaming death bed at the age of 34 had kicked a big shot of adrenaline into her brain and she was all go.

'I went to Liberia to confirm something. I got a call, from Bache at the London branch, she took over from me when I went to Greschner. Told me that the interferon had not been getting to West point, that Florence, that's Florence at, at….'

'Yes honey, go on, Florence at where?'

'At….'

She couldn't bear to remember any more. The act of remembering her husband's death rendered images too vivid to bear. The visualisation was blinding. So she switched on the tape in the machine in her handbag, fast forwarded it to where she had got to unaided and listened, more detached, more analytical. It was bearable. Just. 'At the field hospital, Florence Obanga, she had a brother in Monrovia with a government position and a free satellite phone. Edwin Obanga, her husband, had contracted Ebola a few weeks previously and was dying. Just like me now, except without painkillers and intravenous fluids. Said... she said the drugs weren't getting to Liberia... weren't even getting out of London. Greschner cheated Jo, they promised me they would honour the contract....'

'What contract Duncan?'

A pause. As she listened to the scratchy recording she remembered that it was at this point that her husband suffered some sort of seizure and had arched his back and contorted his face into such a hideous mask that she had nearly fainted at the sight, this had lasted about ten seconds and then his body had relaxed in the pool of sweat that was his hospital bed. She had yearned to hold him but the mesh screen was there for a purpose and his dying would be all the worse and all the more pointless if he left her infected and dying too.

35.

As night fell over this outpost of the British Isles the wind picked up. As if in anticipation of the gathering drama, the weather seemed to want to provide a fitting backdrop. Jo and Driver shivered in their unaired beds, two unhappy but highly paid men shivered in a black Hummer on the mainland.

'Right. The sea is over the road Kirkpatrick. We should go and find a bed.'

'Wrong, twat. We find two fuckin' beds. Ah'm no sleeping wi' you yu Austrian cunt'.

'You Scottish are so funny. What time does the road become passable?'

'Fuckin' 1.10am. No point in getting a hotel or B&B. Might as well just sit it out here.'

'You are joking. This thing is going to be like a fridge. I can't keep the engine running, we'll run out of fucking petrol.'

'Ah, shut the fuck up. Get some sleep. It could be an early start.'

36.

Michaela Tuitt disliked driving. Her stature was not conducive to long journeys behind the wheel and she made several stops at service stations. She would not make the funeral service and anyway had no intention of going near it. Simmonds had worried her. She had broken a golden rule a few nights previously and had slept with him. Flattered, she supposed. Not many made a pass at her these days. She had started putting weight at the age of 20 and had not really looked back. But it was not that that had worried her. It was that Simmonds had decided to involve others. He had been genuinely worried by what he had seen at the Greschner HQ. In particular by the name of the registered owner of the Hummer; there wasn't one. The Police national computer had drawn a blank. This meant that the registration number was for some reason blocked or that the number had not been issued. He had decided on the former explanation and this meant that the vehicle had some very powerful owners.

She had expected very scant communications, but not total bloody silence. She had a map reference and the phrase 'priory box'. And that was it. She knew what it was about alright, well, enough to know that it was well worth the trip. She had talked to the woman and was impressed by her composure under what must have been somewhat difficult circumstances. She telephoned her from a call box somewhere between Newcastle and Berwick to give her the location of what she knew would be a basis for a front page. She had understood her caution – Mrs Byers needed to get clear. She could not be caught. Tuitt understood very well. She had a long, dark drive. And now she had to watch out for Simmonds.

37.

Must try to get some sleep. Must try to get some sleep. Must try to get some sleep. Jesus this is hard. Got to be professional. She's in danger. Got to break cover. No. Keep out of it. Surveillance only. No compromise. But... what's the point? If she gets hurt, what's the point in that?

Wait. What the fuck am I doing here? Take a step back. Look at the bigger picture. I'm here because I... need to be here. Nothing more. Yeah. That's a bit of insight. Truth hurts. Well, it looks like I'm going to have to come clean.

They aren't really..., well they're there but they're not if you see... look, I follow her because I sense something. I'm under instructions. I'm keen to strip her. Strip her.

Bitch! Sending me mad like this. My God I cannot wait for morning! Wait until she hears what I've got to tell her. At worst I should get a few quid out of her. At best... well, who knows? At least it's nearly over. Thank God the nightmare is nearly over. But he'll know where I am, oh yes, part of the deal, and he'll be keen to know what I'm doing up here in the middle of nowhere in this beautiful place.

Right, 0600 hours. Got a bit of sleep in the Manor House Hotel, 50 yards from the Anchor. Doesn't feel like it though. Okay. Open the log. Ground assigned, Lindisfarne Village, Holy Island. Single crew, No coms. Weather poor but visibility good. Approaching Anchor Hotel on foot. Target car parked up. Maintain static observation from ruins of Priory.

38.

She slept fitfully and woke at 6. She rose and peered out through the dirty window. Had they got onto the Island? Had they followed her? But there was nobody. Just that fool in the red car that overtook. Nobody else. The tide had gone out during the night so they could be here by now. But they hadn't seen where she had put the disc, had they? That little job had been done at high tide. It'd been pitch black. The Priory ruins were deserted when she saw the dilapidated old donations box attached to the ancient drystone boundary wall. She had unscrewed the padlock hasp within seconds, secreted the disc then re-attached the hasp and lock. It had been freezing in that damp little room overnight and her breath still hung in the air. No central heating in this neck of the woods.

She shivered in her underwear and wondered about a hot shower. The small basin in the corner didn't look very promising. She stripped and soaked a flannel in the tepid water that dribbled from the rusty tap. She stood soaping herself, soaking the floor in the process. She rinsed the flannel and began removing the suds from her body.

There was a faint, nervous tap on the door. Shivering, she wrapped the small towel around herself. Too small, she had to clutch it above her breasts, causing it to barely reach her navel. She tiptoed to the door and opened up, bending so that her lower body remained out of sight.

'What want for breakfast?' Raymond backed away as he said this, hardly able to look at the tall woman. He is nervous, frightened even.

'Bless him,' thought Jo.

'Oh,' she said. 'Thank you. Er, I'm really not hungry. I don't think I'll have any. Thanks all the same.'

She was then immediately stunned by the grief-stricken look on the little man's face. What had she done? Would he be beaten? George Niles had seemed such a gentle man. Raymond's bottom lip began to quiver and huge tears welled up in his eyes.

'On second thought... er yes. Have you got any eggs?' She had heard hens clucking at dawn.

'Aye. Eggs. Right.' As Raymond said this he backed off

again. His expression had changed. He looked quizzical and the woman sees that his eyes have dropped. She realised that she had opened the door fully and was standing, bottomless, in full view of a man with the mind of a child who had probably never seen a naked woman in his confined, sheltered life.

'Oh, I'm so sorry,' she reversed back out of sight. 'Yeah, eggs would be great. Thank you.'

39.

07.41. Light on 1st flr rm to the lft of door. Movement. Target ID positive. Target looks out of window. Target out of sight. Target seen to open door. Towel around upper body. Comment. Appears relaxed, choosing to leave curtain open. Tgt dresses. Dark tracksuit. Ties hair back. Loss.

40.

Kirkpatrick and Hasleberger were getting along just famously.

'Tide's oot.'

'So what?'

'Are wu gonnay have a look?'

'What at?'

'What the fuck d'ye think at? The fuckin' island. Wuv got a target on the fuckin' island that we're getting paid tae fucking' sort ott!'

'Has it crossed your mind, my good friend, that the sun is down, there is no moon nor stars and driving around on a sleeping island in this thing with headlights may just attract attention?'

'Ah think that's very clever. But ahm no ya dear friend, as you put it. Fair enough. We'll wait. Suit's me.'

'And it'll suit Muller, and the one with the chequebook.'

'Jeez ah'm feckin' freezing.'

41.

The Castle Hotel in Berwick upon Tweed on mainland Northumberland is a three star establishment which was just about nearly good enough for the delegation. The management and staff are polite and unobtrusive. There were plenty of vacant rooms for the three men and one woman to choose from. The restaurant is surprisingly good, if a little limited.

Muller and Ellis met at the breakfast table at eight as arranged. Blanchette had finished her muesli and was sipping orange juice whilst flicking through a magazine. Her overdeveloped neck and shoulders gleamed in the pale light of the window. She had just run a gruelling five miles, done 50 press-ups and showered before breakfast. Her job was to plan operations and she had done that down to the last detail on the laptop which remained by her side at all times. Roche, the communications man, is still in his room, waiting for an update from Lytolis and Voillet. Subject to this Blanchette had prepared for the briefing. Ellis always insisted on a formal briefing.

'Ten minutes to briefing,' mutters Ellis, having just swallowed a forkful of Tweed salmon and scrambled eggs.

'Why do we bother? What's the news from Hasleberger?'

Muller regarded his fellow countryman as the leader of the surveillance team; Kirkpatrick an irritation.

'Find out at the briefing,' Ellis is offhand, matter of fact. He scans the FT as he eats and speaks. Muller steams.

42.

Make your mind up time I suppose. Policy decision time. Target under control. Out of sight but under control. Target vehicle in sight. Path leading to rear exit covered. Intelligence update. Target believed to be under surveillance by hostiles. Target vehicle lumped with hostile device. Target therefore in possible danger whilst on island... decision – get alongside target. Confront at first opportunity. Hostiles may have crossed onto island overnight at low tide. Highest vigilance.

43.

Muller was still livid as he and Ellis walked into Blanchette's hotel room. She had been updated by Roche and now projected her briefing notes from her laptop onto the bare wall of the room. She had removed a cheap Monet print to make this possible.

Ellis perched politely on the edge of the bed and gestured for her to begin.

'The red Fiat saloon seen crossing onto the island is significant. The registered keeper is one Godfrey Driver and he is undoubtedly following our target.'

She pauses. Muller was alarmed.

'What? Who is he? Who does he represent?'

'Muller,' sighs Ellis, 'give Ms Blanchette a chance. She will, I am sure, take questions at the end of the briefing.'

'Driver is a 52 year old white male who lives near the target.'

'What? What is a...,' Muller is stretching Ellis's patience.

'Oh, for God's sake man, shut up and listen! Carry on please.'

'Lytolis and Voillet entered and searched the address at 0400 hours. The man is obviously obsessed. Large quantities of images of the target. It would appear that he spends much of his time following her. These are the sort of pictures he takes.'

Blanchette projected images of Jo Byers onto the wall. They are like surveillance photographs; mundane events shot at a distance without foreground.

'The images are the product of a combination of wet film and digital technology. Driver's apartment is where he works from and it would appear that he works for himself. There are no items of correspondence in the flat that would tend to suggest otherwise.'

Blanchette paused to adopt an exaggerated quizzical expression. She places her hands on her narrow hips and raises her face to the ceiling as if in search of an appropriate phrase. Her muscular throat is exposed. She holds this pose for three seconds before relaxing and looking back down to her audience to deliver the answer to an un-asked question.

'He's a stalker. Nothing more.'

Predictably, Muller was first.

'Explain this... this stalker; is he a pervert?'

'He has no previous convictions for sexual offences. Our government contact does report, however, that Driver has what may be an interesting background in surveillance. He is an ex-MI5 Watcher.'

Muller and Ellis are motionless. As executives of a company involved in politically controversial business they have made their business to be aware of the powers and capabilities of Her Majesty's Government. MI5 Watchers are the most highly trained surveillance operatives in Britain.

'How old is he? Why is he no longer with MI5?' Ellis asked these questions as if they were on a bulleted list. The need to answer the second being dependent on the response to the first, Blanchette understood the significant link between the two queries and answered accordingly.

'He left MI5 ten years before he was due to retire. We cannot find out why.'

Ellis seemed keen to wrap things up. 'Okay, so we've got an unhinged ex-spy catcher inconveniently between ourselves and the elusive Mrs Byers. Presents us with an interesting conundrum, don't you think Mr Muller?'

'Presents us with the need to act decisively is what I say. Thank you Miss Blanchette, we'll end the briefing at this point.'

Blanchette is not to be stopped. She has more problems for her employers.

'There is something else, actually, something that you should know about.'

'Go on my dear,' Ellis, ever courteous.

'Lytolis and Voillet seems to have, er, disappeared, I can't raise them on their phones or radios. They sent the images and report up on a landline from Driver's address and now they've just gone.'

Ellis and Muller remained silent, as if waiting for more. When nothing more came and it was clear that Blanchette awaited instructions Ellis sighed and said,

'Bloody contractors. I bet they've gone to sell elsewhere. Shit.'

Muller didn't miss this opportunity for a dig.

'Yes, and we'll have our lovely widow in your Sunday papers no doubt.'

Ellis ignored this and continues to think aloud. 'We have to assume that Lytolis and Voillet have broken loose and we have to assume that they have stolen property from Driver's apartment. I think this is rapidly becoming a damage limitation exercise.'

Muller cannot contain his glee. 'Yes, that's what I've been saying all along, now, please, can we have some executive action?'

Ellis nods gravely. His voice is flat, resigned.

'Yes Muller. Go on then. Do your stuff. You've come prepared.'

44.

OK. This is it I suppose. What we've been waiting for. It's got to be the bump. She's in danger. I've got no back-up. It's got to be the bump. Get alongside her and bump her. If she doesn't turn then so be it. At least I'll have compromised them. Whoever the fuck they are. She's got a lump on her car and they're probably on the island by now. If not they'll be waiting for her to leave before they pick her up again. Who are they? My old firm? Nah, never in a Hummer, and I would have recognised them. At the church you know. Mind you; it's been a while. A long while. But that can't be right. I would have picked them up before now in London. It has to have something to do with the death of her husband. He was a scientist. He puts in long hours and she goes to the gym. That's about all there is to it. Except that I'm usually behind her. Right behind you baby. Until now that is. Anytime now I'm going to have to get in front of you. Right in your face.

45.

Kirkpatrick sat in the driving seat. He had heard Hasleberger's phone go off. The tone had been unfamiliar. The Austrian's reaction had been interesting. Significant. He had got out to take the call, his Scottish partner feeling suddenly left behind, small. Then the grinning face of Hasleberger appeared at the driver's window. Kirkpatrick swallowed hard. He sensed what he was about to be told. He felt sick. Surely not. Not a woman. He knew that grin. The Austrian opened the driver's door, exposing the Scot, making him feel even more vulnerable. 'Time for action. I've had a very important call. Come and see what I've got in the back.'

Kirkpatrick tried to imagine, vainly. He felt drained. Drained by the cold, by lack of sleep and by the fear that he would not be able to handle what he was about to be expected to take part in. As recently as six months previously it would have been no problem.

But things had suddenly become different. The Austrian had a direct line to high level through his fellow Hun. He was in the driving seat now, the favoured one.

Kirkpatrick walked stiffly round to the back of the Hummer, bracing himself.

Hasleberger was holding a black briefcase open. In it was a gun. Also ammunition; three small pink-feathered darts nestled in the custom built padding, the barrel of each clearly containing something.

Numbed, Kirkpatrick just wanted to get the point, despite himself. He tried to act casually.

'Didn't know we had a problem with rhinos.'

'These wouldn't harm rhinos.' Hasleberger was smug, totally in charge, loving it.

'What the fuck am I expected to help you with?' Kirkpatrick wanted to get to the bottom of this and deliberately concedes any parity to the Austrian in order to get his answer quickly. What he then hears he can scarcely believe, but does.

'Each dart contains a small quantity of liquid containing a virus. We have to know this so that we will protect ourselves.'

This explanation follows because such detail would not normally be made available to operatives.

Kirkpatrick nods slowly, affecting an expression of world-weary sadness.

'Aye. Aye, ah git it. We kill the woman in a way that'll make the police think that she caught it aff of her dyin' husband. Very, very slick. I'm so proud tae work feh such a professional organisation.'

This was all lost on Hasleberger who simply closed the box of terror and re-stowed it beneath the false floor of the Hummer.

46.

Ellis already had his future in Pharmaceuticals mapped out for him. Consequently he was enjoying the final months of his ten years with MI5. Having graduated from Oxford before doing postgraduate work at University College London he had been recruited as a high flyer. And he had flown – making it to rank of Branch Director in eight years. There was no real prospect of him going higher so he looked at his family's empire as the best future for him.

So he was relaxed, had nothing to worry about, at peace with the world.

47.

Kirkpatrick's thoughts were venomous: Fuckin' loves it, he does. 'Das big professional killerman'. Huh! He would pay to do this job. If I didn't need him I'd slot the bastard. No fuckin' problem. What is this cowboy outfit doin' teamin' a fuckin' Rangers supporter up wi' a fuckin' Austrian Tim? Eh? I ask myself. Look at him, examinin' the fuckin' gun like he'd never seen one before. Just a big kids air rifle anyways. Nuthin' special. Three wee darts. Short needles so they fall oot after injectin'. Nice touch mind. He wants the first shot, as usual. Let him. Safe as houses anyway, no danger until impact – then... squirt – in goes the gear.

'Hey, Adolf, you fancy a drink?'

'No. And don't call me that.'

Having been deployed as the driver he had had no need to know about the darts, and had baulked when the reality of the situation was revealed to him. But here were personal reasons for that initial queasiness. Now he was getting used to the idea. Kirkpatrick had spent his life trying to get used to ideas – not always successfully. Having joined the Coldstream Guards at 16 for a three year kicking he then transferred to the RAF Regiment in which he thrived on the professionalism and comradeship of a top class outfit. After six years he left the military and became a civilian – well, not really – he joined the Royal Ulster Constabulary. His nine years of military service, including five tours in Northern Ireland, had not prepared him for the impossibility of being a copper in West Belfast. His driving and ability as a helicopter pilot had got him through it, not his combat or policing skills. A wily Scot he knew a lot about getting people out of trouble in the nick of time with limited resources. Then, heli-telly. The only RUC helicopter pilot on duty that day, he had got a call to take his observer over a funeral parade in Andersonstown. His observer had to look at what they witnessed because he was filming it.

Kirkpatrick had not had to look, but did. As he saw the rampaging crowd strip and murder two Signal Corps squaddies whose car had strayed into the cortege something snapped inside him. What was the point? He went sick the next day and was soon pensioned off. That had been the end of him. Drifting from one job to the next he wandered around England and into Germany where his marriage to a stripper lasted six months. He'd even worked for a short time as a stunt driver for a film company before being sacked for threatening to silence a whinging luvvy.

48.

'We fulfilled the contract, sent them the recce material. That's all it was for remember? Non-evidential.'

Lytolis had already planned his next move as he drove Voillet out of London on the Westway. She sat in the passenger seat and stared straight ahead.

'Just drop me at the airport. We'll never work in this country again....'

He was unrepentant.

'We won't have to. We'll have a buyer for this lot by tomorrow night. You wait.'

'I'm not waiting for anything. I'm getting the hell out of here, and I want my money for the job first. From you.'

'You'll have to wait. The upfront lot went into my account yesterday. I can't get to it tonight, can I?'

'Wire it to me. I'm out of here. You've screwed up big for both of us Lytolis.'

The big Volvo they've hired glided through the dark drizzle, pulling off at terminal three.

49.

A freezing wind whipped Ellis's coat collar against his face. He walked along the pier. The North Sea pounded the rocks below. Finding shelter behind the lighthouse, he pulled out a phone and thumbed a number.

'Situation please 1306.'

His face, although receiving a severe battering from the flapping collar, is calm and concentrated as he listened to his employee.

'Excellent 1306. I'll be in touch tomorrow.'

Pocketing his phone Ellis set off back along the pier and to the hotel.

Kirkpatrick rolled a cigarette as Hasleberger did some target practice. The dummy darts thwacked into the piece of driftwood with alarming force and accuracy. Ten yards, twenty yards, thirty, forty. The Austrian clearly loved it. There are ten dummy darts in the kit. They are identical to the three in the gun case save that they are not loaded with a liquid containing enough virus to kill the population of an average size city. Kirkpatrick had seen the likes of Hasleberger many times before. They were everywhere. Dangerous big kids with guns. Often commit suicide in the end, when faced with their future. Can't live without being near to death – preferably that of others, but not necessarily. The Scot thought back to Angola when he had seen Hasleberger invite another mercenary to shoot him. The lad couldn't do it so Hasleberger had shot him through the knee to get the company to fly him home. It was as if one of them had to go and the German did not mind who or how. Kirkpatrick could only respect the German for his total disregard for his own life. But he feared him for his disregard for others' lives.

50.

'Mrs Byers?'

It did not come as a surprise to her. She expected it and consequently rather welcomed it. Reassuring. She turned around slowly, casually, to face her caller.

'Mrs Byers?'

Impressive. Would pass for a birdwatcher any day. What a nerd.

'Yes?'

'Can we talk?'

'What about? Who are you?'

'Can we talk in private?'

She looks around exaggeratedly at the deserted island village.

'Doesn't get more private than this.'

'Up on the dunes please.'

'My God, do you think I'm mad; who the hell trained you?'

The nerd drew close. He smelled of soap.

'Nobody trained me. You're in danger'

'No doubt I am but I don't really care much. You can do what you like to me.'

'What... you think... listen Jo Byers, I know everything about you. I am your guardian angel.'

She stared at him, incredulous; he stared back, plainly suffering from some sort of emotional trauma.

'I came from London. I was outside the church. They put a beacon on your car. You're being followed Jo.'

'Obviously – by you!'

'And by them, by your husband's firm or whoever they are.'

The woman paused, looks the nerd up and down, half smiling, smirking.

'Okay, let's go to the dunes.'

They trudged off, he intense, protective. She quizzical, annoyed, irritated, mildly amused.

Dawn was braking across the vast sky, gulls screamed warnings and a freezing gale gathered pace, as if urging the rising tide across the causeway.

51.

Ellis was in his hotel room smoking, against the rules. He dialled a short number on a mobile.

'Come up to my room will you?'

He continued to smoke, his eyes closed. There was a single knock on the door.

'Come in my dear.'

Blanchette entered and stood before her boss in the 'at ease' position and with a very straight back.

'Sit down for God's sake.'

'I'd rather stand, sir.'

'And stop calling me sir.'

'I thought you said it was alright when we're alone.'

'Yes, but... oh, never mind. Look, I want you to do something for me....'

'You usually do, sir.'

'Receive a message. Receive a message from London. Can you do that?'

'I can do anything you tell me.'

'Go on then, here it is.'

He handed the woman a piece of paper, folded.

The athlete took it, nodded and left the room, leaving a swirl of smoke in her wake.

Ellis closed his eyes again and smiled, before talking to himself.

'Oh I do love beautiful women – even when they are built like brick shithouses.'

52.

'Okay?'

'Yeah.'

It did not matter which of the two spoke first. For once, they spoke as one. They knew it was time and that there was only one thing going to happen. They were about to murder a beautiful and unarmed young woman. Kirkpatrick and Hasleberger, two misfits, nutters, pieces of scum, whatever you want to call them, came together. Their relationship was seamless, a perfect if temporary marriage. The Scotsman drove. There is enough light to see by now and the Hummer raced across the causeway without headlights. Hasleberger loads the rifle with one of the three lethal darts. The other two remain in his pocket. The tide had been out, and was now returning – they did not have long.

53.

Jo and Godfrey Work Together

'You are one sad little fucker.'

She said it without malice or disgust. Just a statement of fact.

'I don't think of it like that... it's..., we..., look, we don't have time for this. Are you with me or against me? I'm your only chance. I know the business they're in, they'll be coming to get you now. Fucking now!'

The woman glared at the geek and sprung to her feet from where they were crouching behind a low dune. She turned and stared intently at the causeway, by now a pale dark line across an expanse of watery sand. She saw it, the Hummer, and knew it was them. It was crossing the causeway, towards to the island.

He was up beside her. Seeing what she saw he swung her around and down by her arm.

'*My* car.'

'What?'

'*My* car. They know yours and it's got a lump on it.'

She was his.

He took her hand and led her, half running, half walking, back to the outskirts of the village where the little red Fiat was parked. She made for the passenger side.

'No', he had thought this through.

'Here's the key, get into the driving seat and stay here and watch for them to pass into the village. Give me your car keys. Wait for them to pass into the village then go for it.'

She knew what he was doing. And she knew that he did also. Perhaps not so sad after all. He took the key to her Beemer and sprinted back towards the village harbour and hotel where it was parked. The tide was coming in and boats were beginning to free themselves from the oily mud, moving and creaking as they rose.

54.

'She's on the move.'

Hasleberger had his eyes on the tracker monitor.

'Heading away from the causeway. That is good. Very good for us.'

The Scot concurred.

'Aye, let's hope she's going to try to dig in somewhere. Then we do this in private.'

The big vehicle hit the halfway point on the causeway with a splash. The tide was coming in fast, already covering the lowest section of tarmac.

'Fuck. Shit, we're just in time, skin of our arses. At least we know she won't get off now.'

The Hummer reached the Island and turned right along the mile long stretch of road running towards the village between dunes and rising sea. Kirkpatrick moved through the gears, hunter's eyes searching for the woman's car.

'She's stopped moving.'

The Austrian had his eyes on the tracking screen.

'Far end of the Island, past the village, the harbour.'

The woman watched the Hummer from behind the small dune. Behind her, equally hidden, was her escape vehicle, a little red Fiat with rusty door panels. There are three factors for her to take into the calculation. The distance between her and the Hummer; the distance between the Hummer and her own car, and the tide. The tide was the biggest factor – she had to beat the tide and it was rising fast. She leapt to her feet and slid into the Fiat. It started first time but the wheels spun madly, throwing up twin plumes of sand.

'Keep an eye out for the stalker – we have to finish him too. He'll be near her. In a red Fiat.' This from Hasleberger, looking forwards and sideways.

Kirkpatrick's bulging eyes were on his nearside rear view mirror. He could see the Fiat struggling to get out of the sand about 200 metres behind them.

'Fuck! We've passed it! It's behind us!' He jammed on the brakes and the Hummer went into a long arcing skid. The Scot brought it out of the skid and controlled the wheelspin until the vehicle gripped the road and accelerated, fishtailing in the direction from which it had come, and in pursuit of the little red car that had just managed to get out onto the road and head for the causeway.

'Come on,' shouts Haslberger, 'before he gets to the mainland.'

Unaware of the turn of events, Driver took the woman's BMW down onto the harbour side, slowly, willing the beacon to transmit clearly to the pursuit vehicle, or to those directing it. He parked up and waited. One minute, two minutes, any minute now, any second now, surely....

Jo moved the Fiat frantically up through its screaming gearbox, max revs before each change. She hit the causeway and put her foot to the boards, the mainland about half a mile ahead, the halfway point marked by a wooden shelter on stilts – and water, water on the road, spilling around the stilts, the lowest point on the causeway, the first to be submerged. Then she saw the Hummer. Gaining on her, but still 200 metres behind. If she could just get. . . seaweed, a strand of bright green damp seaweed is strewn across the tarmac. The Fiat hit it dead square on. Jo could not believe it – the little car jumped about a foot into the air and then hit the ground without slowing. She tore ahead when she expected to skid off the road. Eyes in the mirror again. The Hummer is still gaining on her. It hit the seaweed and veered to one side, allowing her to gain a few vital metres.

'Fucking shit.'

Kirkpatrick wrestles violently with the steering wheel as the Hummer hit the slimy green debris. It began to go into a spin but the Scot was too good for it, pulling out but losing time.

The Fiat hit the first water too fast. Much too fast. The little engine with its exposed wiring and open air intake got a generous dousing of North Sea and within seconds was spluttering and choking. Jo slowed right down and the car seemed to recover. But vital time has been lost and the black Hummer was closing.

Perhaps they wanted to talk. Perhaps they don't need to kill me, she tries to kid herself that everything was really okay and that... then she bursts into tears as the Fiat dies.

Crying hysterically, she staggered out of the car. The water is up to her shins and she tripped forward as she made for the wooden stilted shelter about thirty metres away. She could perhaps fend them off until help arrived. Help? What help? That geek was sitting in her car on the island. It would have made it through the water! Christ – the BMW would have made it! That fucking geek!

But realizing what must have happened, that same geek was taking emergency action. The sight of the harbour brought it all back to him; the training in Plymouth, the deadly diving courses, the misery of endless freezing nights on senseless exercises. He chose the boat easily; a fourteen foot skiff with a big Johnson outboard which started first time. The BMW could stay where it was; the Royal Marine was back at sea.

Hasleberger shrieked with delight as he saw the woman's plight, Kirkpatrick slowed the Hummer and started whistling the Billy Boys. There's something strange about reluctant killers; they're only reluctant when they're thinking about it, but when the smell of blood is in the air something else takes over, for a while, anyway. They were about 40 metres behind their target who had started to climb the ladder to the elevated shelter. The box on stilts about 10 feet above high tide level, which made it about 20 feet for her to climb from the side of the causeway, now under 4 feet of water and sinking with each sweep of the ravenous, wind-driven waves. Kirkpatrick stopped the Hummer before it reached the deepest water. He ground his teeth. Does he really want this? The chase was over and the reluctance had returned. Did he really want to see his companion put a poison dart into a woman's backside? But the Austrian's torso was already out of the Hummer's front passenger window; he was sitting on the window frame and taking aim with his elbows on the roof. The seagulls wheeled and screeched, sensing the drama. The wind howled louder. The tide gushed in.

Jo climbed the ladder. She could hear no shouts, no attempt at communication. That meant only one thing and her panic rushed in like the flooding tide. She expected a bullet and freezes on the ladder, tensing up, mind blank. The gulls screamed and the wind whistles in the wooden framework of the shelter. Duncan, here I come.

Hasleberger's trigger finger was tightening when the bow of the skiff hit the side of the Hummer. Neither killer saw it coming. The light craft barely budged the huge vehicle but the loud impact was enough to distract the Austrian, he swivelled to assess the source of the disruption. In one motion, Driver killed the outboard motor and leapt up to grab the gunman, who could not get his weapon round fast enough. Driver was all over him, the rifle went flying and the two men fell backwards, bouncing off the bow of the boat before plunging together into the swirling brine, the gun disappeared. Kirkpatrick could not get his door open, the rising tide saw to that; he had to scramble across the passenger seat to follow his colleague out of the passenger window.

Hasleberger roared with rage, tearing his terrified assailant off of him like he was ridding himself of a cloying cobweb - the water was up to their chests - he looked up and saw his target had disappeared into the wooden box atop its stilts. Driver tried to hang on to the Austrian and was just about to sustain a hard fist to the face when Kirkpatrick intervened, launching himself into the melee through the churning water.

The Scot had made a decision, enough was enough, there was no telling who would arrive next, the water was now too deep for even the Hummer to escape and he didn't want to be caught trying to swim away from the scene of two murders. He got enough power behind a punch which caught Hasleberger on the point of the chin; the stunned Austrian got the message, turned and began swimming awkwardly away, towards the island. Kirkpatrick tried to grab Driver, but the geek was by now out of reach, thrashing back to the boat which had begun to drift off. Kirkpatrick followed him as best he could but the ex-marine hauled himself on board the bobbing craft and was yanking the outboard motor starter rope, the engine failed at first pull, giving Kirkpatrick enough time to get to the propeller shaft and wrap himself round it, glaring up at Driver as he did so. 'You're not going without me!' he yelled and Driver, realising he had no choice, pulled the Scot up and into the skiff. Another pull on the starter rope and the engine roared into action, Driver steered it round the Hummer and made for the foot of the ladder up which Jo Byers had just climbed to safety. 'No,' shouted Kirkpatrick above the noise of the rushing tide and Johnson engine, 'leave her there, we're feckin' getting' oota here!' The Scot was crouching but his left hand gripped Driver's shoulder and his right hand gripped a very sharp looking knife. 'Make for shore! Now, or ah'll cut ya feckin' throat!'

55.

Ten miles south on the A1 dual carriageway Simmonds and Casey speed north. It had taken a lot of doing to persuade his boss to do this trip and had taken a lot of doing for Casey to persuade his bosses to free up the money. Modern policing is all about money.

'The Hummer was in Leeds and in Newcastle yesterday. Northumbria Police emailed me a photo of it on the Tyne Bridge, great technology eh Guv?'

Casey was rolling a fag.

'Did you put an interest report on it?'

'Yeah, course – 'do not stop – report sightings etc., etc.'

'Good lad.'

The two cops entered the kill zone. Although unaware of the near farcical life and death struggle on the causeway, each felt that the air was somehow pressure-laden. The north Northumbrian landscape had become most inhospitable and the cold northerly wind buffeted the car.

'Yeah, thanks guv, but what the hell do we do now? This is the middle of nowhere, might as well check local pubs and hotels, see if anybody's seen the Hummer, can't be many of them in these parts.'

Casey shrugged, 'Okay, suppose so, we'll get some breakfast first, pubs'll not be open for hours yet.'

Unbeknownst to them their plans were to be soon interrupted. About five miles further south was a large black lady. Feeling a similar anticipation, Michaela Tuitt looked at the clock on her dashboard. High tide in twenty minutes. She had not told Simmonds everything, but he had the Hummer; that would be enough, they had the technology to follow it and her worry was that they would inevitably bump into each other. Not that that mattered too much, as long as she got that disc. She hoped Jo was okay; why shouldn't she be? Bright girl, could look after herself.

56.

Blanchette did not dial the number Ellis had given her. In any case there would have been no point – the phone was completely waterlogged, a fact that had not prevented its IMEI code from transmitting a weak signal to Blanchette's hand held decoding tracker, this had helped direct the light helicopter in which she now sat as passenger.

Driver had managed to crawl onto the top of one of the concrete defence blocks. Freezing, aching, exhausted he was the happiest man on earth. He had saved her. He knew it. She was in that wooden box on stilts which the sea would not reach. The warmth in his heart did not stop him from shivering violently. His teeth chattered with such ferocity that the sound of it was deafening. Then he heard something else; a similar chattering noise, but metallic and at a distance; a helicopter.

The two cops had stopped in the village of Belford, on the

A1 about five miles south of the causeway turnoff. They were out of the car and looking for a café. Casey's eyes were diverted skywards when he heard the chopper. It was travelling north eastwards over them northbound A1 and therefore towards a point on the coast north of their current position.

'Did Northumbria Police say anything about air support?'

'I never asked for it.'

'Must be coastguard or navy or sumthin'.'

'Yeah, no markings though, looks, black or dark blue to me.'

'Could be any colour if it's a police chopper, it'll be hired, that and the pilot, just like they do in the Met, eh?'

The pilot and passenger in the Schweizer 300 had missed the action. At a thousand feet the wind buffeted the small aircraft and John Nance just wanted to fulfil his contract and get home. He had been flying for the company for eight years now and they had been good to him. For his co-operation and discretion in sensitive times, they said. He had trained with the Royal Navy and had gone on to fly surveillance fixed wings for the Security Service. That had been good but the money was crap and then this little number came along. Easy hours, if a bit erratic, fantastic pay and no paperwork. The flight logs were all done for him; all he had to do was sign them. This had been a long one from the tiny company airfield in Ruislip, west London, with a stop for refuel just outside Wetherby in Yorkshire. And now all he wanted to do was fuck off before the weather worsened. His passenger was more committed.

Very committed, in fact.

As he steered his aircraft towards the island Nance watched Blanchette out of the corner of his eye. He feared what was coming because he had seen her load a small handgun with which she was evidently unfamiliar, before stowing it deep in her clothing. It looked like a kid's pellet gun, but Nance was not fooled by its appearance; it would be lethal, that was for sure. The black-clad woman had been looking intently at the beaches through high powered binos, whilst also referring to what he knew was a tracking app on her iPhone screen. Nance knew to head for the causeway and give a low once over. He would know to hover over the wooden box too. The pilot knew that Blanchette had found her target when she ordered him to set her down behind some dunes on the island 300 metres south of the end of the causeway. The wind and uneven ground made landing impossible and Blanchette had to jump from the craft from a height of 20 feet, but the sand was soft and she rolled away comfortably, hugging herself, grinning, enjoying every second. This was what she had been waiting for.

57.

Oh shit no. Jo's in the box and they're coming. They're coming. They'll bomb it and burn it and she'll be killed. Aw no, aw no. Aw Jo, I can't do anything more to help you. Help me now, I can't think.

He started thinking out loud; 'I can't think, I... can't think properly, if I get down I might be able... fuck you Jo... you hate me Jo, why should... I saved you once, eh? Why should I do it again and again...?'

'Aw shut the fuck up ya whingin' cunt! Git doon here oot a thu way, oota sight ya cunt!'

Driver looked down from the top of the six foot concrete cube.

Kirkpatrick sat with his back resting against the block; he was also exhausted but could muster the energy to give Driver his orders. On a personal level he couldn't have given a fuck for the idiot's safety but a hostage or human shield could always be useful if the need arose.

Driver obeyed and rolled off of the block to fall awkwardly in the sand a few inches away from Kirkpatrick. Having commandeered both the boat and its master, the Scot had got them to the beach on the mainland, but not before he had taken his phone out and hurled it into the sea. The pair had then hauled the boat up onto the sand.

The road from the main A1 to the mainland end of the causeway is a winding country affair, frequently wide enough for only one vehicle. Michaela Tuitt wrestled with the steering wheel whilst hoping vainly to reach the island before the causeway was submerged. As she rounded the final bend and came over the brow of a hill she saw that she was too late. The causeway was under water with only the rescue box visible. And the tops of two vehicles. What had happened? Then she heard and saw the helicopter as it swept in an arc with the rescue box as its focus.

Already half frozen, when Jo heard the chopper she went rigid. She had somehow cut her left breast badly during her desperate fight to reach the safety of the wooden box and her left hand was gashed with its thumbnail hanging off.

She instinctively knew that the helicopter was not good news and it was not difficult to assume that the rescue box was not bullet proof. Shit.

Then came the cloud. It lumbered across the sky like vast billowing Zeppelin and cast a shadow over the island and adjacent mainland. Then it dumped a torrential rainstorm into a sudden gale force gust. The helicopter searchlight came on and lit up the rescue box like a lone white figure on a huge dark stage. Jo trembled violently inside the box, tried to stop her teeth chattering and cried inwardly at the pain in her breast and hand. The salt water made them ten times worse and Jo began to feel a little sorry for herself. She had lost her husband to murderers who were now intent on murdering her. Her agony had now been prolonged by the interference of a halfwit and she was having to put up with a smashed hand and a gashed tit. Oh for fuck's sake, come on, get on with it.

58.

Tuitt just sat there transfixed. She stared at the chopper now circling the rescue box, knowing that anyone in there was not about to be rescued otherwise there would be a man coming down on a rope by now. Then her rear view mirror lit up as headlights raced up behind her and screeched to a halt. Then the chopper soared upwards, dipped its nose and sped off to the island where it dropped low and loitered for a few seconds before rising again, turning south and disappearing south down the coastline. Jesus, she thought, whoever's in that helicopter was spooked by the headlights. What the hell does that mean? But Nance had not been spooked by any headlights at all. Air traffic control at Newcastle airport had ordered him out of the area to give way to a Royal Air Force rescue helicopter, scrambled from RAF Boulmer, 50 miles to the south. Casey and Simmonds had just found a café when they got news of this development over their police radio. Holy Island? Neither had ever heard of it.

Seeing the unmarked police car race round the corner and pull up behind her, Tuitt tried to compose herself and activate her vehicle's locking system but she was too late. Her driver's door was pulled open and the first thing she saw as it was thrust in her face was a police warrant card. Its bearer was out of sight, his head behind and above her, more interested in the departing chopper than seeing the driver to whom he was about to introduce himself. By the time he showed his face and saw that it was Tuitt, she was saying,

'Yes DC Simmonds, what can I do for you?'

'Wha... What the fuck are you doing here? How did...?'

'Don't worry, I came on my own steam, not on anything you told me.'

Simmonds was aware that by this time his boss was standing behind him and wouldn't believe that Tuitt – the contact – had found her own way to this particular location at this particular time without the assistance of police intelligence.

'Guvnor, this is, er, this is Michaela Tuitt, my, er, contact, Michaela, this is DI Casey.'

Tuitt tried to get out of the car but Simmonds told her to stay where she was. The two men withdrew a few paces and conferred.

'What's going on here?' hissed Casey.

'Fuck knows guv, I'll need to talk to her.'

'Seems like you already have mate.'

Casey walked back to their car; Simmonds moved quickly around the front of Tuitt's car and got in the passenger side.

'Who led you here?'

'Jo Byers.'

'Why didn't you tell me, we've had to follow a fucking Hummer for three hundred miles? To think you knew all along where... Jesus Christ Michaela.'

Simmonds just could not believe this, this woman could have compromised the follow, if those two in the Hummer had seen her too many times they would have thought she was following them, ironic or what?

'Anyway, what's going on? Why's the Hummer in the middle of the fucking sea? Whose is the red car? What's fucking going on?'

He blurted this whilst staring out at the causeway ahead of them, searching for clues in the weird scenario, only the roof of the red Fiat now visible, the Hummer still recognisable. The big low gunmetal cloud was still over them but now the dipping sun was beneath it on the mainland horizon behind them, illuminating its underbelly and casting a golden hue over the dunes and island. The rain had stopped.

59.

I can't really cope with this. I'm sitting here freezing to death with a killer. Alright, he seems to have turned a bit but he's still a killer. Don't know what to say to him. Don't know how much he knows, don't know how much he wants to know, don't know what he knows about me, what the people he works for know about me, what they want to know about me, if they want me dead now or if they want me to... this killer can't kill Jo so they'll have to get someone else, they must know she's in that box, why didn't the chopper shoot her or throw flames at the box, it's only wooden... maybe it was friendly... I'll start a conversation:

'What are we waiting for?'

Kirkpatrick was sat with his back against the concrete block trying to salvage some tobacco from what was meant to be a waterproof pouch.

'Ah dinnae nae aboot you but I'm waiting tae dry oot so ah kin fuck off oota here – and naybody iz gannae stop me – diyah hear?'

Driver didn't respond.

'Diyah hear!?'

'Yes, yes, course. Why would anyone want to…?'

Kirkpatrick turned and glared menacingly. Driver knew that this gentleman was not to be messed with, so he fell silent and concentrated his thoughts on his subject who was alive but very vulnerable in a wooden box on stilts in the middle of the sea.

60.

'She's in that box?'

Michaela Tuitt had joined the two policemen and was sitting between and behind them on the rear seat of their car. Simmonds agreed, sarcastically,

'There's a good chance somebody's in there, with two vehicles waterlogged.'

Casey twisted around to face up close to Tuitt.

'Listen luv, you'd better not be holding back on us here. If you do that and hold things up or cause problems I'll have you prosecuted, do you understand me?'

Simmonds caught Tuitt's eye in the rear view mirror.

'He means it Michaela, give us everything you know. C'mon, let's go for some fresh air, just you and me.'

Once out of the car Simmonds held the woman firmly by the arms and faced her with a lot of emphasis.

'Michaela, me and my boss are up here on a need-to-know basis on the direct orders of a commander, that's about five ranks above us. There's probably Special Branch activity and possibly MI5 involvement. We ourselves might be under surveillance, the local cops know about our interest in the Humvee... what I'm saying is that this could get very big and it all started with you. Please do not fuck about.'

Tuitt was convinced.

'There's an old priory on the island, like the ruins of a

church built by monks hundreds of years ago. There's a little wooden suggestion box. If Jo Byers has been on the island then that box will contain a computer disc. On that disc is evidence of something terrible... *terrible*.'

Simmonds could barely believe what he was hearing, then the adrenalin kicked in and he took a very firm control of the situation.

'Do carry on,' he told her, quietly, tightening his grip on her arms.

61.

Raymond looked down from the little pier at the thing floating upward on the rising tide. A few more minutes and he would be able to kneel down, reach over and pluck it out of the water. He always went for a walk down to the pier at this time in the morning, he had been wondering all day when the lady with the yellow hair would come back. Bag was still in the room and his dad was trying to decide whether or not to make dinner. There had been nobody in the pub yet so they were unaware of the drama or of the stranded vehicles causeway as it was out of sight of the pub and most of the village.

A few minutes later it was in his hand – an arrow. Where was the bow, he wondered? Arrow too short for bow though. It looked very sharp and he knew not to touch that sharp end because that would make blood come out of his finger and he hated the sight of blood. Holding his prize at arm's length he walked slowly back towards his father's little pub.

Two hundred yards further south and hidden amongst the

outcrop of jagged rock upon which the castle rested another figure stirred. Hasleberger lay and shivered, unaware that someone was approaching.

62.

Now what do I do? Jo's in that box, alive I can only hope, I've got a killer who seems to have changed sides. Fucking hope he has anyway. Another killer hopefully drowned. Fucking helicopters whizzing about all over the place. And - and this is a big 'and' - two cars are parked up at the end of the causeway facing the island. They're too early just to be waiting for the tide to go out... well, they are but they're making sure that they'll be first across when it does. Or maybe they got here just a little bit late; or maybe a bit of both. Jesus, my head hurts so much. So much.

The Coastguard chopper made its way toward the island. It had been strangely requested to look for a boat being swept out to sea and having not found such a craft it returned to pluck Joanne Byers from her little wooden box before she died of hypothermia. This was a fair assessment and the crew were attaching sufficient urgency to the fact that she had been in there for over an hour, probably soaking wet and freezing cold. The downdraft of the rotor blades did not improve the situation as Jo sat clutching her knees under her chin with her eyes tight shut not knowing what to expect – a bullet, a knife, a club to the head before being tossed into the drink below. None of these. The lifeguard appeared at the window, suspended on a nylon rope, and beckoned to her. He held a harness and she relaxed, she was going to be dry and warm soon. But for how long? What really awaited her on dry land? Greschner. No doubt about it. There was nobody else. Well, nearly nobody. She had not seen Driver and one of the killers leave the disappearing causeway in the boat. By then she had been rolled up on the floor of the box in no doubt that she was about to die. She let the lifeguard take her and was reassured when he strapped the harness around her trembling body. Within seconds she was flying.

63.

The Scotsman was first to speak. 'Right, that's the job fucked. Those two cars down there, they're nae fuckin' tourists, there's two men and a black woman, they've got sumthin' tae diy wi all this. Right, listen ya little cunt and listen gud, ah saved ya, but ah kin undo that little favour, got it?'

Driver was stunned and just stared at the Jock. 'Ah says have ya *got* that?!'

'Yes, yes.'

'Right, we've got a boat and ah bet those three are in a hurry tae git tae the island, you're gonna help them – and you've never seen hide nor hair of me, got it?'

Driver nodded and looked at the boat a few yards away on the sand between two dunes.

Kirkpatrick continued, 'Take the boat out and along there, give them a shout, and offer them a lift over, a wee ferry service….'

'But….'

'But fuckin' nothin', you won't see me again, now come on, ah'll help yiz launch it.'

The outboard engine started at the first time of asking and Kirkpatrick gave Driver one last hard glare before giving the boat an equally hard shove into deeper water, Driver took control remarkably well and set off along the coastline towards the two parked vehicles and their occupants at the mainland end of the causeway.

64.

Blanchette crawled between the tufts of dune grass at the top of a low dune and looked down to where Hasleberger lay in the sand. He had found a sheet of canvas and had wrapped himself in it in an attempt to get warm and dry out. This was going to be too easy, she thought, and was actually disappointed. She broke cover and walked down the side of the dune towards him. He heard her and swivelled round to look up at her.

'Where's the other one?' Her question was matter of fact. Hasleberger made no reply; he had never met Blanchette but sensed extreme danger. He tried to unravel himself to stand and face her, but she was on him and in a trice and had him pinned down, still in his canvas cocoon. She pulled a hunting knife from her belt and held it against his face.

'There's two of you, where's the other one?'

'Probably drowned, like I nearly did, who the fuck are you?' 'You're a liar, and a failure,' and with that she slit his throat, hard and deep. Being sure to sever both jugulars. His body arched as the blood spurted from his jugular; she held on and forced her gloved fist into his mouth to stifle any attempt at a scream. She looked down into his bulging eyes. Too easy, she thought, and watched him bleed out.

65.

'Right, let's get out of here, I'm freezing cold and starving.'

Casey was talking to Tuitt and Simmonds, they were all still sat in the unmarked police car with Tuitt in the back, Casey swivelled round to address her in particular, 'Get back in your own car love and meet us in Belford, about five miles south on the A1, I'll buy you breakfast....'

Tuitt interrupted, 'No, I need to get onto the island.'

Casey frowned, 'The tide won't be out for hours, you can't just sit here waiting for God's sake, that's stupid.'

The trio had watched the RAF rescue Jo Byers but Tuitt had been more interested in the first helicopter that had appeared and then left, after making what had appeared to be a brief landing on the island.

'With all due respect Mr Casey, Jo Byers is safe now, but if we don't get that disc from that priory over there a lot of people will be very unsafe.'

'That's a matter for Northumbria Police,' said Casey as he started the car.

'Go on, out you go, see you in Belford....' He was interrupted by the sound of an outboard motor and the sight of Godfrey Driver steering the skiff hard at the beach before them. The craft skidded up onto the sand and Driver waved at them, keen to attract their attention and avoid their seeing Kirkpatrick make good his escape inland on foot across the fields. He need not have worried; they would not have been interested.

'Who the fuck is that!?' Casey turned to face Tuitt again, accusingly.

'I've no idea,' she replied, truthfully. Simmonds got out of the car and hurried to the water's edge to speak to the newcomer. Casey and Tuitt remained in the vehicle and waited. The tide was now high and the causeway invisible, save for the now empty rescue box on its stilts and the top of the Hummer. Driver's little red Fiat had disappeared completely.

66.

'One down, one to go.' Blanchette spoke to Ellis whilst hurrying to the top of a dune to get a better view of the island; she was breathing hard and hoping for some sort of guidance from her commander, knowing that a job half done was not done at all.

'Keep looking my dear, just do your best, and then we'll send the chopper back to pick you up.' Ellis's tone was calm, fatherly, his eyes were on a screen before him on which three green dots showed on a map of the island and adjacent coastline. He assumed, correctly, that the transmitting phone of the fourth was underwater and that, incorrectly, its Scottish owner had drowned. Hasleberger's signal was of course stationary and Ellis could see that of Blanchette moving slowly across the island. But he was more interested in the third green dot on his screen. He tried making a call to its source phone but the line was dead, obviously waterlogged, its circuitry capable now of only sending the weak tracking signal.

Ellis frowned; what was that fucking idiot up to? This was

the problem with 'free radicals' as he called the likes of Driver; useful at times but all too often unpredictable loose cannons. He closed the laptop, just as Muller walked into the room.

'What are you doing?' asked the German.

'Clearing up your fucking mess, old chap.'

'We have to assume she's left the disc on the island, I....'

Ellis did not allow Muller to finish,

'Don't worry, I've got it covered.'

Muller knew the game was up for him, his men had failed and had humiliated him, and now Ellis was going to make the most of it. The German left the room quietly, eyes downcast.

Ellis called Blanchette. 'You've got a boat coming across, probably only one occupant, but can't be sure from here. Have a look please darling, there's a good girl.'

The killer paid no attention to the patronising tone, she just grunted agreement, cut the call and crawled to the top of yet another dune. She saw the boat immediately; there were four on board and it looked like it was being expertly handled.

67.

Jo Byers was by now 50 miles south, being cared for deep in the bowels of Newcastle General Hospital. Aside from her gashed breast and hand, she felt physically fine but had no intention of discharging herself until she was as sure as she could be that it was safe to do so. There was no telling when Greschner would locate her whereabouts and she had to assume that it wouldn't be long. She was under observation for hyperthermia and to make general recovery, it was a busy ward with lots of nursing and auxiliary staff; much safer from her point of view than a private room. She'd seen the movies – killers always got into private rooms. But they'd be wanting her bed soon and then she'd be out and alone again, vulnerable; they would be waiting for her.

68.

Blanchette watched as the boat hit the island beach and its incongruous occupants clumsily dragged it up onto the sand. Two of the males, one young and one middle aged, were dressed in suits and overcoats, the fat black female in slacks, woolly jumper and brightly coloured trainers. Only the steersman appeared to be appropriately attired in a dark hiking trousers, fleece and boots. She assumed he was some sort of pro, with his apparent seamanship and crewcut. He was short and wiry and looked at home. The others were completely out of place. Having got their craft clear of the water the three passengers trundled up the beach and onto the tarmac road which led from the end of the submerged causeway to the village at the southern point of the island which featured the ancient ruins of the priory. The crewcut remained with his boat. The killer figured that the civilians, as she had decided to call them, had a good 10 minute walk to the island village ahead of them; time for her to think, communicate and take instructions. She called Ellis.

'Okay my dear, well done. Right, interesting, let me think.'

This development had Ellis stumped for a few seconds; but only a few seconds. He issued his orders clearly, as if they had been prepared for hours.

'Let the passengers go. Approach the boatman. Tell him I sent you, give him my phone – and then use that gun I gave you.'

Blanchette gave her usual grunt of acknowledgement and killed the call. She watched as the three passengers walked up the narrow beach and onto the road. The boatman was preparing to re-launch, she had only a few seconds before he would be gone. She broke cover and sprinted down the dune and towards the water. Driver had got the boat back into the water but was having trouble starting the outboard motor; he looked up from what he was doing and saw her rapid approach. He froze, like a rabbit in the headlights - who the fuck is this, he thought?

As soon as he was within earshot she hissed, 'It's okay, I work for Ellis,' and with that she thrashed into the water and leapt into the boat. Driver just stood there, hands still on the motor, and gaped at his new passenger.

'Come on, get the fucking thing started and get us back across there!' She pointed at the mainland.

Driver knew to obey, the engine roared into life and within four minutes the pair had abandoned the vessel and were clambering out of the water and up onto the mainland beach. Blanchette made for the cover of a large clump of dune grass and sat down in the sand. She took off her boots and trousers. Driver was mesmerised by her heavily muscled legs but had no intention of following suit; he would rather freeze than have her see his skinny pins. He sat and watched as she rung out her legwear and filled her boots with sand to soak the moisture out of them. She was a highly trained survivalist.

'Did Kirkpatrick drown?' Her hands were still busy but she looked at him carefully as she asked the question.

'No, he's gone, that way,' Driver jerked his head towards the fields behind them and he hugged himself, shivering.

'You've got to dry out, come on, strip off, I'll show you.' He reluctantly complied and she helped him get most of the water out of his clothes. Then her hand went to the inside pocket of her padded bomber jacket, she pulled out a buzzing phone and answered the incoming call.

'It's for you,' she said, almost conversationally, and handed it to him.

'Yeah?'

'Godfrey dear boy, how are you?'

Driver recognised the voice. 'Fine, sir.'

'Good, now listen carefully, you're very nearly there.'

69.

It took only a couple of tugs and Simmonds had the lid off of the old wooden suggestion box, from which he then withdrew a three inch compact disc sealed inside a waterproof plastic envelope. It was unmarked.

'Is this what you're looking for?' he said to Tuitt. The

journalist held out her hand to take it.

'No,' Casey said, unnecessarily. Simmonds had no intention of parting with the find. 'That's police evidence of some pretty serious crime, if what you're telling us is true.'

Tuitt was alarmed, 'But I led you to it, I should have the first option.' Neither cop replied, Simmonds put the disk into his pocket, looked around and started walking out of the priory grounds and into the village. Casey followed with Tuitt, who was still protesting.

70.

Kirkpatrick sat on the bus and began to dry out properly. He was on the A1 heading to Newcastle on the hourly bus from Berwick which he'd boarded when it had made its scheduled stop at Beal, ten miles south of Berwick and fifty miles north of its destination. The driver had been somewhat alarmed by the appearance of the new passenger, soaked through, muddy and dishevelled, but the sight of the two twenty pound notes proffered allayed his fears and Kirkpatrick was allowed to take one of the many vacant seats.

Without his phone he had no internet access so meaningful research was impossible. However, he happened to know that there were two hospitals in Newcastle and only one of them had a helipad; the General, to which he was now headed. The journey would take him two hours, plenty time to come up with a plan to finish the job in hand. His only concern was that Hasleberger would get there before him. He need not have worried, of course. So the bus chugged cheerfully southwards, and Kirkpatrick's body warmed through.

71.

He's telling me I'm nearly there. Where is nearly there, I ask him. The end of your mission Godfrey, he tells me, the grand finale, he tells me. What do you mean, grand finale? I ask him. He asks me if he really needs to spell it out, that surely I must understand. It's him who doesn't understand; I'm a stalker mate; we don't do grand finales, we do infatuation and adoration and obsession, but not grand finales, because that would spoil everything. But I don't get time to explain this to him because he's insisting that if I don't complete the mission I'll never work again, not ever, and not only that, Jo Byers will be left terribly exposed if she isn't turned into a victim. A victim of what, I ask him. A victim of the grand finale, he tells me, now go and finish the job Godfrey.

And then... bang, I'm knocked hard against the concrete block by fucking muscle woman, she's firing a handgun at something I can't see, I can't hear anything and there's a searing pain in my buttock, I'm concussed, I shake my head to get some clarity, get my bearings, but I'm lying with sand in my eyes, the phone's gone from my hand, and this crazy woman keeps firing at something, but I can't hear the gun. And then she stops, turns round and bends down, her naked legs like those of Hercules, straddling me.

'I'm sorry, you got some friendly fire, you were in the fucking way, but they've gone now.'

Who's gone, there was nobody else here, what's she talking about? Then the pain in my buttock flares up, and she's on top of me rubbing and squeezing it like it's a bee sting.

'Sorry, you'll be okay, just a graze, the bullet didn't penetrate.'

'It fucking well feels like it did,' I tell her, and she gets her big arms under my shoulders and drags me into some long dune grass, the last thing I see is the sun rays lancing through the fast grey clouds, then I fall asleep.

72.

'How are you feeling Jo?'

The white coated junior doctor was looking at the notes on the end of the bed as he asked the question.

'Not too bad, I suppose,' was all Joanne Byers could think to say. 'Terrified' might have sounded strange. It dimly occurred to her that the medic's abbreviation of her name should perhaps have begged a question, but she let it go.

'Well, I think we can get you out of here and off home soon, do you have anyone to pick you up?' The doctor was now giving his patient a modicum of eye contact.

'No,' said Jo, thinking she didn't have anyone full stop, never mind to pick her up. This realisation turned her stomach; the feelings of loneliness and fear combining to make her slowly pull the bedsheet tightly around herself. The doctor saw this and paused, 'What's the matter? Are you okay?'

'No, I'm anything but okay, but thanks for asking.'

The doctor smiled weakly, turned and tried not to walk

away too quickly. Jo watched him confer briefly with a member of the nursing staff, the nurse nodded and the doctor disappeared.

73.

Kirkpatrick alighted at Newcastle central bus depot and made his way into the nearest phone shop. Five minutes later he emerged with a small box containing a cheap, unregistered mobile which he quickly assembled at the table of a greasy spoon café in which he ordered an all-day breakfast; he was starving. Satisfied no-one could overhear, he put a call in to Muller, not expecting a response. But Muller picked up.

'It's Kirkpatrick, I'm still with her but I don't know where the fuck Hasleberger is.'

'You're still with her? You have her with you?'

'No, not quite, but….'

Muller was suddenly excited, 'Are you in Newcastle?'

'Aye.'

'What?'

'Yes! I'm in Newcastle, near the hospital, it's my best chance….'

'Very good,' Muller could hardly contain himself, he was glad he was alone in his hotel room, his bags packed ready to leave.

The Scot continued, 'I need to be sure which hospital she's

in tho', whether it's the…?'

'Newcastle General Hospital, ward seven.' Muller had already made the enquiry, posing over the phone as a concerned relative.

Kirkpatrick ended the call and wolfed down the fry-up that had just been put in front of him. The bus journey to the cold northern city had taken over ninety minutes but his clothes were not totally dry. The café was drafty and he shivered, keen to get moving again. His stomach full, he paid and left. The job ahead was not going to be easy, and he had some shopping to do before he could even attempt it.

Meanwhile Jo Byers was taking a shower, taking care not to disrupt the sutures in her hand and breast.

74.

The tiny Anchor pub was open but empty as the three incongruent visitors shuffled in. It would be several hours before the tide receded sufficiently for them to walk back across the causeway to their cars. The taciturn George Niles regarded them with open suspicion and his surly service of their drinks made Tuitt in particular feel most unwelcome; she put it down to the distinct possibility that black people were not welcome on this North Sea outpost of England. But that was not the reason for Niles's reticence. He had not half an hour earlier confiscated from his son what he correctly assumed to be a poisoned dart, also correctly assuming that it and these strangers were somehow connected.

'Has this got anything to do with you lot?' Niles's tone was accusatory as he produced the offending article from a shelf behind the bar.

The three visitors all stared at the dart with vacant expressions. Tuitt broke the silence, keen to disassociate herself from something which could worsen her host's racist perceptions.

'Nothing to do with me,' she said, hurriedly. Casey was totally disinterested, more concerned about the dubious contents of his pint glass. Simmonds held out his hand and took the dart from Niles, carefully.

'Where did you find this?' he asked, frowning.

'My boy found it in the sea, about the time those helicopters were buzzing around the island, I expect that had something to do with you lot as well.'

Casey thought he'd better take control and decided to break cover.

'We're police officers from London,' he said and produced his warrant card. 'We know nothing about the helicopters or this thing here,' he nodded towards the dart in Simmonds' hand. 'But if you want to tell us anything you know we'd be more than grateful.'

The response was entirely predictable; this very rural publican wanted nothing to do with the police.

'I don't know anything about anything, only that some visitors bring nothing but trouble and we don't need coppers on our island.'

Then it was his turn to nod at the dart in Simmonds' hand,

'When you leave, take that thing with you.'

The trio moved away from the bar and sat down at a table with their drinks. Simmonds carefully examined the dart. It was just over four inches long, tipped at one end with what was clearly a hypodermic needle; at the other with a bright pink feather flight. The shaft was about a quarter of an inch diameter, made of opaque white plastic which obscured its contents. Simmonds set about carefully wrapping it a makeshift package made of cardboard beermats.

'What are you doing?' asked Casey.

Simmonds did not look up from the task in hand.

'It's an exhibit, and I don't intend pricking myself with it.'

'An exhibit of what?' Casey was unimpressed, back to trying to acquire a taste for the contents of his glass.

'It she's right and that disc contains a formula for some sort of poison, then we have to suspect that this dart contains some of it.'

'Who's 'she', the cat's mother?' Tuitt had to challenge the young policeman, but he did not rise to the challenge.

She went on, 'Remember who brought you here please, if it had not been for me….'

But the cops were ignoring her. Casey was becoming less disinterested, but also quite scathing,

'And who do we get to produce this exhibit if this ever goes anywhere near a court?'

Simmonds looked up and nodded towards the bar, 'He says his boy found it, we should get a statement from him.'

Right on cue, Raymond appeared and walked across to the threesome. The dart was now mostly out of sight, but the bright pink flight protruded from the beermat wrapping.

'That's mine, I found that!' exclaimed the tubby lad, pointing at his confiscated trophy.

The cops looked at him and then at each other.

'We're just going to borrow it for a while, we'll bring it back soon,' explained Casey with a reassuring smile. Raymond appeared satisfied and wandered off.

'That's your exhibiting witness, son,' said Casey with a smirk.

Simmonds took the point. There was nothing in law which prevented a person with Down's syndrome from giving evidence, but the reality of the situation meant that they were never called upon to do so; any opposing barrister would easily discredit their ability to remember and accurately elucidate facts.

Simmonds had a go at sipping his pint. He flinched at the taste and put down the glass. 'I suppose the same applies to the disc,' he mused, staring at the table top.

'Yeah, it does son, without a written statement from the person who put it in that suggestion box we have nothing to prove its provenance.'

'All the more reason why we have to find Jo Byers.' Tuitt said this with an air of authority; as an investigative journalist she knew the basics of continuity of evidence.

The three of them looked out of the window. The causeway was still submerged.

75.

'No! Call him off, we can't risk a bloodbath in a fucking public hospital you idiot!' Ellis's urbane exterior had at last deserted him.

Muller was taken aback but convinced he was doing right. 'The woman has to be taken out, we don't know where the disc is but without her to state where it came from it means nothing!'

Ellis recovered some composure, 'I'm aware of that and you're quite correct, she's the only witness as to the origin of the disc and yes, the poor girl has to go, but not in a matter that will provoke a full scale murder enquiry!'

His voice was raised again, he could scarcely believe the stupidity of the German.

'Call off Kirkpatrick, I have a contingency plan in place, and if you keep out of the fucking way it'll work!'

76.

Nance had been looking forward to a long weekend off and had parked up the Schweizer 300 on friendly farm land near Newcastle. The small helicopter was safe there and Nance had booked into a nearby Travelodge from which he had planned a few evenings drinking beer on Tyneside. So the call from Ellis had not been welcome but he had no choice but to accept this additional assignment – the money was good, and to turn Ellis down might not be good for business, going forward. Nance knew the sort of man Ellis was; understated power personified, not to be messed with.

It did not take long for him to spot Driver and Blanchette, the co-ordinates transmitted from the woman's mobile device were accurate to within two metres. He set the craft down in the middle of a field just inland of the dunes, scattering a dozen or so sheep with its noise and downdraft. Other than that the chopper went unnoticed; the sparse population of the region paid little attention to that which did not directly impact on their rural needs.

'Go on, get on board,' urged Blanchette, and Driver complied. There was only room for one passenger.

The little chopper leapt skywards, amplifying the growing feeling of euphoria that its passenger had been experiencing during the thirty minute wait for its arrival. The sky was clearing, it was noon and the low November sum was as high as it would get. Driver put his elated mental state down to altitude and anticipation. He did not connect it with the dull pain in his buttock.

Blanchette stood in the middle of the field and watched the aircraft rise, turn and head off south. The adrenaline drained from her nervous system. She felt an emptiness envelope her which the imminent words of praise from Ellis would do nothing to alleviate. The air pistol beneath her left armpit seemed suddenly heavy and the knowledge that she had enough pellets in her pocket to trigger a catastrophic epidemic of Ebolapox was an equally impotent antidote. In a rare moment of self-awareness she realised that as a human being she was woefully deficient and incapable of acting without orders. Head down, she dumped her weaponry under a thick hawthorn hedge and began her trudge towards the main road and a lonely journey back to London.

77.

I'm flying alright, in more ways than one. I've been up in choppers before but it was never like this. It's like I'm enjoying being out of my depth, but this is nothing compared to what I'm heading for.

Fuck me, it's windy up here, this little thing is no Sea King. The pilot is talking to air traffic control, probably at Newcastle, I don't know the call signs. He just wants somewhere to set down and chuck me out, and I'm freezing. But at the same time I feel kind of warm and really full of energy. I should be exhausted but I'm ready for anything, like I've got something inside me, driving me forward. My doubts and fears have gone, I'm eager to get the job done, finish the mission. I have to get to her before they do.

78.

Jo Byers put on her dry clothes which had been warming on a radiator near her bed. The screen curtains were pulled round to give her some privacy and, once dressed, she lay down on her back to think about what to do next. She closed her eyes and wondered about the train back to London. Deciding to check online she groped for her iPhone at her side. Then one hand gripped her wrist tightly and another came down firmly over her mouth. Her eyes snapped open to see Driver's face, its expression one of urgency and fear.

'Now shush, we're getting out of here now, it's not over yet, they're still coming.'

She took no convincing; this guy had already saved her once in the last 24 hours; he was proven. She nodded quickly as best she could beneath the weight of his hand, which he then removed from her face, but he held on to her wrist.

'Okay, you can let go of me, I'm coming!' she hissed. 'Have you got your car?'

Driver thought of his Fiat for the first time since he had told her to leave the island in it.

'No, it's still where you left it.'

He still had her wrist as they hurried past the nursing station.

'Er, Mrs Byers, we need to...,' but the ward sister's protest was ignored as Jo was taken into the stairwell by her highly focused visitor.

79.

Kirkpatrick emerged from the kitchenware shop next to the bus station with his newly purchased item safely concealed. The street signs to the hospital were clear and it was a small city; he did not need a cab. He knew that scheduled visiting hours were a thing of the past and patients at most hospitals could receive visitors pretty much around the clock. His main concern was doing the job, and getting out when it was done. And where was he going to go? He had plenty cash and a loaded credit card, but if the impending deed kicked off a frantic police search the airport and railway station would be on lock down. He pondered these familiar logistics as he walked through the main entrance of the hospital building. When he looked up at the ward direction signs he saw them coming down the escalator; that weirdo had got to her first.

Luckily for Kirkpatrick, Jo Byers and her guardian angel were distracted by their own urgent conversation and did not notice the killer watching them. He ducked behind a coffee machine and let them pass. This was good, he would not have to do it on a busy ward, but he would have to be quick. He followed them, catching up. They half walked, half stumbled down the concrete stairs leading out of the automatic entrance doors. Kirkpatrick took the wheelchair friendly slope, heading them off, and met them at the foot of the steps. He decided to take the woman first, to prevent the inevitable scream before he dealt with Driver. The knife came out and he lunged forward but Driver was too quick.

80.

Well, it wasn't me being quick as much as being prepared. I'd seen him you see, but I didn't say anything; I didn't want to panic her and I didn't think he'd seen us, otherwise I wouldn't have taken her out through those doors. But knowing he was there had put me on guard, and guard was what I did – with my life. I didn't feel a thing, not like I'd been stabbed anyway. It was more like a punch that knocked the wind out of me. Her scream sounded distant, all I knew was to hang on to him, for her dear life. The first I knew of the knife was when he was trying to get it out of me, but he couldn't, so strong was I hugging him. It must

*have looked like we were embracing long lost friends, or –
given the location - like bereaved relatives comforting each
other.*

'Run Jo,' I shouted, 'run!'

81.

As Jo Byers screamed she backed away a few paces, drew
breath and screamed again, but she did not run. People
stopped to stare and two cops began to approach the
fighting men, gathering speed. One shouted 'Oi!'
Kirkpatrick broke free and raced off. The cops did their job
and prioritised the injured party who was now on his knees,
holding his stomach. In a trice Jo was on her knees too, her
arms round his torso, trying to help him hold in his spilling
guts.

The last thing Driver saw were Jo's hands, crimson with his
blood, the dressing on her injured thumb saturated,
glistening in the cold sun.

Within seconds paramedics were upon them, Driver was
stretchered and Jo escorted. They were taken through to
Accident and Emergency and placed on gurneys, Jo
protesting that she was okay.

'I'm okay, I've just been discharged, Just look after him. I
want to stay with him, he just saved my life.'

'You weren't discharged Mrs Byers, you discharged
yourself.'

It was one of the nurses from the ward Jo had just left.

'You're coming back in, come on, we need to keep an eye

on you.'

'No, you need to keep an eye on *him*, fucking loads of eyes in fact, are the police going after that man, the one with the knife? He tried to kill me, he....' She pointed to the gurney disappearing though the automatic doors,

'Fucking saved me, I want to be with him, I owe him my life....'

The bossy nurse was determined to take control.

'No come on. Let's get this blood off you, love, come back up to the ward, you need some more rest.'

82.

Why all the masks? Why am I looking up at people wearing masks over their noses and mouths, and worried looks in their eyes? They're not talking to me, I'm on a bed or a trolley and now they're moving me, quickly, why so quickly. I feel like I've died and woken up in someone else's body. The speed of this thing, and noise of the wheels, I don't like the way they're looking at each other, through big swing doors, the ceiling whizzing past, the décor's changing, cleaner surroundings, lots of polythene curtains, then they hand me over to others, others wearing some serious gear, full face masks with plastic visors and yellow overalls, I swivel my head to see some are still getting ready, getting dressed, up, what are they going to do to me? They won't talk to me; the sheet over me has me pinned down. Now I can't hear anything, can't feel anything....

83.

'He's been taken into ITU, you can't go in with him, just wait here then, but don't try to get through there, I'll be back in a minute.'

The nurse left Jo seated in a lobby, content that she was settled and certainly not about to decamp again. She bustled along a couple of corridors to the intensive care unit so that at least she could return to Jo with some hopefully calming information.

Jo sat and shivered, after a few minutes an auxiliary came to her with a bowl of warm soapy water and some clean dressings for her hand and breast – such was the crush in A & E the reluctant patient was going to be cleaned up in a waiting area.

'It'll be alreet hinnie, yuh'll see yuh boyfriend in a little while, let's get yuh cleaned up just now.'

Jo was familiar with the Geordie accent; she'd been married to one for long enough. She relaxed and let the girl attend to her, all the while watching the door in case some mad bastard came back at her.

About ninety seconds elapsed and job was nearly finished, the auxiliary was on her honkers and leaned back to admire the handiwork that was Jo's new clean dressing. An internal door was barged open by two young medics in full chemical hazard suits,

'Don't touch her, get back!' shouted one of them at the Geordie lass.

84.

I'm spinning backwards, reverse somersaults, in time and distance, especially time, back to the school 'playground', 'play', that was it, go out and play they said, except that I was the plaything, the toy the other boys played with, hey Ginger, fuckin' Ginger, skinny little fucker, show us your dick, come on, let's see what you've got you little ginger cunt. Oh, great fun it was, that play stuff. I didn't know how to deal with it then and I still don't know now. Not a bit. And now I'm going back into it again, with each revolution, reverse revolution, I see it closer coming back at me, Jesus no, I'm plunging back there, please let me die now. I thought I'd got through it, pulled myself up and out of that horrible life, found myself tools, 'coping mechanisms' they called them, got really fit, passed the induction, became a man, got called brave, bold, fearless – but I never was. It was all fake, I was a fake. Became a Marine though, and then a spy catcher, and then it all started falling apart. A Special Forces operative with the mind of a pubescent boy, that's all I've been all these years. It's getting faster, the spinning and the falling, and darker, I'll never shake this one off, it's the worst it's ever been, by far. Dropping down, darker, colder. Black.

85.

Florence Obanga attended the funeral of her husband and several others that morning, a group affair at one of the six emergency crematoria on West Point from which the smoke had been rising skywards – like the death count - continuously for several weeks. Florence also expected to die and was looking forward to the release that death would bring. Release from the grief of her loss and from the overwhelming feeling of guilt she felt for bringing children into this filthy life. She walked slowly south through the slum town that was West Point, towards the neck of its peninsula which joined it to the rest of the sprawling city of Monrovia, itself little more than a giant slum with the odd hotel and shopping mall for visiting Yanks and Europeans, not that there were many of them these days; embassies were on lock down and incoming flights were at a bare minimum, such was the fear of Ebola.

Although embracing death she still wanted the answer to a question; why had they been deserted by the rich west so suddenly? In the foregoing days she had seen an exodus of the NGO volunteers, even the rag-tag Liberian troops had been withdrawn, the so-called medical centres were now barely staffed by Liberians who themselves had virtually given up hope of escaping with their lives. She had noticed that the disease had become more virulent of late, the symptoms had changed and people were becoming infected more quickly, and were dying more quickly. It was like the virus had mutated.

With her were her two children, aged 4 and 5, they carried a few belongings each and Florence carried nothing; she felt weak and light-headed, totally unable to comprehend how life could be, and end, like this. How death could descend on a whole population and dismiss it with an almost casual sweep of its hand.

She trudged through the shit-filled canals that were called streets, fresh air blew in from the Atlantic, she was hoping to take her kids into rump Monrovia to see if she could get help, help of some kind, she knew not what. The crowd thickened as it approached United Nations Avenue, the main thoroughfare separating West Point from the main city. The density of the shuffling exodus grew. Then it slowed, and finally stopped. Word soon got back to Florence and those around her that the peninsula had been closed off; quarantine.

The clatter of a helicopter attracted her attention skywards, it was low and she could read the lettering of the aircraft's livery - CNN News. It hovered noisily like a giant blowfly assessing a dung heap. She thought she could see the cameraman leaning out from the fuselage, his lens pointing downwards. Then the chopper turned, dipped its nose and sped off southwards.

86.

The mantle of evil weighed heavily, painfully on Ellis as he watched the CNN news bulletin. He knew what he was being party to and the incoming CNN bulletin hammered the knowledge home with bruising force.

A reporter in protective gear – facemask, gloves, overshoes – stood on the south side of United Nations Avenue, Monrovia, facing south. Behind him troops guarded a hastily erected fence of mesh and razor barbed wire, ten feet tall, supported by steel poles in concrete-filled forty gallon oil drums. Beyond the fence were hundreds, probably thousands of anguished, poverty stricken human beings. They were shouting, crying, pressing against the wire tentatively, pleadingly, knowing that any attempt to breach it would precipitate action from the trigger happy boy soldiers who were equally scared and confused. Beyond the massing crowd was the West Point peninsular which jutted northwards into the Atlantic Ocean, now a colony for the infected.

'No-one really knows why this strain of Ebola has suddenly become so virulent,' screeched the reporter through her facemask, 'All we've been told by departing medical volunteers is that they've seen nothing like it. One doctor just told me a few minutes ago that the disease was spreading like wild fire, that the symptoms had changed and that the infected victims were, after only a few days incubation period, dying rapidly and that nothing could be done to save them. This is Julia Prex, CNN News, Monrovia, Liberia.'

Ellis snorted at the irony of the reporter's New York accent. Fitting, he thought; Liberia was Africa's only US colony, set up in the early 19th century to receive emancipated slaves from America's southern states. Now descendants of those slaves were being used in a mass experiment in the race to develop... Ellis forced himself to think of something else; attend to more pressing problems.

87.

No sooner had the startled auxiliary worker been shooed away Jo found herself surround by a team of medical staff wearing biohazard suits and concerned expressions behind their thick plastic visors. She was virtually manhandled onto a gurney and, speechless, was suddenly on her back staring up at corridor ceilings racing past and above her. The gloved hand of one medic held her wrist firmly in an attempt at reassurance, 'This is just a precaution Mrs Byers, nothing to worry about.'

'Oh, really?' replied Jo with all the sarcasm she could

muster. She was completely overwhelmed - something had gone very wrong and the connections her brain was making were terrifying.

The gurney crashed through a swing door and heavy polythene curtains, wheeled abruptly around and shuddered to an abrupt halt, like a car being parked by a stunt driver. Jo's wide eyes took in the peripheral scene; the masked faced, the hands removing her clothes and wound dressings none too gingerly.

'Small scratch,' said a medic, and Jo felt the needle go into the back of her uninjured hand. And then nothing.

88.

Ellis watched it break. Sky had the scoop, as usual, and their crew were at the hospital in double quick time.

'A knifeman attacked two innocent people outside this, the Newcastle General Hospital, not 30 minutes ago. The victims, a man and woman who appeared to know each other, have been taken inside the building and are receiving medical care right now. Their attacker escaped on foot and a police manhunt has been activated. We have been told that the male victim received serious abdominal injuries whilst the woman was not seriously injured. This John Haines, Sky News, Newcastle upon Tyne.'

Muller had walked into the room halfway through the bulletin.

'Looks like your man fucked up royally old chap. You failed to call him off, and now he's failed to nail the target.'

'Who was with her? One of your imbeciles?' Muller had long suspected Ellis of running a shadow operation.

'No,' denied Ellis. Driver was deniable.

89.

Muller left the room and Ellis made a call. Whilst reasonably confident that things were more or less under control, he hated not knowing. His call was to Scotland Yard, his contact there would glean the relevant information from Northumbria Police who would, surely by now, have investigators at the hospital but, Ellis hoped, not at Driver's bedside. Nor at that of Mrs Byers, for that matter. He hoped the two were together, and as close as possible, but the situation could suddenly spiral catastrophically out of control if his luck didn't hold. His second call was to Newcastle General Hospital and he asked to speak to the doctor in charge of Accident and Emergency. He had to warn them and to do so adopted the persona of a concerned scientist – he knew the jargon to use.

'Do keep your two most recent patients isolated Doctor, I believe they've been infected with a most deadly and highly contagious virus for which there is not yet an antidote.'

'I've no idea who you are,' replied the stressed out junior doctor. 'There is a police investigation going on here so I cannot comment.'

Ellis had to rub it in. 'My name is Doctor Ballard, Ian Ballard, I work for the Soissons Institute at the London Hospital. I have very good reasons to believe that your patients have been infected by what is a hybrid of smallpox and Ebola which is extremely contagious at the level of a pandemic scale. You can call me back if you wish.' Ellis gambled on the offer not being accepted. He won.

'We're already aware of that, the male patient is exhibiting very worrying symptoms and the female has had bodily fluid contact with him, they've both been isolated.'

'Good, best of luck, call me back if you need any help,' said Ellis, before ending the call.

Driver's 'very worrying symptoms' included sporadic loss of consciousness, blackening of the skin and internal haemorrhaging; it was classic Ebola but seemed more invasive, more debilitating in that the patient appeared lobotomised, unaware of his surroundings. A run of the mill Ebola patient is totally aware and lucid throughout. Driver appeared to have lost sentience. His abdominal wound had clearly caused shock trauma, but the medics had virtually lost interest in that and were frantically calling upon experts to examine the patient and make an accurate diagnosis.

Jo Byer's loss of consciousness was at first down to the heavy sedative that she had been injected with upon admission; a hysterical woman carrying a lethal contagion was not what a busy general hospital needed. At first she had been out in her own room, but when she decided to exhibit the same outwardly visible signs as Driver her gurney had been wheeled in alongside him. The two were side by side in an isolation unit staffed by increasingly anxious specialist nurses. They had all received proper training, but nothing could have prepared them for a situation in which they were required to do nothing but protect themselves and the public from these two patients; it went against their core instincts – they were supposed to be carers, not imprisoners.

90.

It was a difficult journey from Berwick to Newcastle. Only sixty miles; but a long sixty miles. At least he had not had Muller as company; the German had already gone to the Greschner fortress in Ashington from where he would be helicoptered to London. Ellis had only his taciturn communications operative-cum-driver for company and the man was characteristically silent. So, rather than have to maintain polite conversation with an ex-squadie, the Greschner operations director was prone to some rather unwelcome introspection.

The big Lexus ploughed south along the A1 and the bleak Northumbrian landscape rushed past, as if it was late on its journey north to Scotland. Ellis was confident that everything was under control, but just needed to see the evidence. He was not looking forward to the experience. Not that he was squeamish in the least, and not that he felt guilty – he had always known what this job would sometimes entail. But he had noticed that, with age, he'd developed a semblance of a conscience, and within the next hour he would be called upon to deal with it.

He presented his credentials at the hospital reception, together with his confident charm. He was taken by a nurse through a maze of corridors and into a very silent anteroom. He was solemnly asked to wait, and the nurse disappeared back the way they had come.

Ellis just stood there, after thirty seconds he took out his phone; no signal. He looked around himself, nothing on the wall, no NHS leaflets scattered about on the broken plastic chair, no Help to Stop Smoking posters, no coffee machine, not even the mandatory hand gel dispenser. There were two doors; the one through which he had entered the anteroom with the nurse and, facing it from the other side of the anteroom, a very secure looking door with a keypad mounted on the wall beside it.

He kicked his heels and walked around the anteroom. It measured about 12 feet by 16 feet; quite a lot of space for seemingly no useful purpose. The only feature was a pair of large plastic wheelie bins with swing lids. He looked inside one of them, it was empty, the same with the other one.

The security door opened with a sudden loud click of the electro-magnetic lock. Two people walked out through it and Ellis was momentarily stunned by their clothing and, when they had removed their hooded helmets and Perspex masks, their expressions; traumatised. A male and a female, they paused to regard Ellis and exchange glances with each other. They continued to busy themselves with taking off their bright yellow Hazcem suits, revealing underneath featureless green surgical theatre garb. No sign of name tags or badges of rank. Last to come off were their rubber gloves and then, heads down they made for the exit door.

'Excuse me,' said Ellis, having no intention of being ignored, 'I need to know what has happened to Mrs Byers and her companion.' He produced his Security Service I.D., an impressive affair with a metallic badge mounted on black leather. The two medics regarded it carefully and then looked at each other again. The female turned to Ellis and stared at him for a full three seconds, the time it took her to make the decision.

'Within the last ten minutes, in both cases, life has been pronounced extinct. The bodies are in high contagion lockdown. They suffered almost simultaneous embolisms, exacerbated in the case of the male by severe abdominal injuries. In the case of the female, Mrs Byers as you call her, by pre-existing shock. They both exhibited extreme symptoms of some sort of haemorrhagic fever, we've never seen anything like it. Please come this way, you shouldn't really be here.'

The female medic then stood back to allow Ellis to follow her colleague through the door, she then followed him. Ellis said nothing and allowed himself to be escorted along the corridor and into the real world of the bustling hospital.

So accustomed was Ellis to fulfilling his appointed role in his life of justified ruthlessness that he barely noticed a light tug at his trouser leg. But it was there, and he looked down, nothing, and then another, he looked down again, nothing; just the cold wispy breeze. Were he possessed of a scintilla of humanity, of imagination, he may have discerned a little brown hand. A little brown hand at the end of an arm thrust through a fence across a causeway between a place called West Point and another called Monrovia.

**

Bad Books

(Translation by David Dougall)

1.

Eat. Food, food. Somethin' tae drink. Must get some fluids intae me. That's maest important. In training, if ye lose fluids ye can easily go intae shock. Eat. Drink. First job. Always first job ae the day, night ah mean – get to mah feet.

Get the numbness oot. Work masell free ae the fuckin' cauld. Loadsa feet. Must be gettin' late. Sleepin well, s'pose. Stiff as a board tho. Pubs've turned oot, next the restaurants, then the leftovers, the fuckin' slops. Tha'll dae fur fuckin' me. Thae boatles. Hunners ae 'em. Charlotte Street first. Fck, Aye. Charlotte Street first. Then the late slop shop in Goodge…

OOMPH!

Ahh fuck! That was a kick. Shite! Anurrar wan. Roll up. Tight in a bawl. Cover mah heed an eyes - AAH! fuck, no. That's piss. Pissin' oan me. Naw. Please. Ah'll fuckin' freeze. Whit tha fuck dae ye mean 'Dirty ol' fucker'? Aye, ah am noo cos youz cunts've pissed oan me. Go on my sons. Hae a fuckin' guid laugh. Go on, aff yeez go noo before a polis comes - AAGH!!

That's the last wan. The finale. The last wan is ayeways the hardest. Anyways, nae blood. Just piss. That's it. Noo aff yeez go lads. Goat to get up noo. Goat tae dry aff before the…. Whit's this?

2.

Whit's this? Mah n… mah name in the… in the shoap

windae. Someboady huz the same name as me? Someboady writin' fuckin' books. Making loads ae money. Lucky bastart. Hey! You in therr Bernard fuckin' Ackrose ma arse! Tha's *mah* fuckin' name. Who said yeez could hae it? Eh? Who said you could fuckn have it to write all thae fuckin' books under. Hunners ae fuckin' books, look. An' they're all the fuckin' same. Oh. Aye. No, just hunners o the same fuckin' book! Copies! A best seller display in a fuckin' bookshop! Either that or ah've goat multiple fuckin' vision! Bernard Ackrose, who said yeez could use ma fuckin'… Jesus the fuckin' piss is runnin' doon mah fuckin' back, thae cunts. Thae fuckin' cunts.

Hey, oi! Youz in therr! Whits yer fuckin' book aboot, eh, Bernard fuckin' Ackrose?

Bet you dinnay hae' tae put up wi' this, eh? Bet youz dinnay get kicked an' pissed oan in shop doorways, eh. Bet your fuckin' fancy book which ye've hud the fuckin' audacity tae write in mah fuckin' name, is nae in any way aboot me, aboot this poor cunt getting' kicked an' pissed oan ev'ry fuckin' night by all an' sundry drunken' bastarts. Eh? Fuck me, ah kin hardly staund, thae must hauv kicked me harder than ah felt. It's gittin' worse. As the cold wears aff the pain gets worse.

You either hurt or you get cold an' ye can die o the fuckin' cauld but ye cannae sleep when ye're hurt so it therefore follows, like, thon pain saves yer fuckin' life.

Eh? Did'yu hear what am sayin' Bernard fuckin' namesake fuckin' Ackrose? Military trainin' mah son. Mair than ah bet ye nae aboot, yu fuckin' English poof. Look at that poster, "The Matriarchy by Bernard Ackrose – the book they tried to ban!"

Bet yerra fuckin' poof, eh. A poof using ma fuckin' name tae write a book under. Jesus fuckin' Christ that's nae fuckin' piss its fuckin' blood, ahh Jesus, whit the fuck, hey Bernard in therr, this is yer fuckin' namesake oot here, tell me, tell me whit the fuck the Bernard oot here did tae fuckin'

deserve this fuckin' deal an, while yerr fuckin' at it ye can tell me az weel whit the fuck did ye, The Bernard Ackrose In Therr, dae tae deserve your deal. Eh? Eh…?

3.

Fffff… JESUS! Huh? Christ ahm fuckin' paralysed. Starved. Starved an fuckin' paralysed. Fell back tae'sleep, must've. Never goat any food. Nae fluids. Big mistake, that. Oh! mah back. Mah neck! Freezin. That piss. The fuckin' stinkin' piss husnae dried yet. Ahm goanni stink aw fuckin' day long. A serious handicap, that. As if ah didnae hae enough serious fuckin' handicaps. Look at yon cunt ower therr. Any spare change please any spare change please. Professional fuckin' beggar. Up early this morning pal? Bacon an' eggs for brekky wis it? Cunt. Fuckin' wanker. Prob'ly huz a bath in the mornin' then pits oan fake filth. Prob'ly shares a Big Issue pitch wae his fuckin' wife then goes back t'the flat in Brixton af a night. Noo before pickin' up the kids frae school mind. Eh? Try an turn oan ma side.. aah… pain, pain, pain, is therr never, ever anything fuckin' else?!

An noo ahm lookin' through this fuckin' shop windae again. Seein' two o m'sel' no, dozens o m'sel', best seller, aw the same, wae ma fuckin' name oan them!

Eh? Eh… you again. You wae ma fuckin' name ya cheeky copyin' cunt! Didny like yer ain name so ye thooght ye'd hae mines eh? Tell ye whit. Ye're fuckin' welcome tae it! Bernard Ackrose. Be ma fuckin' guest! Write as many books as yeh like under ma name. Mah handle.

4.

Hello, here we go, the shop proprietor no less, time tae move. Waky wakey rise 'n' shine. No before a wee snatch up yir

fuckin' skirt tho lass. Just a quicky. Wow, eh, power. Look at aw thae keys janglin.

Mornin'. Nae reply. I said Mornin'. Nae reply wis the answer. Must be a fuckin' lesbian. Hey, sweetheart, ah'll huv yeez know that beneath these rags an' aw this shit an' piss lives the body of an Adonis. Not tae mention a cock like a fuckin' donkey. Here, look at…. Naw, better no. Not that auld' sketch. Kickin' every oor oan the fuckin' oor for that little misdemeanour. Old Bill do not appreciate the humour and art behind such a stunt. Mornin' lass. No be long. Willny chase away aw yer customers. Those book-buyin' intellectual customers of yours. Don't speak then. Obviously shy. A shy lesbian. Poor cow. Ma heart goes oot to yez lass. Stretch… crane the neck.. lessee – yes! Gottya. Bingo! Wearin' the tackle! Red knickers! Whitta start tae the day. Fuckin' hell. That wis better than Anne Summers' door. Aye they're wise to it at that place noo, mind. Move yeez before openin' up.

Mmmm, feelin better aalready. Better than breakfast that. Prob'ly huv tae replace breakfast mind. Wae me stinkin' o piss an' aw. Hmmph! Thassit. Oan ma feet noo. Staun here furra a

minute. Get the blood gaun' roon. Right then. Must get gaun' or ah'll be late furrra oaffice. Ha! Be late fur breakfast at the fuckin' Dorchester. Eh Bernard? Bernard over therr inside that cosy fuckin' shoap windae. Bet tha's wherr ye're huvin yere fuckin' brekky eh? Salmon an' poached egg at the fuckin' Dorch ya cunt. Hae some for me. Wonder if ah showed mah dole card with mah name oan it if they'd let me in? Ah'd prob'ly just get nicked for usin' ma ain fuckin' dole card, eh! Ironic eh?

Right then. Next joab, after a wee can fur breakfast that is, tae git a copy o that fuckin' book. Nae bother that'll be. Ah'll just walk straight in an' teck a fucker. That's it. Nae fuckin' probs.

5.

Here we go noo, one, two three, hup, lift an oot! Aye, they don't mess wae ol' stinker here. Any other twat, part time fuckin' vagrant tried that they'd make some sort of citizens arrest an' call the fuckin' polis. Not wae me though, No. No.

They widnae even come near me. Vonny ma wee lamb ye wid be proud of me. At last ah huv achieved greatness. Actually excelled at somthin'. Vagrancy. I scaled the heights of depth. I huv plumbed the depths of shite! A poet an' ah didny know it as weel! Aye Vonny, ye an' the kids'd be proud of uz, nae doubt abbot that! Ye see, if yer goana be a dosser be a fuckin' dosser an' doant fuck aboot, like. There's nothing more fuckin' irritatin' than part-time tramps. Designer Dossers, I caw thaem. Beggars – 'spare some change please'. Cunts. I hae tae admit I tried it wance or twice mind, the auld beggin'. But I aye was found ah wis too over qualified. A bit ripe. A bit of spare fuckin' change wiz never goany dae *me* any good. Fuckin' hell, a fuckin' wanner would hardly put a scratch oan *me*, never mind a few pence o spare fuckn' change. So they didn't bother.

Another possible reason wis that I dinnae like to shout. Ye

see like ah say ah've always embraced filth. Nae point in tryin tae keep clean if yir a dosser. Otherwise ye just spend yer dole money oan soap an stuff when it could be goin' oan Special Brew, Tennants or Full Strength Kestrel. So ah suppose ah've always been a wee bit high in mair ways than wan!

This is a handicap when it comes tae beggin' cos it's hard tae politely ask fur money from somebody who's aboot tae spew at the stench of ye an' who's trying to gee ye ah fifteen yard berth withoot gettin knocked doon by a fuckn bus cos they've hud tae walk oan the fuckin' road! Ye can try an shout, like – 'GOAT ANY SPARE CHANGE PLEEEZE!!!' - but that can getye nicked an' a hose doon in the back yard o' the polis shoap. Nae guid.

6.

That wiz a guid joab well done. In. Oot. Goat it. Alarm be fucked. Bleep bleep. Whit thae goanna dae aboot it. Cannay sell the fuckin' book noo. Ha. Bet it fuckin' stinks already! Right. Let's hae a look at this then... Jesus Christ. They've ma photo oan the back. It's me. ME! From when I wis... that wis taken when ah joined... for ma oaffice pass. Jesus Christ, how'd they get that... I'm bein' stitched up. I didnae write this fuckin' book. Ah've never written any fuckin' book. Whit's this – aboot the author – believed living in France – fuckin' news tae me pal. Yeah anyway, Ah'd huv gone tae fuckin' Brazil if ah'd written this book... fuckin' hell. Three failed in-junk-shons in court tae stoap publication. And it's written by fuckin' *me*!!! Published by Dobbins. Bill Dobbins Publications it sez here. Right ya cunts. The Matriarchy eh? That's aboot right eh. It was that awright, never a truer word said, except that ah never said it. Never wrote a word aw the time ah was therr. Hud ah been a clever cunt, aye, mebbies. But me, ah wiz a techie. Recruited from the old mob because of certain skills and experience. Hah! No the Liam Neeson kind a fuckin' skill, just skills an' experience in keepin mah fuckin' mooth shut, aye that's aboot right.

Photos. Black an' white. Where the fuck did they get these from. How did whoever wrote this book get these?! An' they're blaimin' me! Stitch up! Ah'll git fuckin' done fur this! Prob'ly auld by noo but it's still under the OSA. Official Secrets fuckin' Act. Another photo o me! With... no.... Vonny, why did ye gee them that! And Harry and Florence. No Vonny, what did ye dae that fur? Ye had enough tae live oan, ah made sure o that, didnae? Didnae? DIDNAE?! ... bitch, Vonny, bitch!

7.

Right, in tae a phone box, goat a wee bit a change fur wance.

Posh voice noo.

Hello. Hello. Is that Bill Dobbins publications? Yes? Right. I want to speak about this book called The Matriarchy.

Anybody. Not bothered. Preferably the person

who decided to publish it... Bernard Ackrose... BERNARD ACKROSE. Look here I am the bloke who you lot have stitched up for writing this book.... Hello. Hello. Put that fuckin' music aff!... Eh? Who? Right! What... Eh? Don't fuckin' thank me, mate, for ringin'

Look here. I am probably a bluddy wanted man because of you lot. I never wrote that book and you lot surely know this!

Whaat? Not fuckin' likely mate. I'm meetin' nobody aboot

fuck aall!… Bollocks! Ah'll turn up an ye'll hae the fuckin' Old Bill waitin' furmee, more's the like. Eh?… Eh?… How much?… Jeezas fuckin' Christ! No it isn't fuckin' good! Nay fuckin' good at aw. What the fuck ahm ah goany dae with aw that? Not only ah'm ah noo a traitor an' a fuckin' spy, ahm aboot to get ma fuckin' dole stoaped into the fuckin' bargain! Eh? No. Wait! What did you say your name was? Goodynuff? Eh? Are you taikin' the piss? Ah'll find ye if ye are! Right. Right then Mister Edwin Goode-fuckin'-nough. Ah don't want yar fuckin'

money. Ah want a front page apology in the papers tommorruh.

No. Ahm not fuckin' jokin'. Ev'ry newspaper with the words BERNARD ACKROSE DID NOT WRITE THE MATER-IARCHY AND BILL DOBBINS PUBLISHING APOLOGISES, eh? Matriarchy then, so fuckin' what, ye no what ahm… are ye taikin' the fuckin piss oota me?

Better no be, eh? What dya mean ya cannay dae it? Cunt. It is true! AH DIDN'T WRITE THE BOOK. AH HAVVINT EVEN GOAT A FUCKIN' PEN!!! Furfucksake. Mah moneys run oot.

Bastard. He's fuckin' laughin' at me. Ah'm goan tae read this book the night. Every bluddy page. Then ah'm goan tae contact them. Again. Direct. Gonnae go therr, it's just roon' the corner. Tell them it wisnae me that wrote it. Whit a bunch o bastards that did this. Maikin' a fuckin' fortune oota me like this. Whit I cannae, just cannae, understaun' is *why*? Why fuckin' why? *Me*. C'mon Sleep. Ma best friend Sleep. Take me aff oota here fur a while. This is aw too much at the minute. Mebbies a'ave been asleep aw this time an aw this is jist a dream. A bad fuckin' dream. Ah think. Ah think ah'll jist go doon tae that oaffice in the morra an staun therr, like, an' gie it fuckin' laldy.

8.

Here I am! Bernard fuckin' Ackrose! Come oan an get uz. Now ya bastart! C'moan! Or ah ciud just turn up at the nick. Or the court ...or somewhere. Then ah'd just say right oot, hey it's *me*, the cunt that wrote thon fuckin' book yer aw oan aboot! Wid they believe me? Like fuck! Hose doon. That's aboot aw ah'd git – fuckin' hose doon ... in the back fuckin' yard. Ring the press? Complain? *A book has been written in my name to protect the identity of the true author!* Why would anyone want to do that? Thae cunts wid say. Mmmm Aye! Good question. Answer. Because ah could huv written thon book. Could huv, quite easily, written that fuckin' book! Then why fuckin' didn't you, they would then say! If you could write like that, then why are yoo a filthy drunken dosser wae maggots crawling oot aiy yer fuckin' arm? EH? *EH?!*

Mmmm. Good question. Answer. Cos writin' that book puts you, the writer, like, in very great danger o drawin' serious bluddy porridge wi' a kickin' ev'ry fuckin' day. So the best thing you can do is put the blame oan some other poor bastart for writin' it an' grab aw the money fur yer fuckin' *BASTART SELF!!!*

9.

Jesus Christ ah bet ahm bein' followed anaw. The Watchers'll hae me well boxed. Twenty, thirty, forty – mebbies a hunnerd o' them even. Ah used tae be able tae spot a Watcher. Bet ah still can – except ah'll go stark starin' fuckin mad in the process. Yu see ye've goatae assume that therr aw watchin' ye, then work back frae therr. Ah reckon ah'll start wae some counter-surveillance techniques. A few re-cips anna wee bit o windae work. Nae bother. Just tae begin wi'. If thae wur just goanna huckle me thae wid've done it by noo. Kings Cross dole office. Cannae be many Bernard fuckin' Ackroses aboot, eh? Feel ma collar, whizz me in, loads o questions and nae fuckin' anssarz, that's whit wid've happened. Then whit? – Nae confession from me means nae bluddy evidence that ah wrote the damn book means nae evidence that ah broke the bluddy Act - an even, even if ah did, it's only two years. Doddle fur the likes o me. Naw, they think things thru better than that. Far fuckin' better. Goodenough'll hae refused tae co-operate other than tae say that he received the manuscript, decided tae publish but couldnae ever get a haud o me, tae pay me. Bollocks. He's defeated the fuckin' courts oan publication. Clever lad. Must hae plenty aw backers.

But the Service ... must surely be efter me tho. The Office. Thames fuckin' Hoose. Different kettle o fish. No interested in the fuckin' Official Secrets Act. Interested in spies tho. Very interested in spies. Fuck! That's another fuckin' thing! Some spies might now be very interested in me.

Noo then. Let's consider ma position here. One - ahm a millionnaire if ah want to be, or so it would seem. But that would entail me coming oot o the woodwork and taikin' flight like a fuckin' blowfly. Ah widnae last five minutes. That wid be the same as confessin' tae writin' the book and then ah wid be targetted. Not many Benny! All thae people wantin' to speak. Ahd get ill again. Like ah wis. Ahd fuckin' top mesel nae bother. Ah canny even bear thae twats at the Kings Cross dole oaffice trying tae be nice an chatty while makin' a phone call oot in the back oaffice.

10.

Aye well. Another day. Another day in the life o a famous author. Eh? A famous public-enemy-number-wan-to-be author! Great eh? Dole day the day. This is the day we'll see 'em. The Watchers. Mebbies ah'll no see 'em, mind. Been a long time

been a long time been a lonely lonely lonely time ...

bam bam on ye blether blah fuckin' blah fuckin' blah.

Jeeezas Christ whitssat?! Ahm fuckin' stuck! Cannae move. Lie back. Relax. Try again in a minute. Now this can get messy! If ah struggle tae get up too much some helpful cunt'll think ahm hae'in' a fit an' call a bluddy ambulance an' then mah day's well and truly fucked.

Except ye'd think ah wid enjoy bein' pampered in a hoaspital. Not likely pal. Thae female nurses at University College Hoaspital willny come near me. Oan account of somethin' ahm meant ta'huv done a while back in thon casualty department. Ah heard them callin' me a pervert when ah woke up. Noo ah dae not wan little bit mind bein' called a pervert. Nae problemo. Whit I dae mind is noo remembrin' whit led tae me bein' awarded that wee soubriquet an' whether ah enjoyed it or no.

D'ye see this Vonny. Ye must've helped them. They must've called. Thon photo in the book. How much did ye get ferrit, eh? Coupla grand at least. The kids must know an' aw. Getting teased and bullied at school, eh? Dads a spy, a traitor? Are the other wimmin' speakin tae ye? EH? Better fuckin' no be Vonny – or ah'll bully yeez!

11.

Right noo, that wis a nice wee walk. Here it is, here we are.

Charlotte House. Home tae, amongst other things oan the various floors, Bill Dobbins Publishing. Receptionist gein' me an odd look through the windae. Ahm used tae that. Clockin' ma interest though. She'll pick up the phone if ah start hangin' aboot.

And… aboot turn quick – there that's wan. A Watcher. And another. There'll be a car in a minute, aye, and mebbies a bike. Okay. Time tae shuffle aff. Ah'll away doon tae Centre Point. Even they willny come doon therr. Even they couldnae avoid a compromise in yon fuckin' snake pit.

Ah remember… ah remember the time… the time when ah seemed tae be getting' oan well. Gettin' some respect fur whit ah did. The bit that ah played, mah contribution. But no sooner hud it begun tae take shape than it started tae unravel. Self-fuckin'-destruct, like, aye that's me. Always been the fuckin' same. Like ah was scared o something. Feared that ah would end up haein' too much tae hing oan tae. Mebbies. Maybee. Ah don't really know? So ah guess, ah make this wild guess, that ah've unwittingly made masell into a very valuable item. Nil ambition. Nil ego. Nil self-respect. Nothing tae lose. And - and this is the important bit – nothin' tae gain! Mah 'gain thingy' disnae work any mair. Fell aff years ago after a long but steady process o blissful atrophy.

So. Therr it is. Now they think ah've done the dirty. Turned! So they've goat some major sport oan therr haun's now. The Assessors'll be haein' a fuckin' field day. Am ah biding mah time for a pay day? Maybe. Am ah dain' this tae set them up, a
distraction from the real problems? Maybe. Should they wait and see if ahm pitched, thereby using me as a barium meal against the Opposition. Maybe. But this is aw

assumin' that ah wrote that fuckin' book. Which ah did not! So! Who the fuck did then? The publishers've goat away wi' publishin', obviously oan the basis that nae real harm has been done tae the public good. Which is probably right. Ha'ein now scanned this item of fuckin' literature pretty fully ah can say there's loats o secrets in it, but only the wans that everybody knew anyway. It's aw been written before.

12.

OK. Here goes. Look at her face. Not yer day lass, eh!

Can you help me? Yes you can help me. In case that wis what you were going tae ask, my dear, before you started gaggin'. I want to see your boss, Edwin Goodenough. NOW!

Don't give me that shite. Bill Dobbins Publishin'. In big letters on that list. Get him here. NOW! He publishes books and he's gonnae be in mah fuckin' bad fuckin' books if he disnae get his poofdah arse doon here now!

You whit? Ye goannae call security? Security? Security? Ah could tell ye a few things aboot security lass. Ye havnae even goat very big tuts!

(See whit ah mean aboot self destruct?)

Awright, awright, be careful or ah'll shit masell, an' then ye'll all hae a job. Whit? Get the fuckin' polis then. Ah'll git their uniforms shitty an'aw! Where's Goodenough? Bill Dobbins Publishin. Nutter? Whadya say? Nutter? Aye right, whatever you say. Whatever.

Think ah'll go furra a walk now. Wan o' mah long ones.*

13.

Aff the manor. Up Kings Cross. A bit o fresh fuckin' air. Awa' from aw thae fuckin' people. The gasometers. They reckon HG Wells walked aboot therr when he was writin' the Time Machine. And now another great writer will follow in his hallowed fuckin' footsteps! Or so they'll huv it. Great, eh? A bet he didnae dae this but. Ha.

Here ah am, in the graveyard using ma special wee place. Good vantage point fur keepin' a lookout. Whoever relocated thae gravestanes like this must've been a dosser, though. Or a fuckin' genius. Close together bunched arouon' a tree. All up against each other but wae gaps wide enough tae take the shit. Just right. So therr ah'll squat. Under mah tree in the gravestanes hae'in' a shite. Luxshry! Fuckkin' – oooh - luxshry.

Who's that? Cunts. Bastards. Watchers. They'll be followin' me therr anaw. Whit ahm ah meant to be fuckin' goanna dae!?

Ah'll say ahm hae'in a shite ya bastards!!! Tha's aw. A shite. Even fuckin' traitors huv tae hae shites. Especially dosser traitors whit write fuckin' books. That'll git rid o' thaem.

It was ayeways goanna be this way Vonnie. Ayeways in decline. Ah wiz never happy wis ah? Eh? Only when ah wis wallowin' in self-pity. That was aboot it, right? That's whit you used tae tell uz anyways. When ah came oot the mob with ma wee pension an' we moved uz an' the kids away. Then the joab came up at the Oaffice and we moved them back again. We knew it wis a mistake but it wis a joab and a joab's a jobe. A steady joab, respectable and secure. Specially wi' mah health oan the blink a bit. Needed a secure joab. Then they filleted me. Ah wiz getting' sidelined after aboot a year and a hauf. Getting' bad reports an' things. Past mah shelf life. Sidelined. Cunts – sorry – ah shouldny swear, I dinnae usually swear when ahm talkin' to you Vonnie. I talk to you every hour of every day. An' ah huvvnae even seen you for two years. Ah speak t'ye now mair than ah did when we wiz taegether. An ah miss thae kids. I ache fur thaem, Vonny. Ache mair than the cold an' the kickins make me ache. The cold an' the kickins are nuthin. Nuthin.

14.

And now ye've given some bastard my auld photo from when we wuz oan holiday. Ye've cut it oot but ah know which photo it wiz from. There wiz just the two o us in that picture. Kids must've been asleep. Naw. Wrong. Florence wid hae been asleep. Harry wisnae born then. It wiz by a pool in Greece. The only time when we ever went abroad Vonnie. Aye, an' ye've sold it. You cannay be fuckin' skint already though, but. Christ it's only been two years. Well, two an' a hauff. But surely tae

God, whit huv ye done wi' it aw? They'll be watchin' yeez Vonnie. They'll be watchin' in case ah come hame. No like they're gonna nab me or nothin, it'll be just tae see if ah bring anybody back, get a lift with anyone.

Let's go thru' this again. Some cunt writes a book. The publisher has a hard time getting' it intae the shoaps cos it's aboot the Oaffice, the Service. But it gets thru' the courts and ontae the best seller list. There's no real actual secrets in it, but there is enough detail tae make people feel a wee bit queezy aboot it. It represents a wee bit of a melt doon, or partial melt doon at least, o' the 'mystery factor.' And they dinnae like that. No, because if the walls come doon much mair the game'll be up. Too fuckin' right like.

Anyway, the book thereby attracts a wee bit o' litigation and therefore - unbeknownst tae me because ah never read the newspapers coz ah'm usually fuckin' sleepin' in them - a good deal o' free publicity. Bestsellers' shelves here we come. Now then, the cunt that's written the book, he's just some bastard that's done a deal wae the publisher. Prob'ly an ex-Oaffice wallah that hasnae goat the bottle tae face the wrath o' the right wing media or polis or the courts, wants tae keep his heed right doon, like. So he scouts aroon' fur a scapegoat, for ah, well, the likes of yours truly. Ex-service, gone missin', mebbies even deed but, in any event, somebody wae a past that hus actually existed and then done a disappearin' act. Then bingo, we hae a mystery. The mysterious Bernard Ackrose, disappearing traitor. Ching go the tills. Mair money.

15.

That's wan scenario. Another scenario is that the Oaffice is behind the entire thing. Wants tae flush me oot and use me.

That's really fuckin' spooky! They write the book, set up the publishin' company, publish the fuckin' thing and wait fur me tae phone in moanin' like a fuckin' drain. Then plot me up and well, we'll see whit happens aboot that particular fuckin' theory. Nice wan. Very neat.

Number three. The Opposition are efter me. Not fur any particular reason – aw ma knowledge is well oot o' date, well mouldy. But the publicity wid be good. Ex-service man defects efter writing a book. Turned! They wid need me tae be seriously in a bad mood wae the Service mind. Mebbies they assume ah am already - coz o' the way ah live and that. Coz ah just dropped oot. Walked away from mah kids.

Jesus Vonny how long is it now? Two, three years since ah walked doon the wee garden path fur the last time. Sayin' that wiz it. Sorry Vonny but ah knew ye wiz awright fur cash. And ye've goat the hoose payed fur. At least ah did that. Ah wiz

so proud o' doin' that. Fuckin' tricky it wiz anaw, gettin' past aw thae money launderin' regulations and persuadin' the Service that ah'd done weel ootay legitimate business deals.

Ye pretended tae be aw innocent aboot it Vonny but ye knew aw that money was hooky. It disappointed me how quickly ye took tae the idea that – me of all people – hud managed tae get

ninety grand intae a private account in Dublin.

Aye, disappointed. Ah thought ye'd kick up a bit, go intae wan, refuse to hae anythin' tae dae wi' it. But naw. Took mah fuckin' haun' aff ye did. A wee bit o' token 'where did this come from?' 'Are ye sure it isnae dirty?' Just token, that's aw. Instead, ye jus' had mah fuckin' haun aff. Ripped mah fuckin' arm ootay its socket. We could get this an that, buy a bigger hoose, hae a holiday or three…

Not fuckin' likely girl – we're goannae pay that fuckin' mortgage aff and that's the end o' it. And that wiz the end of it. Ye must've realized pretty soon efter that ah hud ma ane agenda. Hidden a wee bit but no totally cos ye must've known also that ah wiz losing mah marbles.

Ye must've Vonny. Must've.

16.

Jeeesuss Christ! That wiz good. Clear the nasal passages, that's whit allowed that tae happen. The trouble is wi' bein'

a vagrant is that ye oaften hae caulds an' blocked hooters.
This means ye oaften cannae drink straight doon for very
long,
cannae tak' a guid lang pull. This is a big disadvantage fur
drinkin' at this endy the market when ye dinnae really want
tae be tastin' whit ye're drinkin'. Aye try tottin' up dregs
frae fifty or sixty bottles at the backay a fuckin' Greek
restaurant – sometimes the result can be surprizin'ly guid -
excellent bookay an' aw that shite – but usually its fuckin'
boggin', 'specially when ye've goat a nose fulla o fuckin'
caked solid snot cos then ye've goat tae breath through yer
mooth an' that makes ye taste the shite yer drinkin'.
Heights o depth, remember? Talkin' of rememberin' this
book hus
made me remember sumthin' else. Where wis it? Page 356,
chapter 19, captured in North Africa. This how it goes:

> *'It was June 1999, I was fixing up an IT radio
> link in Tunisia. We were miles from anywhere.
> The militia pulled us over and the cover story
> didn't impress them. One of them recognized me
> from a previous encounter. I was separated from
> my colleagues and carted off to a shed near an
> airstrip in the middle of the desert. They held
> me there for three weeks. I was interrogated and
> beaten. They poured kerosene on my back and set
> light to me. I rolled around as much as I could
> to dampen the flames but my back suffered very
> bad burns. I thought they would just kill me then
> but they did not. There was a military hospital
> nearby and they actually treated me, told the
> doctors that it had been an accident. I was so
> happy to be alive and too scared to say anything*

*so I actually supported their story. Even though
I hadn't told them anything they wanted me to
live. Then a battalion pulled in and I got
rescued. I was asked to name my torturers but I
did not. I actually owed them my life. So they
got away with it. Funny that. A spy keeping
secrets from his own side.'*

17.

Now that rings a bit o' a fuckin' bell. Like a leper's bell. Mmm. But mah memories are just dreams. Nightmares. Ah suffer wi' thaem a lot. Anyways, the sun's shinin', got tae stay cheerful. Let's hae a wee swig. Mmmm, tha's nice. No bad. There are times. There are times when life is no too bad. The sunshine. It warms ye through, anaw, warms the pavin' stanes up and then yer boady. Tayks away aw the aches an' pains. And, if ye've goatta brew, well, magic, man, magic! Ye can just lie in the sunshine, warmin' through and let yer thoughts tayk ye away oan a nice wee journey.

Anywhere ye want tae go. Then, oan top o that ye can watch the legs. Hunker doon low an' watch aw the legs oan a nice summer's day in the Tottenham Court Road. Wonder if mah Watchers're doin' the same? Who's that ower therr? It's no Oz, he died last month or so ah heard. Same auld coat mind.

Bet it's a Watcher. Watchin' me. Must've nabbed auld Oz's coat frae the mortuary. Stoap at nuthin, thae cunts. Nuthin!

Widnae huv pit it past thaem tae huv killed auld Oz tae get intae his identity. Nick his coat an' pretend tae be him jest so as they can keep an eye oan me frae a distance.

They wid know I never spoke tae Oz. Never speak tae anyone, me. Except tae hurl fuckin' obscenities now an' again at folks. But they wid know that ah wid notice anything
strange, like a new vagey oan the block. So they git wan o' the Watcher crew tae be Oz. Neat. Or ahm ah gittin' intae the realms o' fuckin' fantasy the now? Mebbies ah ahm. Mebbies. Still, just cos ye'are paranoid disnae mean … blah fuckin' blah. Fuckin' hell. Just pondered something, remembered it, like. Ah thought o' this earlier but it must've been too painful 'cos ah then forgot it furra a few days. The worst scenario of aw. The book's a cover. Loads ae stuff goin' on behind the scenes wae the real author workin' actively fur the Opposition. He needs a smokescreen an' the book, plus loopy nutty auld me, provides just that. So, the author is an agent fur the Opposition, he gets a book published in mah name, knowing about mah droppin' oot, an mah history of so-called mental illness. He knows that the Service'll realise they huv a penetration, a spy in the camp, helpin' the Opposition wi' loads o' workin' practices, but no up tae date methods. Still, knowledge of Service workin' practices and protocols is useful tae the Opposition. Very useful indeedy. So ahm getting' set up furrit. Disposable arrent I. Ah've nae proof o' bein' or not bein' anywhere at any given particular time over the last two an' a hauf fuckin' years. So now the Service hus me under surveillance – and the Opposition must guess that tae be the case – then they can stage a meet wi' me at any time, knowin' they've goat a fuckin' audience.

18.

So, ah must not under any circumstances what-so-fuckin'-ever let anyone speak tae me or come near tae me. But then they've prob'ly fitted me up by now anyway. Ah must read the book mair thoroughly, there must be mair clues in it as tae what they're goanna do tae me. Author believed livin' in France! Mah fuckin' arse. There's fuck aw in this book, really. Justa load of ramblins aboot who did whit an' when an' how the government of the day responded to whit an' which an' where – blah blah blah.

Wait a minute. Wait a fuckin' minute. Wits this ahm supposed tae huv said here? Page 399, hauf-ways doon. That creep Kirkpatrick. When he done a runner tae fuckin' Paris an' wrote a fuckin' book aboot the Service. The French widnae extradite him cos it wis a political crime he claimed.

Which gave the French an excuse tae be awkward wi' the British Government, ah s'pose. But Christ whit a cairry oan that wiz. Fuckin' cunt that Kirkpatrick. Fuckin' Fenian. Cat'lic. Ah used tae hate Tims in the Service. Fuckin' Paddies, maist o' them. Working for HMG – cheeky cunts. Service's fault fur tekkin' them oan in the first place. Anyways. Kirkpatrick came back o' his ane free will eventually and stood trial at the Old Bailey. Got aff wae it. An' now he's a member o' the fuckin' SNP! Staunin' tae be a member o' parliament at the next fuckin' general election. Him a fuckin' Fenian anaw! Funny auld world.

Wonder if ah should dae that, then? Come ootay the woodwork. Buzz aroon' like the fuckin' said blowfly for a while, tek a wee bit o' porridge if need be then join a political party. 'Cept yez cannae get elected if ye've served time. That's the killer. Or been convicted even of anything ever. Goat tae tek ah chance there, eh?

So, ah'll say yeah, aye, I wrote the bluddy book, now geiz mah money ya cunts!

Eh? Hang on tho! The Government hud Kirpatrick's money aff o' him pronto. Said it wis tae pay the costs o his prosecution as he'd brought the whole business oan himself. Fair enough. Aye. Fine by me. Fine by me then but disnae fuckin' help me the now. Not now. Coz if ah claim whit isnae really mine by rights then the money'll still get released tae me an' then swiped by the fuckin' government the next second.

19.

Whit'? Get tae fuck! Whit'the! It's mah lovely wee red knickered shoap assistant wi' a fuckin' polis oan her arm! She's tellin' him she's wantin' me fuckin' searched! That ah'll prob'ly still huv it oan me! Whit's still oan me? A book? Whit fuckin' book?!

Aha, but the cop's no really too fuckin' keen oan searchin' me… noo ah wonder why that might be, eh? Undo mah coat officer? An' why the fuck should ah dae that now? Have ye goat reasonable suspicion? Eh? Ah cannae believe this. Ah just cannae believe this. Fuckin' bitch. There's no fuckin' way ahm goan tae undo mah fuckin' coat. Ah'll freeze fur the rest o' the day. D'ye ken what ye're deein', tellin' uz to unloosen mah coat? Ah'll freeze tae fuckin' death - freeze fur the rest o' the day! Nae way ahma gauntae loosen mah coat fellah, nae way!

Now whit ye gaun tae dae? Nuthin. Fuck aw. Stand there'n'stutter in yer fuckin nice big uniform with yer shiny shoes. Cunt. Yes madam, no madam three an' a hauf bags full madam.

Now wit ye goantae dae pal? Eh? Tell uz tae strip? Stoap

an' search in the street? Ah dinnae think so son. No my son. No worth it mate. Not me. Known for aggravation. Uncertain past. Decorated mebbies as a result of distinguished military service then lost his marbles an' a real bastard tae deal wae cos he disnae gie a fuck...

Whit did ye jest say darlin'? Ooooh, "What the hell is he drivelling on about officer?" Fuckin' cheeky cow!

What are *ye* drivellin' on aboot? What are *ye* drivellin' on aboot? Fuckin' cow!

What did ye say son? She huz alleged that ah stole a book frae her shoap? Is that whit she said wiz it? Does that gie you reasonable suspicion, does it?

Naw, I willnae open ma coat fur the aforementioned health an' safety reasons already given, officer, sir. Not reasonable under the circumstances. Am. I. Speaking. Clearly. Enough?

Whit d'you mean "Whit"? I'll tell you whit! Not! Reasonable! You do not have reasonable grounds under the circumstances. You only have her word for it that I stole a book. You can't

conduct a lawful search of my fuckin' person! I am speaking very clearly in guid fuckin' En-gel-ish!

Whit? You'll dae whit if I dinnae loosen ma coat? Call up fur assistance and huv me carted aff, eh? Aye an' then a hose doon in the back yard o' the nick nae doot.

Whit wis that? "No doubt whatsoever" did ye say? Ah fuck it then! Here fuckin' goes then, the police state fuckin' wins again, no way can ah stomach a bluddy hose doon.

20.

Right, therr's mah coat aff, now mah shirt, now mah vest – whitssamatter, why are ye slopin' aff the pair of yeze, wee bit pongy eh? Well, yeze asked furrit. Therr now! Satisfied? Nae fuckin' book tae be seen.

Eh?!, yer no satisfied?! Ahv'e goat sumthin' stuck doon the back o mah fuckin' pants huv ah? Keep away now, don't ye try tae circum-fuckin-navigate me, ye're no coming near mah arse yah fucker. No fuckin' likely. Fuckin' gays in the polis force eh. Positive discrimination in favour of recruiting poofs. Fuckin' disgrace. Political correctness gone mad is what ah say.

Ah fuck, ah've done it now, the radio's oot, he's calling fur assistance, that fuckin' hose doon's loomin'... Awright, awright aw fuckin' right! You win. Leave yer mates ootay it.

Here we go DAN DADA DA DAAAN - that wiz a fanfare – and wae great fuckin' aplomb ah now produce exhibit fuckin 'A' – the stolen book - correction, the stolen bestsellin' book! Except that ... it's no stolen because it belongs to me pal, this belongs to me! It's legally impossible fur wan tae steal sumthin' that belongs tae wans-fuckin'-self. Coz I fuckin' wrote it! Mah name is Bernard Ackrose. Ah've goat ma dole

card and the fuckin scars tae prove it. Whit you huv here officer is a civil dispute. I Bernard fuckin' Ackrose am the author of this book and therefore have a proprietary right to possession of every copy ever fuckin' printed. Right, here we go. ID... dole card, there it is – Bernard Ackrose. Photos of me in the book, see, if ah huv a shave an' a fuckin' haircut ye'll see it wis me, and scars, oh aye... the scars, here we go, page 356, Chapter 19, here we go, look, "my back suffered very bad burns".

Now take a look at this pal. Let me turn roon and show ye mah back – no mah arse mind, ye're no seein' that – just look at mah roasted back! Bad is it, no? Verifiable fuckin' proof tho' but that I am the one, *the* one an' only fuckin' Bernard fuckin' Ackrose, famous author! The writer and lawful owner of this here book. Now are ye still goan'tae arrest me? Come oan then, dinnae just staun therr gawpin' son, are ye goin tae arrest me or fuckin' not? Let me warn ye though, and talkin' o' books, stayin' oan fuckin' theme, if ye dae such a thing you will most certainly be very much in mah fuckin' *bad* books!

Right then, guid decision. No such a bad lad efter aw. Even if ye ur a poof. An' ah'll tell ye whit ah'll dae, just tae show guid faith, ah'm gonna let ye keep the fuckin' book sweet pea. Hae it! Go on, fuckin' hae it! Take the fuckin' book, hae the fuckin' book and stick it up yer fuckin' red knickered fuckin' arse!

Endy fuckin' stoary!

***

Printed in Poland
by Amazon Fulfillment
Poland Sp. z o.o., Wrocław